Praise for
JACKIE ASHENDEN

'*Book People* is a love letter to people who love books – as well as darling bookshops in charming villages and the passion that book lovers bring to everything book-related. *Book People* is also a pitch-perfect masterclass in writing enemies-to-lovers romance with undercurrents of grief and loss, hope and redemption. Jackie Ashenden is a revelation.
I want to live in this book!'

HAZEL BECK

'Filled with witty banter, loveable characters and bookish fun, *Book People* is a novel for the keeper shelf. The romance was swoon worthy – equal parts charming and spicy – and I loved the small mystery element as well. Jackie Ashenden is one of my favourite authors and I'll read anything she writes'

RACHAEL JOHNS

'Jackie Ashenden shines in her delightful rom-com debut that sizzles. Full of wit, humor, banter, and scorching tension, *Book People* is one you can't miss. Perfect for fans of *Bridget Jones's Diary* and *Book Lovers*, this cozy small town, rivals-to-lovers romance is as stacked full of evergreen tropes as it is of classic literature references. Ashenden absolutely shines'

DANICA NAVA

'Jackie Ashenden's *Book People* has it all, blending the well-loved tropes of a great romance and nods to classic literature into a wonderfully cozy and deliciously spicy love story that will have readers absolutely entranced from beginning to happily ever after'

JENNIFER HENNESSY

Jackie Ashenden has been writing fiction since she was eleven years old. Mild-mannered fantasy/SF/pseudo-literary writer by day, obsessive romance writer by night, she used to balance her writing with the more serious job of librarianship until a chance meeting with another romance writer prompted her to throw off the shackles of her day job and devote herself to the true love of her heart – writing romance. She particularly likes to write dark, emotional stories with alpha heroes who've just got the world to their liking only to have it blown wide apart by their kick-ass heroines.

She lives in Auckland, New Zealand, with her husband, the inimitable Dr Jax, two kids, two cats and two rats. When she's not torturing alpha males and their stroppy heroines, she can be found drinking chocolate martinis, reading anything she can lay her hands on, posting random crap on her blog, or being forced to go mountain biking with her husband.

To keep up to date with Jackie's new releases and other news, sign up for her newsletter at **jackieashenden.com** or find her on Facebook **/Jackie.Ashenden** and Instagram **@Jackie_Ashenden**.

BOOK PEOPLE

Jackie Ashenden

HEADLINE
ETERNAL

First published in 2025
by HEADLINE ETERNAL
An imprint of HEADLINE PUBLISHING GROUP

1

Cataloguing in Publication Data is available from the British Library

Chapter illustrations by Mallory Heyer

ISBN 978 1 0354 1801 5

Typeset in 11.04/16.56pt Adobe Garamond Pro Std by Jouve (UK), Milton Keynes

Printed and bound in Great Britain by Clays Ltd, Elcograf S.p.A.

HEADLINE PUBLISHING GROUP
An Hachette UK Company
Carmelite House
50 Victoria Embankment
London EC4Y 0DZ

The authorised representative in the EEA is Hachette Ireland,
8 Castlecourt Centre, Dublin 15, D15 XTP3, Ireland (email: info@hbgi.ie)

www.headlineeternal.com
www.headline.co.uk
www.hachette.co.uk

To Eileen and Rebel Heart Books. The perfect inspiration.

Chapter One

I confess that I did not think much of you at first.
I thought you were arrogant enough to shame the Devil.
How wrong I was!

C

KATE

He's doing it again.

I scowl across the narrow, cobbled street at the window of Blackwood Books, the bookshop directly opposite mine. Today the owner – the insufferably named Sebastian Blackwood – has clearly decided to make a big deal out of the latest Booker Prize winner. He's got stacks of the book displayed prominently, along with excerpts of glowing reviews that he's blown up and laminated, all arranged around some giant red letters that say 'Booker Prize Winner'.

There are no exclamation marks after 'Winner', of course.

It's as if he's making a point that there's no need to shout. Yet his display practically screams: 'Booker Prize winner! So much better than other books! *Especially* the books across the street!'

I may be projecting, but I'm sure he's doing it to spite me, and, look, I've got good reason to suspect that's what's going on.

It's been six months since I moved to Wychtree – the most picture-perfect of English villages, with a river on one side and woods on the other – and I opened Portable Magic four months later (why, yes, the name *did* come from a quote by the great Stephen King about books being 'a uniquely portable magic'), and Sebastian Blackwood has willingly talked to me exactly zero times. You'd think that, since he owns the only other bookshop here, he'd have been thrilled to have another book person to talk to, but no. Apparently not.

I did try to introduce myself before I opened, because I wanted to do the right thing. I wanted to say hi and, yes, I know I'm opening a bookshop opposite yours, and you could see me as competition, but I'm not. I know Wychtree is small, but people read different things and it should be plenty big enough to support two bookshops – at least I hope it will. We're aiming at different markets, and the people who shop at Blackwood Books aren't the same as the people who shop at Portable Magic, etcetera, etcetera.

Except he didn't want a bar of it. Every time I went into his shop, he was apparently 'very busy', either with customers (fair) or 'putting out stock' (if you could call fiddling around intensely on his computer putting out stock).

Every. Single. Time.

I kept trying, because I didn't want us to get off on the wrong foot. I even resorted to cheery notes slipped under his shop's door. But he ignored those too, so in the end I gave up.

I assume it's the competition thing, and he's pissed off I'm here. Honestly, I get it. But he could at least talk to me about it, instead of giving me the cold shoulder or a being passive-aggressive dick with his shop window.

Turning away from all his Booker Prize nonsense, I glance over at my window instead. I spent most of yesterday arranging a nice little collection of romance novels, along with boxes of chocolates (the boxes, not the chocolates – I ate the chocolates) and mugs of fake tea, and cushions and blankets, and a cheerful, bright sign that says: 'Indulge in some "me time"!'

Yes, there's an exclamation mark. It's jaunty.

I actually get a lot of pleasure out of doing shop displays. I find planning and arranging them restful. It's a mindfulness thing, and I was pleased with what I'd done yesterday, but now I'm frowning at it and second-guessing myself.

Perhaps I shouldn't have added the exclamation mark. Perhaps it makes the display look low-brow and trashy.

I growl under my breath, because how annoying to even think that, and all because of that 'better than you' window display across the street.

The bloody man did the same thing last week too, when I'd put out some cosy mysteries, countering with a lot of weighty true-crime nonfiction and a *very* serious sign that said – pointedly, I felt – 'TRUE Crime'. As if the caps on the word 'true' suggests that a cosy mystery is somehow not as worthy because it's made up, and usually has an animal in it. Then, a week before that, I'd put a lot of effort into a special display for a new shipment of graphic novels. A day later, he'd basically turned his front window into a paean to the classics and 'Books everyone should read in their lifetime'.

And I'm sure he'd underlined the word 'Books'.

I shouldn't take it personally, but being ignored when you're only trying to introduce yourself and be nice is insulting. Especially when I'm not *actually* his competition. His shop is very literary and high-brow, and he has a collection of rare books too, so it's a *totally* different market to mine. I'm all about escapist reads, thrilling thrillers and romantic romances. Cosies and fantasies and science fiction. Also a bit of nonfiction, with family-friendly cookbooks, down-to-earth biographies of famous sports people, and a few travel and home-and-garden, coffee-table-type books.

It *has* to work and it will.

Anyway, good thoughts, good thoughts.

I came to Wychtree to find my joy again after my mother's death and four years in an awful relationship, and being angry is *not* what I want.

Happy is what I want to be. Happy and optimistic, and loving each day because I'm living my dream.

Yet as I turn away from my shop window, I can't help glancing reflexively at his again, and it's terrible timing, because suddenly his tall figure comes into view. He's leaning over to delicately place another copy of the Booker book on an already towering stack, and there must be something in the air because, with an abrupt turn of his head, he glances out the window *straight* at me.

And, really, all this – 'all this' being him – would be so much easier to deal with if it wasn't for one thing: Sebastian Blackwood, snob extraordinaire, is *hot*. Legitimately, incontrovertibly, and supremely annoyingly hot.

He's tall – I've always had a thing for tall men – and he wears his black hair cut ruthlessly short. His face is sharp and hawkish, and he has the bluest eyes this side of Paul Newman. Whenever they look at me, they're always cold and distant, but sometimes . . . Sometimes, they're not. Sometimes I'm certain I see sparks in them, though I'm not sure why. Not when he clearly doesn't like me just as much as I don't like him. Whatever, it's not at *all* what I want, so I try to pretend those sparks aren't there. Ignore the Paul Newman-blue eyes.

But despite the street being between us, I can see them now as his gaze meets mine, and for some inexplicable reason my face feels hot.

I'm blushing. What the hell?

Ordinarily I'd have been tempted to stand there and engage him in the mother of all scowl-offs, but I'm not doing that with my face on fire, so I turn very slowly and pointedly away and walk – unhurriedly – back into my shop.

Bloody man.

After Jasper, my boyfriend of four years, outed himself as a manipulative narcissist, I swore off men completely. And in the six months since I've been here in Wychtree, I haven't changed my mind.

I don't miss them. Men.

The most important thing is that I have my shop, and each and every time I step into it, all my anger and my sadness, my betrayal and my grief, melts away. It does so now. The delicate sandalwood scent from the scented candles I burn infuses my very bones, making everything inside me relax.

This is my dream job and has been ever since I was seven and Mum took me to my first bookshop. She was a single mother and we never had much money, so I'd never been in one before. But it was my birthday and Mum wanted to get me a present, so she told me that I could have whatever book I wanted. I was mesmerised by all the beautiful covers, the pictures of kids doing exciting things, and all the dragons and witches and fairies. It seemed so magical. I spent at least half an hour trying to choose the book I wanted, because choosing just one felt impossible. But eventually I decided on a book about a witch *and* a fairy – my first chapter book – and, when I got home, I read it in one sitting and all by myself.

After that I was hooked. Books became my escape, my happy place. Mum had a second job at a pub at night, and she'd often leave me on my own. But I didn't mind. I'd curl up with a book, because with a book I was never lonely, and with a book I was never afraid. With a book I had friends and adventures, and I lived in a castle or in a tree or in an underwater city, and not in a dodgy flat next to a betting shop. Or a bedsit above a Chinese takeaway. Or the spare room of a friend of Mum's . . . you get the idea.

Owning a bookshop of my own had been a secret dream

for years, but with a childhood that was anything but stable, I wanted security. So I pushed it aside in favour of university and an entry-level publishing job in London with a steady pay cheque, and a man who worked in finance.

Then Mum died and my prince turned into a toad, and nothing felt steady any more, let alone happy. So I ran away.

I didn't want to stay in London. When Mum died two and a half years ago, she'd left me a property in Wychtree, the village where she'd grown up but which she left when I was a baby. She'd had a falling out (never explained) with her own mother and had sworn never to return. She kept that vow. I'd been resisting making a decision about what to do with the property for a number of reasons, but, after Jasper, I was desperate to leave the big city. So it was to Wychtree I went.

The building had been standing empty for years, so it was a bit dilapidated. But after scrabbling around, trying and failing to find a bank who'd lend me some money, I redid my sums (*sans* the cost of labour, since I have two working arms and can slap paint on things) and eventually managed to claw a small amount out of a local building society.

So, I renovated it, aka I put some paint on the walls, and then dedicated the downstairs shop area to, yep, you guessed it: books. It took me a couple of months to get the space ready, and once it was done, I opened the shop.

Starting my own business, especially during tough times for the book trade, was daunting, *especially* in a village that had a bookshop already. But I was determined to make mine work, and, two months on from opening, I'm still as determined. No matter how much of a nuisance the competition just across the high street is turning out to be.

I hum under my breath as I neaten up a stack of thrillers, enjoying the peace of my little shop. I've gone for clean white walls and white shelving so as to best display all the lovely covers. There are white tables – with a bit of vintage distressing – where I lay out my new arrivals, and there's also a section that I curate myself with a brightly coloured sign that says 'Kate's top reads'.

Down one end is a big couch covered in colourful throws and there's a nice rag-rolled rug on the floor. A place for people to sit while they peruse their potential purchases. More brightly coloured signs have been stuck to shelving, some whimsical, i.e. 'Happy reads for when you're feeling sad!', and some more serious: 'You might want to grab some tissues!'

I wanted it to feel like you might be in your own living room. A place to grab a book, find a comfy chair, and then sit down and read and relax.

People like that. I had lots of villagers coming in initially to see what 'the Jones girl' was doing, and to have a general nose about, though now everyone knows I'm here, interest has died off a little. But I've had the nicest comments from customers. They're so pleased someone is living in the building again. Some of them even said they never went into bookshops because they didn't have the kinds of books they liked, but now they'd found Portable Magic, they were going to come in every week.

And they do.

I'm fiddling around with one of the displays on the table by the door when one of my regulars comes in. It's Mrs Abbot, a retired district court judge in her late sixties. She was widowed a few years ago and loves romance novels; she can't get enough of them.

I give her a smile and a 'Good morning'.

'Good morning, Kate!' she responds – she's always cheerful and everything she says sounds like it should have an exclamation mark after it, which *definitely* makes her one of my customers. 'I love your window this morning!'

'Oh, excellent.' I beam at her. 'Because I arranged it with you in mind.'

'Well, you've certainly sold me on at least two of those titles!' There's a hint of wickedness in her brown eyes. 'You know I like a hot read!'

Oh, yes. I know. And the spicier the better.

'Speaking of,' I say. 'Those three other titles you ordered have come in. Do you want to pick them up now?'

She nods, and while I go behind the counter to retrieve them, she wanders over to the romance section and plucks a couple of titles off the shelf. Then she comes to the counter and puts them down, waiting while I ring up her purchases.

'You must be looking forward to the festival next month,' she says conversationally. 'I always hope for fewer literary sessions, but sadly I hope in vain.'

I frown. I'm not sure what she's talking about. 'A festival? What festival?'

'Oh, All the World's a Page. You've heard of it, yes?'

A shock goes through me. I'd heard it talked about when I worked for James Locke Publishing. It used to be one of the oldest literary festivals in England, beginning in the fifties and running up until the early nineties. 'Yes, but I thought it was shut down years ago?'

'It was,' Mrs Abbot says. 'But Sebastian decided to revive it this year.' She gives me a slightly puzzled look. 'Surely he's talked to you about it? I'd love it if we could have some more sessions aimed at readers like me.'

I'm trying to pay attention, I really am. But it's very difficult, due to the sudden uprush of fury coalescing in my veins. Because, no, Sebastian hasn't talked to me about it. Sebastian never talks to me at all.

So, to sum up: there's a literary festival happening. A literary festival *he* is reviving. A literary festival that is happening in approximately one month and that he *deliberately* hasn't told me about. And it has to be deliberate. There's no other reason he wouldn't tell the owner of the only other bookshop in the entire village.

My smile might as well have been cut out and pasted on, it feels so stiff. But I manage to keep it there as Mrs Abbot chats a bit more, then pays for her books and I put them in a bag for her. Then I wait for the minute it takes her to leave the shop before I'm striding out myself, banging my door closed and sticking on it the piece of paper I keep to hand that says 'Back in ten minutes'.

I'm not normally confrontational. I prefer to pour oil on troubled waters. I *don't* create the trouble myself. At least, that's what I spent most of my time doing in my relationship with Jasper. But this is my dream we're dealing with here, my dream of a successful bookshop, and I will fight to the death anyone who dares to threaten it.

So I stride in an absolute rage, my good thoughts forgotten, straight across the street to Blackwood Books.

It's a ridiculously picturesque shop. Located in a half-timbered, historic Tudor building, the inside is like something out of Dickens. Old wooden floors and panelled walls. Built-in shelves that look like they've been there for centuries. The ceiling is low, with big, exposed beams, and there are enough Persian rugs to carpet the entirety of Persia. There's even an ancient staircase that leads to a second floor, where all the rare books are kept in a special climate-controlled room.

It's beautiful, but I don't want him ever to know that I'm jealous of his perfect little bookshop.

What I *do* want him to know is that I'm livid.

He's standing behind the huge, antique oak desk that doubles as his counter, and he's looking down at the slim, black laptop he's got open. He doesn't glance up as I enter. He's wearing a plain black shirt and black trousers, and has the most affected, hipster-looking glasses in the history of the entire world sitting on the end of his Roman nose.

Even while I'm furious at him, he's still hot. His profile looks like that of an emperor, though I would literally die if he ever found out that I thought that.

'Hello? Yes,' I say, coming to a stop in front of the counter, 'I need to talk to you.'

He doesn't look up. 'I'm a bit busy at the moment,' he says, with frigid politeness. His voice is deep and I hate that I find it sexy.

I ignore his busyness. 'It's about the festival. The festival *you* didn't tell me about.'

'The festival is a literary event,' he says, sounding absolutely insufferable. Then he deigns to lift his gaze from his laptop screen, staring at me coldly through his rimless glasses. The lenses make his amazing blue eyes even more amazing. 'It's got nothing to do with you.'

He said that. He really said that. The . . . *audacity*.

My fury is growing, sitting in my stomach like acid, but I'm not going to be rude like him. I'm better than that. I'm going to take the higher ground, I decide, and continue my offensive by being aggressively pleasant.

I try a smile, though I'm pretty sure it's turned into a feral grimace. 'I am a bookshop owner. In case you didn't know. And since this is a book festival, I'd say it has a little bit to do with me.'

His eyes glitter behind his glasses, and for a long moment he just stares at me. And for a second I think I can see those sparks again and it makes my heart give an odd little jump. Then, slowly, he raises his hands and, with deliberate precision, takes his glasses off, folding them up carefully and laying them down on the counter, the epitome of a very important man graciously granting a poor idiot a couple of moments of his precious time. 'It's not that kind of festival,' he says, as if explaining to a child. 'As I said, it's a *literary* festival.'

'Books are literature,' I snap.

'Not all books,' he says, patiently.

Of all the . . . Anger grabs me around the throat and for a second I'm so furious I can't speak. Ever since I opened, he's ignored all my gestures of friendship, all my attempts to get to know him, and he's rebuffed every single olive branch I've tried to extend. He's even been passive-aggressive with his window displays. He clearly thinks he's better than me, and now he's trying to cut me out of a festival that could very well be good for both of us.

'Give me a reason,' I demand, my pleasantness slipping through my fingers no matter how hard I try to hang on to it. 'Just one reason why you didn't tell me about this festival.'

'I believe I just did.'

'No, the real reason.'

'That *was* the real reason.'

'It wasn't.' I glare at him. 'You deliberately didn't tell me.'

He lets out a breath and shifts on his feet, as if he's got more important high-brow things to do. 'Why would I do that?'

'Because you're an insufferable snob,' I say, before I can think better of it.

He merely extends an arm and looks down at the heavy watch around his wrist. 'Is that all you have to say? I've got some orders to process and they need to be done fairly quickly.'

'So you're really going to stick with being an arse? I've tried to introduce myself for the past two months and all you do is ignore me.'

'I'm sorry, I've been very—'

'Yes,' I interrupt. 'You've been very busy. I heard you the first fifty million times you said it. But what I really want to know is why you can't even have a conversation with me?'

This time something sparks in his eyes. 'Are we having a conversation? Or are you just here to harangue me?'

'I wouldn't harangue you if you hadn't been ignoring me.'

'Why would I ignore you?' This time his tone is slightly less measured and slightly more impatient.

'I don't know, *you* tell me.'

For a moment we glare angrily at each other, tension filling the space.

Then, finally, he says, 'I've spent the last six months putting this festival together and it's opening next month. It's too late to do anything about it now.'

He sounds just a little bit smug, making me want to smack him. It would feel *so* good to really lose my temper . . .

But, no, I've left anger behind me. I've left tension and stress and grief and bloody *men* back in London, and they're not following me here, they're just not.

So instead I take a deep, silent breath and let the tension go. Then I smile at him, very, *very* sweetly. 'That's what you think,' I say.

Then I turn and, with extreme deliberation, I stroll out.

Chapter Two

You were such an angry little thing.
A real termagant. Did I ever tell
you how much I liked that?

H

SEBASTIAN

I do not like Kate Jones.

I do not like Kate Jones.

I do not like Kate Jones.

I have to say it to myself three times as a calming mechanism, because otherwise I'm going to charge out of the shop door after her to continue our argument, and that would be a very stupid thing to do.

I don't want her to know how angry she makes me. I don't want her to know how she gets under my skin. Like a splinter of glass you can't see to pull out, slowly working its way deeper and deeper, hurting like a bastard.

Instead, I watch her through my front window as she strolls casually across the road, the hem of her frothy pink skirt lifting in the light breeze, revealing a flash of pale thigh.

She's ridiculous. She dresses like a Barbie doll, not a book-seller. Every gesture she makes is over-exaggerated and it's the same with her expressions, every emotion on her face writ large enough for everyone to see.

I can't stand how open she is.

I do *not* like her.

So I have no idea why I can't take my eyes off her.

I do *not* like that either.

She walks with a confident swing of her hips, approaching that ridiculous space that I refuse to call a bookshop. Her hair is long and gathered into a low ponytail at the nape of her neck, spilling down her back in a fluffy golden cloud. She's wearing little pink sandals that match her pink dress and she looks like the Sugar Plum Fairy. Sparkling and sweet, a delicious confection. Light and airy, without substance.

I don't want anything to do with women who lack substance.

I don't want anything to do with women full stop. Or at least not women who live in the village. I go elsewhere if I want female company.

Yet still I watch her as the breeze lifts strands of gold from her shoulders and she pauses to smooth them back. Does she know I'm watching her? Is she trying to prove a point? And, if so, what particular point is she trying to prove?

She was right, I was an arse to her just now. I know that. She had every right to call me a snob. I *was* being deliberately provocative. But I wanted to make it clear that I didn't want her or her books anywhere near my festival.

And it is *my* festival. I've spent months organising it for the benefit of Blackwood Books and Blackwood Books alone. Though, it's more accurate to say I revived it, since it was my great-grandfather who conceived the initial festival, then ran it successfully for years until my grandfather took over. He, unfortunately, didn't have the same interest in the shop that my great-grandfather did, and his lack of passion hurt the festival, and so it became less and less successful over time. Then my father took over and he ran it into the ground.

Which is the story of Blackwood Books in many ways, since it's also my father's fault that the bookshop is struggling now. Too many debts. Lack of financial oversight. Too few books being sold. Too much online competition. Too few people reading. The problems are myriad, but I'm determined to overcome them.

Blackwood Books has been a village icon for over half a century and I certainly won't be the Blackwood responsible for the business going under. Dad might have given up on it after Mum died, but I haven't.

Pretty Miss Jones pauses before the doors of her ridiculously named shop, and glances over her shoulder.

No doubt she can see me standing here, looking at her.

I should pretend that I'm not looking and turn away, abashed. But I don't. I'm a deliberate man. I want her to see me staring after her. I want her to know that I was serious when I said I didn't want her at my festival, that I will brook no argument.

We've already had a silent battle of wills once today. Why not another?

I don't want her at my festival.

I don't want her in my town.

I don't want her pretty, flirty skirts, her pale thighs, her tangled blonde hair, her sunny, friendly smiles, and her wide grey eyes anywhere near me.

She's too far away for me to tell whether she blushes, but she doesn't turn away. She sees me, I know she does, and she's looking right back.

I turn calmly and without haste, glancing down at the laptop I have open on the counter, and resume pretending to check through my stock ordering.

If a customer were to come in now, all they'd see would be a bookseller calmly working at his laptop, nothing but professional and pleasant.

Inside, though, I'm feral.

She's a persistent woman, and this I know because she's been persistently courting me ever since she arrived in Wychtree. Not courting in a romantic fashion but in a business sense. She wants me to be okay with her bookshop, with her taking some of my business away. She wants us to be 'friends'.

But I don't do 'friends', and certainly not with her. And

while it's true our shops are aimed at different readers, there's a proportion of my customers who have abandoned me entirely. They used to put orders through me and now they don't. It's a problem, I can't deny it.

She called me a snob and no doubt thinks that I'm some kind of intellectual puritan. While it's true that I've played up to her expectations because I'm angry with her, I'm neither of those things. I believe all books should exist and every genre has its place. But she's directly threatening my livelihood, and that's why I'm angry. That's why I organised the festival. I need more customers, and if large numbers of people in the village now get their reading material from her, then I need to reach beyond the village.

I want the All the World's a Page festival to become the new go-to of literary festivals, the way it used to be back when my great-grandfather started it. I want Wychtree to become the new Hay-on-Wye. I've already had massive issues with the printers about the posters that were supposed to go up last month, and now Miss Jones is meddling. I can't have her insinuating herself and taking all my potential new customers and orders. Blackwood Books will be the sole supplier and that's final.

Books are a serious business. They deal with deep issues. They are subversive. Political. Religious. They deal with humanity at its worst and its best, and while I believe in fun escapism too, that's not what my bookshop is about.

I glance out of the shop window again, irresistibly drawn to Portable Magic across the road. Her window dressing is absurd. Piles of romance novels, and mugs of tea and choc-olate boxes and cushions, and a huge sign that reads: 'Indulge in some "me time"!'

The exclamation mark is an affront. The bright colours are an attack. And I'm a fool for indulging in this ridiculous window-dressing battle we have going on, yet I can't help myself. I filled my window with James Wyatt's latest Booker Prize winner, *The Bay at Midnight*, in response to all the fluff in hers. She's got me stooping to her level and I resent it with every fibre of my being.

I shouldn't let her get to me, but the debts are already piling up due to the festival and I'm hoping to God that it will be a success, because the bank won't give me another loan.

No. It will be a success. I'll make it a bloody success.

James Wyatt himself is the headliner, a coup I managed to pull off through a colleague who manages Wyatt's wife's favourite bookshop. My colleague put in a word with the wife, who then convinced Wyatt not only to come to Wychtree, but also to give a reading and a talk right here in Blackwood Books. I've got a few other authors, some journalists and some poets too. Ticket sales have been brisk.

Kate Jones and her 'me time!' window be damned.

The rest of the village love her, think the sun shines out of her pert rear end, but I refuse to buy into that. She's the com-petition, the new kid on the block, and all I have on my side is the history of Blackwood Books, but it's enough. The village loves its history and Blackwood is part of that.

My great-grandfather, who started the bookshop back in

the thirties, was a Sebastian Blackwood and so am I, and I will
not let his legacy vanish.

I try to concentrate on the stock ordering, but I can't get
the look on Kate Jones's face as she left my shop out of my
head. She was angry with me, but I also spotted determination
in her grey eyes.

I don't trust that determination. I don't trust it an inch.

The bell above the door chimes and old Mr Parsons comes
in. He's a retired English professor with a fondness for
nineteenth-century classics – he's a particular fan of Proust –
but I'm trying to introduce him to some modern authors. And
when I say modern, I mean written after 1950. I got him to
take a chance on Faulkner and Rushdie, so now I'm hoping
he'll like the Wyatt too.

The Bay at Midnight is set in an old pub in Ireland over
the course of one night and it's a modern classic. A rich
tapestry of life in a village, redolent with history, fraught
relationships, and a searing commentary on the loneliness
of the human condition – at least, that's what the *Times*
review said.

I haven't read it. I don't need to read about villages and the
loneliness of the human condition. I know all about that
already. My reading tastes run to . . . other things, that I will
never reveal to anyone.

Most especially not to Miss Kate Jones.

'Blackwood,' Mr Parsons says in greeting.

'Mr Parsons,' I say cordially back. 'I have the Shakespeare
edition you were after. It came in yesterday. The *Coriolanus*.'

He's a tall man in his mid-seventies, straight-backed and severe. A bit like my great-grandfather, which is why I bear his little moments of pettiness. At seventy-six, you're allowed a few pettinesses.

'Excellent,' he says, rubbing his hands as he approaches the counter. 'I've been looking forward to it.'

I pick up the Wyatt from the stack beside me and put it next to the Shakespeare. 'You might like this,' I say. 'If you like Rushdie, you should give it a try.'

He looks suspiciously at the book and I tap the 'Booker Prize Winner' sticker displayed prominently on the front. 'It won the Booker,' I say, just in case he missed the sticker. 'And the author will be coming to Blackwood Books for the festival next month.'

'Oh, I see.' Mr Parsons picks the book up and gives it a cursory study. 'Will he be doing a reading?'

Mr Parsons does love a reading.

'Yes,' I say. 'And a Q&A.'

Mr Parsons does love a Q&A.

'Hmm.' He puts the book down on top of the Shakespeare. 'I'll take it. But if the first two pages don't grab me, I'm bringing it back.'

Mr Parsons also loves his two-page rule. I do *not* love it, especially when he brings the books back to return them. But I don't argue with him when he does, because he's a loyal customer and the books he likes to buy are expensive.

'Of course,' I murmur, and ring the books up for him.

As he's paying, Beverly from the Wychtree Arms comes in and, after Mr Parsons has gone, we go over the details for the poetry-reading event for the festival. That event in particular hasn't sold as many tickets as I'd like, despite me managing to snag Augusta Heroine (a pseudonym, obviously) reading from her epic verse novel *When We Were Heroes*, a retelling of *The Iliad* from the point of view of a gender-swapped Odysseus.

Her readings are usually sell-outs in London, so I'm hoping there will be more takers. There's still a few weeks to go, after all.

After Beverly leaves, we enter the long hours of the afternoon lull. I find myself yet again looking out of my front window and across the road to Portable Magic.

Miss Jones is adding a few more books to her window. The covers are brightly coloured, with cartoon people on them, and she arranges them picturesquely on the low table, next to a cup and saucer and a teapot.

A group of teenage girls assemble in front of the window, looking at the books, and Miss Jones straightens and gives them a smile. Then she picks up the books one by one and shows them to the girls, who grin and point and nod.

I stare balefully out at them, thinking what a ridiculous pantomime it is. And when the girls all pile excitedly into her shop, I'm incensed.

She treats her front window like it's a department store display, like a toyshop. She thinks she's the Pied Piper of Wychtree, luring all the children into her shop, and once they're inside, they never come out again.

As the girls make their way in, Miss Jones straightens in the front window and throws a jaunty salute my way.

My jaw clenches tight, my teeth grind.

I turn back to my own shop and stare at it, trying to find my usual clear-eyed calm.

This place has always been an escape for me, ever since childhood. My father took it over when my grandfather died and I grew up among the shelves, my toys scattered about on the rugs. I learned to read in this shop, learned all about the world in the pages of these books, and, when my mother died, it was my escape. She loved this place too, just like my great-grandfather did, and it's for her as well that I want to keep it going.

I need to keep it going.

For the rest of the afternoon, I try to concentrate on yet another festival publicity budget, but I keep being distracted by people in costume all disappearing into Miss Jones's shop.

At first I think it's only children, but it's not. There are adults among them too.

I'm going to have to talk to her, I realise. I'm going to have to make it absolutely clear that she's not to be involved in my festival in any way. Or sabotage it or subvert it. As she might.

The village grapevine worked overtime when she first arrived here, and not only because she's the great-granddaughter of the first Kate Jones, who used to own a teashop where the bookshop now is. There was something about a relationship breakup and a redundancy back in London. She'd been doing some kind of corporate job.

She's probably ambitious – you can't be in the corporate world for too long before you have to start walking over the backs of people – so I really wouldn't put it past her to do something to insinuate herself into my festival. I wouldn't put it past her to organise some kind of sabotage.

So, just before closing, I walk out of Blackwood Books, cross the road and approach Portable Magic.

I've never set foot in this shop and I've never wanted to. It's galling that I'm now having to take this step, but it has to be done. She has to know that I will not have her hijacking my festival, not in any way, shape or form.

I step inside and am immediately assailed by a roomful of people all dressed up like cartoon characters. Or superheroes. Or video game characters or something. I can't tell which it is.

I don't like it, not any of it. They're all talking loudly, leaving no space for quiet reading of any kind, and they're passing around comics and graphic novels indiscriminately. Some kid pulls a toy gun from a holster and pretends to shoot me with it.

I scowl at him and he moves on to shoot his friend instead.

'Mr Blackwood,' a feminine voice says. 'Fancy seeing you here.'

I turn to see Miss Jones standing behind the counter. She's not wearing her pink skirt any more but a sleek, silver jumpsuit, with knives in holsters strapped to her shapely thighs. She has a black utility belt around her waist.

I tell myself she looks preposterous and do not let my gaze stray from her face.

She raises a golden brow. 'What brings you to finally darken my door?'

'I need to talk to you,' I say.

'Oh? What about?'

'The festival.'

Her smile becomes sweet, almost saccharine. 'What festival? Which one? Oh, the one you didn't invite me to be a part of?'

I ignore the circus going on around me the way I also ignore her sarcasm, folding my arms and staring at her coldly. Her attention drops briefly to my chest, which is interesting, though not at all welcome. Definitely not.

'You know which festival I'm talking about, Miss Jones. All the World's a Page. There's a reason you weren't invited and it's because I want Blackwood Books to be the sole supplier of books for the festival. So I'm here to reiterate that I don't want you or your bookshop to be involved.'

'That's fine,' she says. 'I've just started planning my own festival. It'll run concurrently with yours, though of course there'll be different events and different authors coming.'

A shock of anger pulses through me, so intense that at first I can't speak.

'You can't,' I finally splutter. 'A month isn't long enough to organise an entire festival. Even six months was pushing it.'

She lifts a shoulder. 'It's enough time when you have a lot of thirsty readers.'

'No,' I say.

'No?' She raises both brows this time. 'I'm sorry, did Wychtree install a dictator while I wasn't looking? Or maybe appoint you to be the book police? Who died and made you God, Mr Blackwood?'

My jaw is so tight it's aching. 'You can't have a festival at the same time as mine,' I force out through gritted teeth. 'The village isn't big enough.'

She leans forward, both elbows on the counter, looking up at me from beneath her golden lashes. 'Of course it is. Like I told you before, we cater to different readers. The world is plenty big enough for the both of us and so is this village.'

I don't want to reveal the extent of my shop's losses. Dad was the main culprit, it's true, but I don't like what it says about me as a business owner. I want her to stop poaching on my territory, but she thinks this is a game, a battle of front windows, intellectualism versus the mainstream, and it's not.

It's my livelihood.

Someone approaches the counter and she allows her saccharine-sweet smile to linger on me for a moment longer before she directs her attention to her customer, a gangly adolescent boy with blue-dyed hair, wearing some complicated and elaborate harness around his shoulders.

The smile she directs at him is so warm and genuine that he blushes.

Suddenly I'm even more furious.

Furious that she should be so pretty. Furious that everyone likes her. Furious that I know exactly how long it's been since a woman smiled at me like that. Furious that I don't think I've *ever* had a woman smile at me like that.

I stand there fuming as she talks with the kid, exchanging a bit of banter and gently teasing him as he buys his little stack of manga. And I should probably leave. I'm in no fit state to speak to anyone – not even a woman I don't like – when I'm in this kind of mood. But I don't move.

When the boy finally walks away, she gives me an exasperated look. 'What is it, exactly, Mr Blackwood, that is making you quite so angry about my shop?'

'My falling sales,' I blurt, unable to stop myself.

She blinks as though this is a shock to her. 'Falling sales?'

'Yes, falling sales,' I bark. 'What? Did you think there were no romance readers here until your little shop opened? Did you think people only started reading thrillers and mysteries when you miraculously came down from the heavens and waved your portable magic wand?' I give her my coldest stare. 'They were always here, those readers. And they used to order from Blackwood Books.'

She blinks again. Yes, this is clearly news to her.

Slowly she straightens and the shock fades from her eyes. The look she gives me now is as cool as the one I'm giving her. 'Then perhaps you should have done more to keep them.'

It's a little knife she's got, but it slides in and wounds all the same. I stiffen. 'I don't run a bad business.'

'No, you don't,' she agrees. 'But you don't run a warm, welcoming business either. You took for granted the customers you had, so don't blame them if they wanted to go somewhere else where they're not looked down upon.'

Another knife wound.

'I don't look down on anyone,' I say. 'Everyone should be able to read what they want. But Blackwood Books has a history and that history should be treated with honour and respect.'

Her grey eyes flash with temper and, like the cliché I'm rapidly becoming, I find her even prettier when she's angry. 'Are you saying that genre fiction is disrespectful?'

'No.' I uncross my arms and put both hands on the counter, leaning on them. 'I'm saying that Blackwood Books is in a historic building. It's a small local business, and you and your corporate nonsense are in danger of running it into the ground.'

She puts her hands on the counter too, and leans in, invading my personal space the way I invaded hers. She's looking angrily up at me, not at all afraid that I'm so much taller and broader than she is. 'Corporate nonsense? Next you'll be comparing me to Amazon and proclaiming that the death of the independent bookseller is nigh.'

'It is, Miss Jones,' I bite out, staring down into her pretty eyes. 'It is nigher than you think.'

We stare furiously at each other and only then do I realise that her eyes are almost crystalline, lighter in the centre, with a darker ring of charcoal around the outside. Her skin is smooth and velvety, and slightly flushed, and she smells as sweet as she looks. Her mouth is slightly open and her lips are full and soft-looking.

I want to take a bite right out of them.

I want to take a bite right out of her.

'Um,' an adolescent voice says from behind me. 'Maybe you two should get a room?'

I curse under my breath and shove myself away.

Then I turn and leave that hellhole without another word.

Chapter Three

J really shouldn't be telling you these things. It's far too forward.

C

KATE

'It is nigher than you think.'

Oh my God. Sebastian Blackwood is a stupid man who says the most unbelievably stupid things, and that makes me even stupider for taking his bait.

I crash around my tiny kitchen, stacking the dishwasher noisily and coming near to breaking several glasses.

It's been a couple of days since that moment in my book-shop and I can't stop thinking about him putting his hands on the counter and leaning in, his blue eyes piercing me right through.

I was shocked he even deigned to set foot in Portable Magic. Then incensed that he only did so to warn me away from his stupid festival again. Then furious that I inadvertently glanced at his magnificent chest as he stood with his arms folded, looking around at all the people having fun for Cosplay Day as if he couldn't think of anything more stupid in his entire life, and basically being a human energy sink.

Then enraged that he leaned in, pinning me with that cold stare of his, telling me I was responsible for the drop in sales of his bookshop and basically accusing me of being Jeff Bezos.

The gall of him. The absolute *gall*.

I'm so tired of men telling me I'm the problem when they're not exactly blameless themselves. Jasper, for example, always used to complain about how busy I was, that I never had time for him, when in fact it was the opposite. I was always rearranging my time to suit him, because he was the one who was so busy.

The annoying thing about the argument with Sebastian Blackwood, though, was that I felt bad for him. And the *really* aggravating thing is that I still do.

I researched the village when I first arrived, though that mainly consisted of looking at the other businesses here and the villagers. I didn't do any research about its history. I decided I'd get to the history part – including my mother's family's history – once I'd settled in with the bookshop.

More than a few people have tried to talk to me about my great-grandmother, the original Kate Jones, and what a strong personality Rose, her daughter and my grandmother, was. But I didn't know Rose. My mother, Rebecca, left Wychtree when I was three months old and she never went back.

I didn't know much about the history of this village, because I never knew my family's history *was* this village. Mum never talked about it, and I never asked, because it seemed as if the subject was a painful one and I didn't want to bring anything up that might be hurtful. My distractible, optimistic, bright mother had enough to deal with being a single parent; she didn't need to be doing battle with her history too.

Anyway, all that to say: I didn't think a great deal about the historical significance of Blackwood Books. I didn't think I'd feel bad about taking some of his customers away, either. But . . . I do.

I'd told him – and myself – that it was good old healthy competition, yet in that moment, when I looked up at him and there was fire in his eyes, all I felt was guilt.

The times I've seen him around the village – in the corner shop, the butcher's, the little bakery, the café where all the tourists and the locals like to get their coffee, the post office – he's seemed cold and distant. Not a man who cares too much about anything or anyone, and, yes, I've made some assumptions. Assumptions that were upheld every time he looked past me or through me, never acknowledging me, not even once.

Yet, just a few days ago, he looked straight at me and I saw the fire inside him. He wasn't as cold as he seemed. He cared about his bookshop and, dammit, no matter how much I didn't want to, I related to that hard. And I felt bad for taking his customers.

Infuriating man.

He hasn't changed his shopfront window since then. I took down my romance theme after a new shipment of witch books came in, and had huge fun setting out tarot cards and crystals, a black cardboard cat and an old-fashioned twig broom. I even managed to beg a cauldron prop from the Wychtree Dramatic Society.

I thought he'd respond, put some kind of science-y books out and maybe a few biographies of Nobel Prize winners, but he hasn't. The only prize winner in his window right now is that same stack of the Booker book that's been there all week, and I don't know why that annoys me so much, but it does.

No. I know why it annoys me.

I felt guilty for taking his customers, and now he's decided to stop playing our little game with the windows, I'm disappointed.

I hate that I'm disappointed.

I hate that I feel guilty.

I was supposed to come back here to find joy, to find happiness, to think good thoughts, but Sebastian Blackwood is threatening my quest and my dream, and that is *not* what I want.

I slam the dishwasher shut and turn around, reflecting on how much men suck as I survey the tiny but cosy flat above the shop.

It's an open-plan living area and kitchen, with a small hall that leads to a small bedroom and even smaller bathroom, but it's plenty of room for me, and I love it.

I loved the flat I shared with Jasper, too. It was big and

airy and got lots of sun. Except it was his and he never let me do any redecorating – he had no patience for my cheerful clutter.

Damn. I don't want to think about Jasper. He doesn't deserve any of my thoughts, and I've thought of him too many times lately already.

Anyway, the important thing is that I have a whole building that's mine and a business that's mine too, and no one can take those things away from me.

Most certainly not Sebastian Blackwood.

The mini-festival I planned in a frenzy the day I found out about his was petty, I know, and he's probably right: I probably can't plan a festival in a few weeks. But I'll be damned if I don't try.

I've already got a little social calendar of things I do with the shop. The romance book club. Tarot night. Yoga mornings. Role-playing weekends. Board-game Fridays. The bi-monthly Jack Reacher discussions.

The events were initially meant to attract more customers and get the word out there about Portable Magic, and they've proved very popular. It's really going to come in handy now, because I can tell people to tell their people and those people to tell theirs about my mini-festival.

It may not compare with Sebastian's in terms of attracting out-of-towners, but I bet we'll have more fun. And judging from my Cosplay Day attendance, there are plenty who'd like to come.

Also. *My* events will be free.

I let out a breath and go over to the sofa, sit down and switch on my TV, channel-surfing for some distraction.

The flat wasn't furnished when I arrived, and, since I didn't have the money for brand-new stuff, I had to get second-hand. Yet while most of the furniture is old and run-down, it's still perfectly serviceable.

I like the shabby-chic vibe. I've covered the old moth-eaten velvet sofa and the worn leather armchair by the window with a couple of pretty throws. A scarf thrown over the ugly shade of the lamp on a side table beside the sofa makes it shed a more muted and softer pink light. A couple of rag rugs I found in Mrs Bennet's craft shop beside the post office cover up the worst of the spots on the cream carpet.

It's cheerful and pretty, and I love being here.

Right now, though, staring at my cheerful, pretty room and scrolling through the nothing that's on TV, I'm aware that grief is lurking in the corners of the room. It's followed me from London and it's waiting in the shadows, and I don't want it. Not tonight. Not after Sebastian Blackwood made me feel so restless and off balance.

I need to get out, go and be somewhere else, be with people.

A village can be insular if you're a newcomer, and while people here are friendly enough, it's also clear that I'm an outsider. It doesn't matter that my mother was from here; I haven't lived here and thus I'm not a local.

I'd always planned to do a bit of digging into my family's history, find out why my mother never spoke of home and never wanted me to either. Learn about my roots.

I've heard a lot of talk about Rose Jones and what a difficult woman she was, but I haven't bothered to discover why and how, and exactly what kind of difficult she was. Maybe I'm afraid to.

I can't let fear stop me, though. Fear bled all the colour from my life back in London, and I swore I wasn't going to let it rule me again. So, yes, I should stop putting off investigating my family history, and I should look at what kind of business Blackwood Books is too, see if it really is the historical icon Sebastian told me it was.

Of course, to do that, I need to find people to talk to and the quickest way to find them is to head to the heart of any village: the pub.

I like wearing pretty things and I feel a bit plain in my current T-shirt and jeans. So I change into one of my favourite dresses, which is white and lacy and flowy. I wrap a wide belt around my hips and leave my hair free. I like to think the vibe is very Stevie Nicks. Either that or like I should have a garland on my head in preparation for leaping over a Beltane fire in the middle of Stonehenge.

Jasper preferred a more polished, corporate look, and he told me so often enough. But since I left London, the one thing I'm *not* doing is polished or corporate.

Grabbing my coat and my keys, I go downstairs and step out into the evening twilight.

The Wychtree Arms is smack in the middle of the village, where all the roads meet in a small, cobbled square. It's your classic historic British pub, with low beams, a smoke-stained ceiling, a giant fireplace and a big oak bar. There are little nooks and crannies everywhere for people to sit in, and apparently in the summer it heaves with tourists.

Tonight, though, in that weird space between the end of spring and the beginning of summer, when the weather can't decide if it's hot or cold so chooses to be rainy and damp instead, there are only locals in here.

Gerry, who owns the butcher's shop and who's been fighting the construction of a giant Tesco on the outskirts of town, is locked in deep conversation with Molly and Lindsey, who own the bakery.

Claire, who works at the post office, is having dinner and a drink with her husband, John, an accountant.

Leonard and his cronies from Len's Quality Construction are being loud with their pints in a corner.

I spot Aisling, who has just taken over the café and is trying to introduce 'plant-based delicacies' to unimpressed villagers who only want a giant scone and some clotted cream, and maybe a sausage roll, with their tea. She's the one friend I've managed to make here and she's lovely. But she's married and has a small toddler, and she too is having a quiet drink with her husband, Ben, so I don't bother them. If it's date night and they have a babysitter, they won't want me barging into their quiet time.

I take another survey of the pub, and that's when I see him in the snug next to the fireplace. Sebastian Blackwood, grimly reading a book.

He does everything grimly, I think, as I stare, which is a

shame, especially when it comes to reading. No one should ever read a book grimly. Yet grim is the only word that springs to mind when I look at him, the carved lines of his face set, his black brows drawn down, his mouth in a line.

He's wearing a dark-blue casual shirt and his usual black trousers, and he gives the impression of splendid isolation, his looks making him appear even more so somehow. Yet, as if defying that isolation and all that grimness, there are his absurd little hipster glasses perched on the end of his very fine nose: a tiny flaw, a sign of his humanity.

It's endearing, which is an odd thing to think about a man so cold and rigid.

Except, he wasn't rigid leaning over my counter with fire in his eyes, furious about my bookshop, furious at the threat to his livelihood. He's protective of it, that's clear. I guess it was pretty cheeky of me to open my bookshop directly across the road from his, and perhaps I've been in denial about that.

I want to explain. I want to tell him why I did it, that it's been my dream to own my own bookshop, and that opening one here, in the building my mother left me, is the only way I could afford to do it. Yes, I truly did think that it wouldn't affect his sales and that readers drew the same lines in the book sand that he and I do, but . . . well . . .

I was naïve, clearly.

I turn to the bar and order myself a gin and tonic from Tom, the publican, and then, when it's ready, I turn back to the snug where he's sitting. But just as I'm starting to rethink talking to him, because he really does look very grim and I don't want to interrupt anyone's reading, he looks up from the pages of his book and his gaze meets mine.

His eyes are ridiculous. The colour of them is astonishing. I see something flare in them, something I can't name because it's gone too fast for me to figure out what it was. It's also too late to alter my course, to go sit at another table. I don't want him to think I'm afraid of him, or embarrassed to be caught staring, or too chicken to talk, so I brace myself and head towards the snug determinedly.

With extreme deliberation, he slips a bookmark into his book, closes it, and puts it down on the table, and by the time I arrive, the book has been somehow obscured by the pub's menu. Which is annoying in the extreme, because now I'm desperate to know what he was reading and what put that expression on his face.

'Yes?' he asks, in that ridiculously deep voice of his, somehow managing to make the question sound bored, annoyed and challenging all the same time. 'Can I help you, Miss Jones?'

He doesn't invite me to sit, so I'm left standing awkwardly with my gin and tonic. If I was still the me I was back in London, I'd give him an apologetic smile, take his tone as a rejection, and slope off somewhere else.

But I'm not that me, and so I think to hell with it and sit down anyway, putting my drink down on the table between us, a declaration of intent.

'What are you reading?' I ask, like the excellent bookseller I am.

'A book.'

'What book?'

'None of your business.'

Off to a great start then.

'I want to talk to you,' I say.

His gaze touches on the book obscured by the menu. 'I'm reading.'

'So?'

'If I wanted to talk to someone, I wouldn't be reading.'

'But you put your book down.'

'I was being polite.'

'Were you? Is that even possible, Mr Blackwood?'

This time his gaze isn't on his book, but the dress I'm wearing. It's a lightning-fast glance, but I catch it all the same, just as I see how his mouth hardens. Does he like it? Does he disapprove? Do I care?

'What do you want?' he demands, all impatience, and desperate for me to leave.

Naturally, I decide to settle in for the evening.

He's turning me into a bloody-minded, stubborn arse, and I find I quite like the experience, especially since I was always giving in to Jasper.

'I told you what I want.' I pick up my gin and tonic and take a sip. 'I want to talk to you.'

'Why?'

'To explain why my shop is where it is and that I didn't intentionally set out to take your customers.'

'I don't need an explanation, nor do I want one.'

'Too bad. You're getting one.'

'I've been told consent is important, Miss Jones. And I do not consent to you sitting at my table and disturbing my reading.'

'You really are a stubborn bastard, aren't you?'

'Pot. Kettle.'

We glare at each other over the table and once again his gaze drops to my dress, and all at once I'm aware that I neglected to put on the cream slip I usually wear with it and that my knickers are purple, and my bra is red, so he can see them.

At first I'm reflexively embarrassed, but then I catch myself. It's not my problem if he doesn't like it or disapproves. It's only underwear and I very much don't dress for men any more.

I grip my drink. 'I had to open my shop there because I inherited the building when my mother died. I had a relationship breakup, and I didn't come out of it with any money, so I didn't have the luxury of choice. I deliberately don't stock any of the books you have in your inventory. Not a single title. There's no overlap. But I genuinely didn't know that people in the village used you to order in titles. I thought they would have gone through Amazon or something.'

He is silent, staring daggers at me over the top of his glasses. He's very fierce and it makes me restless. It's disturbing to be under his gaze. He stares at me like a watchmaker stares at a watch he's taking apart, piece by tiny piece.

'That's all very interesting,' he says at last, as if it's the most tedious thing he's ever heard. 'But I don't care. The fact remains that you have taken some valued customers and now I have to find some way to replace them.'

I take another sip of my drink. 'Tell me about Blackwood Books.'

'Why?'

'Because I want to know. You said yours was an historic local business and it should be respected.'

He crosses his arms over his broad chest, his expression nothing but hostile. 'Tell me, did you do any research at all before you came here?'

Heat creeps into my cheeks. 'Of course I did.'

'Then why are you asking me questions that you should already know the answers to?'

My face is hot. I take yet another sip, relishing the burn of the gin as it goes down, because I do *not* relish the way he's looking at me. It's clear that he's majorly pissed off, not to mention being very judgemental, and he does have a right to his anger if not the judgement. And I suppose I have to give him points for honesty, too. I had precious little of that with Jasper, for example.

'I get that you're angry with me,' I say doggedly. 'And you have every right to be. I . . . perhaps assumed a few things about bookselling that I shouldn't have. But if you want me to respect your business, then tell me why I should respect it. Unless it's a state secret, of course.'

He doesn't like that, not at all. His eyes glitter and his mouth hardens. 'I don't owe you anything.'

It's true, he doesn't.

We're not going to get anywhere if we're too busy sniping at each other, and I don't know why I even *want* to get somewhere with him. He's rude and cold, so why bother?

I'm not here for arguments, for negativity, for bad feelings. I left those behind in London. I'm here to reclaim my joy, to find something good in the wreckage of my life.

I want to be happy again and it's clear that I'm not going to find it arguing with the stubborn bastard across from me, so maybe I won't bother.

Maybe it's better to leave him to marinate in whatever fury he's in and disassociate myself from him entirely.

So I give him a tight smile. 'No, you don't,' I say, and pick up my drink. 'Well, you can't say I didn't try.' I get to my feet. 'Thanks for the non-conversation, Mr Blackwood. I'll leave you to your book.'

Chapter Four

*Of course you can tell me these things. You
can tell me anything you like.*

H

SEBASTIAN

She's leaving and that's a good thing. I definitely don't want
her sitting at this table in that extraordinarily sexy dress I can
see right through. She's wearing purple knickers and a red bra,
and both of them are as lacy as that dress.

I don't want to talk about my shop and I don't want to
hear her explanations as to why she stole my customers. I don't
want to hear any excuses from her at all.

Yet the moment she came into the pub, I couldn't concentrate on my book and I know I won't be able to until she leaves.
Her presence prickles over my skin, then creeps underneath it,
needling me.

I can't think why it does, because she's nothing I want, yet she needles me all the same.

I haven't been able to stop thinking about her since that moment in her shop, when I leaned in and caught her scent and saw the crystalline glint in her eyes. Which was when I realised this dance we were doing was dangerous and that I needed to stop before one of us pushed too far, and everything came crashing down.

So when she changed her front window, I didn't change mine. I left it and tried to ignore her looking in my direction every time she came out of her shop, as if she was waiting for me to respond. Waiting for me to change my window too.

I didn't give her the satisfaction.

I put her out of my head.

And I thought I'd succeeded.

So I don't know why I now say, 'Wait.' Because I can't seriously want to tell her about Blackwood Books, can I?

Her hair is loose around her shoulders, all golden curls, and in her dress with its wide belt around her hips, she looks like a Woodstock escapee. I want to touch that hair, bury my hands in it.

Christ, what a bloody cliché I am.

She hesitates, her drink in her hand.

I don't want her to sit, I don't. And I can't tell her I'm also angry because she's beautiful. I can't tell her that she's ruining my business, that her fiery temper and her bright, pretty smiles make me want to take her to bed and keep both of those things all to myself, and I'm furious about it.

I'm furious with myself for being such a basic male animal.

I'm furious with how out of control I feel around her, because if there's one thing I hate it's being out of control. I felt the same way when Dad told me that Mum was very sick and that there was nothing the doctors could do.

But I have to get some control somehow, because even I don't like my own behaviour. Being repeatedly rude to her isn't the way, especially not when the rest of the village think she's some kind of goddess descended from the heavens to dispense joy and sunbeams to the population at large.

They already think I'm aloof and distant, and since that's better than them feeling sorry for me, the poor little mite who lost his mother so early, I let them think that. But I can't have them also thinking I'm rude. That would be a killer for the business.

'My great-grandfather first opened the shop,' I say, giving her a grain of truth. 'He opened it in the thirties, so it's been in the village for over eighty years.'

Her fair brows draw together and she's still for a second, clearly weighing up whether to stay or go. And I want her to go. Yes, very definitely I want her to go.

But she doesn't.

She continues to sit at my table and she puts her drink back down. 'My great-grandmother used to live here. She probably knew him.'

'Kathryn Jones,' I say. That's well-known history here. 'They say she did *not* like my great-grandfather.'

Kate leans back in her chair and a spark of amusement

glitters in her eyes. 'Can't say I blame her. If he was anything like you.'

My muscles tighten at her humour, at the way she looks at me, but I fight my physical reaction and ignore the comment. 'So are you Kate or Kathryn?' I ask, mystified at myself and why I even care.

'Kathryn,' she says. 'But everyone calls me Kate.'

It's not lost on me, the significance of being named after our feuding great-grandparents.

'You didn't know anything about Wychtree, then?' I pick up my scotch and take a healthy sip. I can't believe I'm actually having a somewhat normal conversation with her, not when everything inside me feels so tight and hot.

'No. Mum never talked about it. The first I knew of it was after she died and I inherited the shop here. Apparently my grandmother owned it before that, and she died in 2018, so Mum only had it a few years herself. She didn't do anything with it, just let it stand empty.'

'Yes, I remember. That shop has had various incarnations over the years, but nothing ever stuck.'

Anyway, it appears we have something in common. We both lost our mothers. I feel an odd tug at that, but ignore it.

'Why books?' I'm unable to sound anything but challenging.

'Because I've always loved reading.' She gives me a little half-smile, as if she wants me to share in something, but I don't know what she wants me to share in and smiling at her is dangerous, so I don't. 'It was actually a dream of mine to open my own bookshop, but I never got around to it. I had a publishing job in London as an assistant editor instead.'

Books were never anything as insubstantial as a dream for me. Books are part of me, they're in my blood. So many people have these fantasies of what owning a bookshop is like, where they sit there all day reading and there's a cat on the counter and tea and lots of people browsing. They can't conceive of the mundane reality of stock control and ordering, and updating computer systems, doing business plans and taxes and managing debts. Of watching your orders go down because of online bookshops and e-books, and losing readers to computer games, streaming services and doomscrolling on their phones.

She was one of those people, I just know it. Building little castles in the air. Dreaming of little bookshops that look like someone's Instagram feed, created from AI. Little bookshops made of pretty pink smoke. Pipe dreams.

'Bookselling is more than just pretty shelves,' I say, knowing I sound like the snob she thinks I am and not caring. 'Bookselling is bloody hard work. It's spreadsheets and debt and knowing your customers better than they do themselves.'

'I didn't think it was easy, if that's what you're implying.' There it is, that flicker of temper in her eyes. A glitter of sparks. 'I inherited the building from Mum, but I didn't have a lot of money when I came here. I had to take on some debt to get the building up to standard. I was going to give myself a year to see if I could make it work.'

Ah. So she has a time limit, has she?

I should feel some modicum of relief at this, that if her

business tanks she'll leave. But I'm not relieved. I feel even more tense.

'What? And then you'll leave Wychtree?' I ask.

She lifts a shoulder. 'I'm not sure. I haven't thought that far ahead.' Her fingers tighten around her glass. 'You'd like that, though, wouldn't you?'

'Yes,' I say bluntly.

'Why? Is it me or the bookshop you don't like?'

There isn't any reason for me to lie, so I don't. 'Both.'

Colour creeps into her cheeks. 'I can understand you not liking the bookshop, but why me? What have I ever done to you?'

'You exist, Miss Jones,' I say succinctly, because I'm not going to explain to her why her presence annoys me so much. 'That's all you need to do.'

Her mouth firms and another silence falls.

'So why books?' she asks, throwing my question back at me.

'Because it was never going to be anything else. Books are not my "side hustle". They're my livelihood. My history. My legacy.' I sound pompous and probably ridiculous, and far too fierce, yet I can't help myself. She should know that her bookshop threatens not only my business but the very core of who I am. I can't take it lightly and I never will.

After my mother died, Dad wanted me to become a doctor, and to please him, I tried. I even got into medical school, but when that acceptance came, every ounce of my being rebelled.

He didn't care about the bookshop. He was running it into the ground, and, while me being a doctor would have been his dream for me, it wasn't my dream for myself. The only dream I ever had was my mother being still alive, and the only way for me to get anywhere close to that was to keep running the bookshop, the bookshop she loved far more than my father ever did.

Kate Jones's eyes get very wide as I hear the pompous words come out of my mouth, and her gaze intensifies. It's as if she's seeing me for the first time, and I don't like it. I've revealed too much.

I should go, so I pick up my whisky and drain the rest of it, preparing to leave, when Mrs Abbot approaches. She's one of the customers who stopped ordering from me when Miss Jones arrived, despite the fact that I'd never poured scorn on her reading material, not once.

She smiles at the both of us. 'Well, look at our two rival booksellers sharing a friendly drink.'

Miss Jones gives her back one of her own warm smiles, and watching it makes me feel restless. 'Just talking to Sebastian about his festival.'

'Oh, yes.' Mrs Abbot turns a faintly judgemental look on me. 'I wondered if you knew about it. I'm glad he's finally bringing you on board.'

Right. So it was her who told Miss Jones about my festival.

If I say I'm not bringing her on board *anywhere* then I'm going to look like an arsehole to a woman who already doesn't think much of my bookshop. And if I agree that I'm bringing Miss Jones on board, then I actually have to bring Miss Jones on board, which will defeat the purpose of my festival.

Either way I'm fucked. I'm going to look like an arsehole and I probably deserve it, but still, as ever, I'm furious.

Then Miss Jones says, 'Oh, yes, Sebastian's been lovely about it. We're just in the middle of organising a few events.' Her eyes sparkle like crystals in the sun. 'I thought we could have a romance panel and extend our book club night to guests. And I'd love to have a cosy mystery evening where everyone can bring their dogs.'

Hell. On. Earth.

Yet Mrs Abbot is smiling. 'What a wonderful idea,' she says, then turns to me, still smiling. 'That's wonderful, Sebastian. I'm so pleased. I'll get my ticket tomorrow. I'll mention it in the romance book club chat, Kate.'

'Oh, please do,' Miss Jones says.

Mrs Abbot, looking extremely satisfied, exchanges a few more words with her before excusing herself and heading to the bar.

'You can thank me later,' Miss Jones murmurs, as she sips at her drink. 'We have twenty people in our book club and they'll all want to buy tickets.'

'I am not having a romance panel,' I force out from between gritted teeth. 'And I am definitely *not* having bloody dogs in my shop.'

'They won't be at your bloody shop,' she says. 'They'll be in mine. And so will the romance panel. And if you don't want them, then you'll have twenty less tickets for your festival, and twenty more for mine.'

She's incorrigible.

She's impossible.

I want to get up and walk away and never speak to her again.

I want to reach over the table, drag her into my lap, and kiss her senseless.

The two desires are so entirely at odds that I'm left paralysed, so I do nothing but sit there like a bloody idiot instead.

Then she does something even more egregious.

She leans forward, elbows on the table, her expression full of entreaty. 'Look. We both want more customers and arguing about who stole what from whom and throwing accusations around isn't helping either of us. We don't like each other, fine, but we're both adults. We're both professionals. We could be helping each other's businesses instead.'

She's so very honest. There's no guile to her, no guardedness. Nothing I can use as an excuse to push her away or rebuff her. If I told her to piss off now, which every part of me wants to do, I would definitely be the bad guy.

I would be the petulant child having a tantrum to her calm, measured adult. She is being the bigger person and I hate it.

It costs me to say it, but I know she's right, so I force it out. 'How?'

This time it's worse, because this time the sparkle in her eyes isn't for Mrs Abbot or one of her other customers that she charms the pants off.

This time the sparkle is for me.

'We can have separate events,' she says, glittering like a diamond. 'I'll do all the genre stuff and you do all the literary high-brow stuff. But we'll get both kinds of readers coming to the event, and all the literary orders can go through you, and I'll do the genre orders. I'd love to be involved in this and I don't have the reach that you do, or the history. And, you know, genre readers do read literary books too. I can send them your way, and you can send literary readers who enjoy a good thriller or romance to me.'

It hits me right in the chest, that sparkle. Like a bullet.

She loves what she's doing, I can see it in her eyes. It might have started as a dream she's been chasing, but it means something to her and I have to concede that she's put her all into her shop.

She's drawn people to her and they like her; they like her books.

It's a tough business, bookselling in general, and even tougher coming into a small village as a relative outsider. And I haven't been welcoming. I've been actively hostile towards her, which isn't fair of me.

Yes, she's taken away some of my customers and I'm angry about it, but now she's offering me an olive branch, and while part of me wants to refuse, I'd be a fool not to take it.

What she says about a shared festival sounds . . . good. For both of us.

How extremely irritating.

'Fine.' I hear the petulant note in my voice and don't like it one bit. 'But there will still be no dogs in my shop.'

She gives me a smile, a real one. Like the one she gave that adolescent boy in her ridiculous shop. Like the one she gives to her customers, as if she's pleased to see them and couldn't think of anything better than to have them in her place of business. Like I've given her a gift she hadn't expected.

That hits me straight in the chest too.

'Okay,' she says. 'No dogs for Mr Blackwood. So noted.' She picks up her gin and tonic, sparkling away like a little star. 'This is great. Let's chat tomorrow about it and we can start to put some more plans in place.'

Her excitement should be infectious but all I feel now is hungry and it isn't for food. I should be able to put it to one side the way I've always done, but it's difficult with her. It's going to be especially difficult if she's going to involve herself in my festival.

I never dip my pen in the company ink – or the village ink, to be precise. It's too difficult here. Especially when everyone knows that Blackwood men can't keep a woman to save their lives. My great-grandfather's wife left him. My grandfather's wife also left him. And I'm sure it was only pure chance that my mother died before she had the opportunity to leave my father.

Luck with the ladies does not run in my family and I have no desire to test that luck anyway. So I take my appetites elsewhere.

Unfortunately, the object of that appetite is sitting opposite me and calmly talking about the two of us working together as if I was a plank of wood with no sexual interest in her whatsoever.

I fucking wish I were a plank of wood.

'Excellent,' I say, meaning the opposite and deciding that now is a good time to leave, since I can't bear sitting here with her any longer.

But then, much to my horror, she reaches out and pushes aside the menu that I used to cover the book I was reading when she came into the pub, and glances at it. 'Oh,' she says. 'I wondered.' Her eyes sparkle even more. 'I didn't spot you for being a science fiction fan.'

I'm appalled at myself for letting slip such a basic secret and even more appalled at my own embarrassment that she found out what I was reading.

Because I meant what I said: I'm not a literary snob. After my mother died I started reading science fiction and dystopian books, because they took me right out of my reality and put me into a completely different one. Where I could forget about my grief at losing not only my mother to cancer but also my father to the bottle that he fell headfirst into after her death.

I still read those books when I need to escape, but it's been my little secret for years. Not that anyone else would care, but I knew Miss Jones would and, sure enough, I can see that she's pleased, as if she's scored a point off me.

I want to show her I could score a point off her too, and maybe in a way that we'd both enjoy, but I'm not going down that path.

Instead, I calmly pick up my book. 'Yes,' I say. 'Sometimes I like to read something different.'

I don't say goodbye.

I get to my feet and stroll out.

Chapter Five

All the village says you're reserved, but you aren't.
There's a fire in you. They don't see it, but I do.

C

KATE

I'm super-excited, I can't lie. Mrs Abbot was a goddess to swan into the pub last night and basically shame Sebastian into including me in his festival. He didn't want to. His reluctance was obvious, his bowing to the inevitable ungracious. But bow he did.

And not only that, but I managed to get some conversation out of him.

That, too, was reluctant and ungracious, and it felt like getting blood out of a particularly hard stone, but he gave it to me nonetheless.

Now I'm in Portable Magic and keen to head on over to

Blackwood Books to have our little planning chat, but the sign on his front door has been turned to 'Closed' all morning and there's no sign he's in there.

It's extremely aggravating and, really, just like him.

Then Aisling comes in with a box of vegan doughnuts and sets them on the counter, giving me a knowing look as she does so. 'I saw you last night. At the Arms. With Tall, Dark and Brooding.'

'I'd rather be Mrs Peacock in the library with the wrench,' I mutter. 'And have Sebastian Blackwood be the victim.'

Aisling shakes her red curls back and rolls her eyes. I've complained to her about him before. More than once. 'Sure, sure. You hate him so much and yet you can't leave him alone.'

I pull a face. 'It's not like that.'

'Of course it isn't. Just like he isn't super-hot.'

I ignore this in favour of flipping open the box of doughnuts and examining them carefully. 'I saw you too, you know. Having a quiet drink with your husband.'

Aisling smiles. 'A surprise date. Ben organised a babysitter.'

'Nice.' I pick out a custardy lemony doughnut. 'He's a keeper.'

'If you think I'm going to be distracted by you telling me what I already know about my husband, you're wrong.' She leans a hip against the counter. 'Come on, take pity on a poor woman with a toddler, a business, a husband and no life. Gimme some exciting single-life goss.'

I met Aisling the first day I came to Wychtree. I wandered into the café she'd just bought, desperate for a coffee, and we got to talking, since we were both starting up new businesses at the same time.

She's an incredible baker and supplies 'plant-based delicacies' to Lindsey's bakery as well as her own café. I've been trying to emulate her approach to the bakery with Sebastian and his shop, i.e. show how businesses can be supportive of each other and not each other's competition.

Most people don't want the vegan treats she makes, so she also provides the more usual ones, but she says that the vegan side of the business is growing, especially in the summer when the tourists come.

I love her doughnuts especially and I can't get enough of them, while, in return, she's a fanatical reader of mysteries, and gets me to order at least ten every couple of months. She also pins bookshop events to her noticeboard in the café and has a little stand of books on her counter that I supply, which does a fairly brisk trade.

She's dry and funny and I like her a lot, but I haven't told her much about my life before I came to Wychtree. I haven't wanted to get into it, even though I know the gossip mill here has gone into overdrive on the subject anyway.

She does know about my family history, though. The locals always do.

'There's no goss,' I tell her, and bite into my doughnut.

'Bullshit,' she says. 'He couldn't take his eyes off you the whole time. Like a wolf with a rabbit.'

I swallow my bite of doughnut. It's delicious as always, but I give her a glare. 'I'm not a bloody rabbit.'

Aisling raises a brow. 'Aren't you? You were certainly giving him big eyes last night.'

I redden. 'I was trying to have a normal conversation with him that didn't involve us arguing for a change. Also, I kind of wanted to know if it was me he didn't like or the bookshop.'

'Both, I would imagine.'

I sigh. 'I get the bookshop, I really do. But I don't understand why he doesn't like me. I'm not that bad. He's not like that to everyone else, is he?'

'You mean, cold and aloof?'

'And rude, don't forget rude.'

Aisling's mouth twitches in amusement. 'I'm afraid he reserves that one just for you. He's not rude to everyone else. Aloof, yes, and reserved. But that's the Blackwoods for you. They've always been like that.'

'Why?'

'First of all they're men. Second, they're emotionally constipated. And third, every woman any of them have ever hooked up with has either left or died.' She gives me a solemn look. 'Mrs Bennet says they're cursed.'

'Mrs Bennet would.' I lean on the counter, fascinated at this insight, because it's news to me. 'Seriously, though?'

'Sebastian's namesake, his great-grandfather, had his wife walk out on him not three years into their marriage. Then his grandmother hated the village, and left his grandfather for London after a few years, and then Sebastian's mother died when he was about ten. I went to school with him, so I remember it.

Village gossip said she would have left his father eventually if she hadn't died.'

I'm appalled. And intrigued.

I hadn't known he'd lost his mother as a kid. That must have been really tough. 'Oh no,' I murmur. 'That's awful.'

'Yeah. Then George Blackwood, his dad, started drinking. It was all bad, really. I don't know the details, but I heard that George was going to lose the bookshop, so Sebastian took over and borrowed massively to keep it going.'

I remember him last night, telling me fiercely that books were his livelihood, his history, his legacy. Making me want to cringe at my burblings about opening my own bookshop. Mine had felt like a cherished dream, while his . . .

His was a vocation. A calling.

He was a priest and his god was books.

'You're getting that look in your eye,' Aisling says.

I redden further. 'What look?'

'The look of a woman who discovers a man's tragic back-story and is now one hundred per cent more interested in him than she was already.'

I make a disdainful sound and take another bite out of the doughnut. 'Come on, Ash,' I say, my mouth full. 'We're failing the Bechdel test.'

Aisling grins. 'Mrs Abbot told me last night that you're now going to be part of the book festival. How did that happen?'

I had a little rant to her a few days ago about how Sebastian left me out of planning the festival, and how annoyed I was, so she knows my feelings on the subject. She also knows that I've been in the process of planning my own.

'Oh, she basically shamed him into it by assuming he'd asked me already and so he had to agree, otherwise he would have looked like a dick in front of her.'

'Did he retract it after she'd gone?'

'No, actually. He didn't. He was pissed off, I saw it in his eyes, but he agreed.' He knew that the ideas I'd given him were good ones, and even now, I feel again the traitorous little echo of warmth that thought gave me.

As if I actually cared about his opinion.

How ridiculous.

'Points to him then, I guess,' Aisling says.

I want to ask her more questions. About the Blackwood family and about what he'd been like as a kid when she'd gone to school with him, but that would render all my protestations that I wasn't interested null and void.

Then just as I'm about to change the subject, a movement out the front window of my shop catches my eye and I see Sebastian stepping into Blackwood Books.

Finally.

I feel the oddest little shiver of anticipation, but I tell myself it's the anticipation of planning. Definitely nothing to do with him and being in his fierce, electric presence.

'Gotta go, Ash,' I say to my friend. 'I've been waiting to talk to him over there about some ideas for the festival, and he's just come back.'

Aisling grins and, after making me promise to tell her all about it later, she disappears out the door.

For a second I'm half tempted to pop upstairs and check the bathroom mirror to see if I've got lipstick on my teeth or something, but then I tell myself sternly I'm not buying into that. I'm done with prettying up myself for a guy, and especially not *that* guy.

However, I do pause beside the Science Fiction/Fantasy section of my shop and peruse the shelves, because after my discovery last night that he was reading a science fiction novel, and after he'd looked so annoyed that I'd discovered it, I kind of want to give him a gift.

A gift that will annoy him, true, but one that he'll appreciate in the end, I hope. After all, genre is my area of expertise and I read avidly from all of them.

I take the latest Murderbot book, by Martha Wells, off the shelf, because it's just come in, and if he hasn't read it already then he should, and then I step out of my shop, cross the road to Blackwood Books and approach the door.

The sign still says 'Closed'.

Of all the . . .

But there's movement inside and, when I peer through the glass, I can see him standing behind his antique oak counter, talking on his phone.

Well, he may not be officially open, but he's there, and I want to talk to him, so I push open the door.

So I'm just in time to hear him yell '*Fuck!*', and aim a kick at the empty wire rubbish bin beside the counter. It bounces, then rolls across the shop floor before bumping gently up against my feet.

I stare at him, absolutely riveted.

I'm not afraid of his display of male fury. What I love is seeing cold and controlled Sebastian Blackwood lose his temper completely.

Then I love it even more when he realises I'm standing there and I've witnessed his little tantrum, and his impressive jaw hardens, a muscle jumping at the side. His eyes burn like twin gas flames.

He raises a hand and shoves it through his short black hair.

'Apologies,' he says stiffly. 'You were not meant to see that.'

'I imagine not.' I pick up the bin and carry it over to the desk. 'But, sadly for you, I'm now curious. What happened?'

'Nothing.' The word is terse as he tucks his phone back into the pocket of his black trousers. He's steadfastly not looking at me.

'Do you always kick bins across the room when nothing happens?'

The muscle in the side of his jaw leaps again. 'Frequently.'

'Did you just make a joke?'

He finally lifts his gaze to mine and I catch the intensity in it head-on. 'What are you doing here, Miss Jones?'

It's annoying how my breath catches, but I try to ignore that. 'I'm here to talk about the festival,' I say cheerily. 'We were going to, remember?'

'Ah, yes. Right.' He glances away again. 'Well, I can't do it now. I have too much to do.'

'Is it related to that temper tantrum?' It's probably unwise of me to ask, but what the hell. If he didn't want anyone to know he was upset, he shouldn't have kicked that bin across his shop.

He glances at me yet again, his mouth in a hard line, and all at once I wonder how I'd ever thought of him as cold, because he's not. He's a bloody house on fire and the flames are licking out the windows.

'Just tell me,' I say. 'You look like you want to chew through a wall.'

He lets out a breath at that and runs a hand through his hair yet again, and I can't help the flicker of desire that shoots through me. Because he was already hot and now, all angry and fierce, he's even hotter, and I like it.

It's honest. It's passionate. And it's an obvious sign that he cares about whatever is making him so angry.

Jasper wasn't honest. He lied all the time and he certainly didn't care. Not about anything, not even me.

'Fucking James Wyatt has pulled out of the festival,' Sebastian finally spits. 'There was a scheduling clash and now he can't come. James Wyatt is—'

'Yes,' I interrupt. 'I know who James Wyatt is, I'm not stupid. I have been staring at your Booker Prize-winning window for the past couple of weeks now.' It makes sense, then, his rage, and I'm not surprised. You don't want your headliner pulling out of your carefully curated event at such short notice.

He glowers at me. 'If he can't come, it's going to be a disaster. I might as well call it off right now.'

I shouldn't smile, that'll only make things worse, but I can't help it. He looks so angry and he's being so dramatic, and it's adorable.

'That's right,' he says shortly. 'Laugh. The death of my bookshop is fucking hilarious.'

I have the oddest urge then to put my hand on his brow and smooth away the lines there, and it's so strong that my fingers itch. I curl them into a fist instead, but I don't stop smiling.

'I hear the Wychtree Dramatic Society is doing *Hamlet* this year,' I say dryly. 'You should audition, Mr Blackwood. I think you'd be a shoo-in after that performance.'

His glower becomes a scowl. 'You don't understand. This shop is—'

'Your livelihood, your history, your legacy. Yes. I remember.'

'Then you'll know why this is a disaster. And it will affect you too.'

He's not, unfortunately, wrong.

James Wyatt would have been a great drawcard and it would certainly have given the festival some of the cachet that we need. As much as it galls me to admit it, you do need a big name to grab the crowds, especially if you're not in a major city.

But just then I have a thought and, quite frankly, it's brilliant. I'm even impressed with myself, and I haven't been impressed with myself for longer than I'd care to admit.

I might have left publishing behind, but I still have my contacts, and while I didn't edit many big names, I did work with one. I didn't acquire her or anything. I was only her point-person when it came to administration, and worked with her on a couple of her later titles, but she was great, and we got on like a house on fire.

Lisa Underwood. She wrote a breakout hit called *Colours*, a sweeping romance that managed to hit the nirvana of publishing: cross-genre audiences. Mainstream fiction readers loved it, so did literary readers, so did romance readers, etcetera, etcetera.

It was the biggest book of the year, hit all kinds of bestseller lists, and garnered glowing reviews everywhere. A movie was optioned and that was a hit too.

In short, she was huge, and we still sometimes email each other, and now I'm wondering if she would want to come to tiny little Wychtree, come to our festival, be our headliner.

She might not, but . . . she might.

I hold up a hand. 'Stop. Wait right there. Don't move.'

Sebastian gives me Blue Steel (if you haven't seen *Zoolander*, I can't help you). 'What?'

'I might have an idea,' I say, and smile. 'I presume you've heard of Lisa Underwood?'

Chapter Six

*You are so beautiful. It's a cliché, I know, but
you quite literally take my
breath away.*

H

SEBASTIAN

Of course I've heard of Lisa Underwood. I read *Colours*. Who in the entire world hasn't? It was a runaway hit and one of my biggest sellers, and despite my initial misgivings when I first read it, it wasn't bad.

But I have no idea what Lisa Underwood has to do with my festival.

A festival that will be a disaster because of *fucking* James Wyatt.

I couldn't believe it when his publicist rang this morning to give me the news. I was less than polite to her. And when he called me just now to give me his apologies personally, I almost bit through my tongue restraining the urge to tell him that he's just *fucked my fucking festival fucking fuck*.

Yes, I kicked the bloody bin.

No, I shouldn't have kicked the bloody bin.

And I was *extremely* unhappy to have Miss Kate Jones, so perky and pretty, witnessing my toddler meltdown.

We're men of control, the Blackwoods. We keep our emotions locked down and it's a point of pride. There's nothing more embarrassing than being out of control emotionally, so we do other things to compensate.

My great-grandfather lost himself in books, the way I do.

My grandfather liked betting shops.

My father liked the bottle.

We all have our vices and mine is to let fly sometimes in the privacy of my own home. Or my shop. When no one's in it. *Privacy* being the operative word.

Now Miss Jones is standing on the other side of the counter looking like the cat who's got the cream, as if my outburst hadn't mattered and hadn't happened, and fuck me but that's a good look on her.

She's wearing (I can't help but notice because I always notice) a bright blue dress with frills and flounces that barely grazes her knee, and silly little high-heeled sandals that are somehow also sexy as hell. Her hair is loose again and I wish it wasn't because it's perfect for gathering into a fist, and she's glittering in that way she does. And I want her.

I'm appalled at myself, the way I was appalled the first

time I saw her six months ago, when she leaned in to peer through the window of what would be her shop. She'd been wearing golden yellow then, a dress that clung to her figure, and her hair had been loose then too, and somehow I'd lost my mind.

It was as if a ray of sunshine had taken human form and I'd been in darkness my whole life.

'Yes,' I say. Tersely. Because I'm always terse with her, I realise now. Because I can't be any other way. I've never met a woman I've wanted so badly and, even now, even amidst the wreckage of my festival, all I can think of is how much I want to kiss her. 'Of course I've heard of Lisa Underwood.'

'Well,' Miss Jones says grandly. 'I happen to know her quite well. I used to work with her in my former job. We got to know each other and I still email her on occasion.' She sparkles just like she did last night in the pub. 'I could ask her if she wants to come to All the World's a Page as our headliner. What do you think?'

I think it's ridiculous. It's outlandish.

It's . . . good.

No. Not just good. It's *fucking brilliant*.

Lisa Underwood is the perfect meeting of genre and literary fiction. A genuine cross-genre sensation.

Literary types might look at her askance, but . . . No one can argue with her sales or her talent. She's not James Wyatt, but then James Wyatt isn't her, and the one thing she has that he doesn't is reach.

Miss Jones raises an eyebrow. 'Well? Are you thinking of

some kind of snobby putdown or are you astounded by my brilliance?'

'Both,' I say, and it's no less than the truth. A snobby put-down to distance her because I *am* astounded by her brilliance and all I want to do is pull her close and kiss her sweet mouth.

I am a bloody idiot. Of epic proportions.

'But I can't deny that it is a brilliant suggestion,' I say.

'Why, thank you, good sir,' she says, and gives the most adorable curtsey.

I am also so, *so* fucked.

At that moment the bell above the door chimes and Dan comes in.

Dan is one of my closest friends – I should say my *only* close friend – and he's the Wychtree GP. We were at school together and we both applied to get into medicine and, while I dropped out, he didn't.

He admires me for it, though I can't think why, since he makes far more money than I do. He always says he went into medicine because he couldn't think of anything better to do and wishes he had a vocation, like me. A vocation, though, is a curse. It rides you hard, sinks its claws in: no matter how badly you want to throw it off, you can't. It's deep in your cells, in your blood, and, yes, like I said, you're fucked.

Dan is smiley and pleasant, unlike me (I would have made a terrible doctor), and he smiles pleasantly at Kate as he approaches the counter. 'Morning, Kate,' he says warmly, then, to me, much more casually, 'Morning, Bas.'

Dan, like me, is single.

I find myself bristling at the way he's smiling at her for absolutely no reason. 'Miss Jones and I were just discussing the festival,' I say, with far more belligerence than the situation warrants, especially with my best friend. 'I'll text you later.'

Dan gives me a surprised look, as well he might since I'm just about biting his head off. 'No drama,' he says. 'Only wanted to see if you were up for a pint tonight.'

'Yes, yes.' I am brisk. Too brisk. 'I'll text you.'

He frowns slightly, then glances at Miss Jones, and *of course* he knows exactly what's going on with me now. This is the problem with close friends. They know you far too well.

Miss Jones is standing there glittering and sparkling, giving him the widest, brightest of smiles. 'Did you get the latest newsletter?' she asks him. 'I've just got a new shipment of thrillers you might enjoy.'

Dan's smile abruptly disappears. As well it might.

So . . . there is a *newsletter*. And he's subscribed to it.

'Traitor,' I mutter.

Dan looks sheepish, while Kate glances from him to me and back again, as if she has no idea what's going on. Then it dawns.

'Oh,' she says. '*Oh.*'

I am rigid with offence. 'You order books from her? Fucking hell, Dan.'

He continues to look sheepish for about a nanosecond longer, then he shrugs. 'The newsletter is how I find out about all the new releases. It's really great. I like a thriller, you know that.'

Miss Jones is watching us and, to give her credit, she's

looking a bit sheepish too. 'Sorry,' she mutters, though who to I can't tell. 'I'd better go. I need to find Lisa's email address and email her.'

She leaves, and I'm sure it's my imagination that my bookshop is a little less bright now she's not in it.

'Okay,' Dan says, giving me a sly grin. '*Now* I get why you've been in such a foul temper the last couple of months.'

I refuse to engage in *that* conversation. 'I'm in debt up to my eyeballs and you're ordering books? From *her*?' I know I'm repeating myself but I don't care.

'Yes.' Dan is unbothered. 'Have you ever tried to find new thrillers online? It's a bloody nightmare.'

I grind my teeth. 'Fine. But you should order through me.'

He lifts a shoulder. 'I order my medical books through you and you know how bloody expensive those things are.'

'Still. You're *my* friend.' I sound like a child. This is what she's reduced me to. It's infuriating.

'You like her.' Dan's gaze is very direct. 'Don't you?'

'Dan—'

'Don't think I didn't notice you being all territorial the moment I smiled at her.' He's grinning now. 'Fucking hell, mate. You're almost bloody in love.'

'*Daniel*—'

'I get it, believe me. She's gorgeous.' He shoves his hands in the pockets of his trousers and looks at the ceiling. 'Maybe I should ask her out for a—'

'Don't you fucking dare,' I growl, rising to his bait despite knowing full well he's taking the piss.

'Really, though,' Dan continues, unfazed. 'The real question is why you're holding back, because it's clear you are. You're a grumpy bastard, Bas, but you've never been this feral.'

No, he's right. I haven't.

I make a conscious effort to release the tension in my muscles. I'll probably have to go for a run later and then have the mother of all cold showers.

'Wyatt pulled out,' I say shortly. 'Which is not helping my mood.'

Dan frowns, because he knows what this means. 'Shit. That's tough. Why?'

'Some kind of scheduling clash. It doesn't matter why, though. He's not coming and I've lost my headliner.'

'What are you going to do?'

It galls me to say it, but I do. 'Miss Jones—'

'You mean Kate.'

'*Miss Jones* has an idea.'

Dan grins at my stupidity. 'Fine. *Miss Jones*, then. What's the idea?'

'She apparently used to work with Lisa Underwood. You know who that is?'

'Yeah, course. *Colours*, right? I read it. Liked it.'

'So does the entire world. Miss Jones is going to email her to see if she wants to come here.'

Dan's brown eyes widen. 'That would be a coup.'

'It would.'

'How well does Kate know her? I mean, would she want to come here? And also . . .' Dan pauses. 'She must cost a bomb.'

I shove a distracted hand through my hair, because I'm only now thinking that. She's a major, global sensation and no doubt charges thousands for appearances. More than James Wyatt. More than I've got.

'I don't know,' I say. 'But, yes, she probably would. And I don't have that kind of money. I've already invested far too much in this bloody festival and I don't have any extra cash to spare.'

'What about the council?'

'They've allocated as much funding as they can. They don't have any more.'

And they don't. They were already generous with what they gave me, because they know how much it'll benefit Wychtree. But I can't ask them for more.

I drop my hand. 'There's not much here I can offer her as an incentive, either. It's not a major festival. It's a small local event and she's not going to do it for free since it's not like she needs the exposure.'

'Maybe a small local festival is what she prefers? Some people like a more personal experience.'

He's not wrong. Then again . . .

'She must get invitations to speak everywhere, at festivals larger and more interesting than ours. Why would she choose to come to us over something else?'

'Good point.' He glances down at his watch. 'Hold that thought. Got to get back to the clinic. Let's discuss at the Arms tonight, yeah?'

I nod and then, after he's gone, I spend some time pacing pointlessly.

Across the road, a group of women are pushing vast prams into Portable Magic, gossiping and laughing. No one is coming into Blackwood Books. No one at all.

I curse under my breath, pacing some more.

There's no reason I can think of why Lisa Underwood would want to come to Wychtree. None. Not even as a professional favour. I don't know her from a bar of soap, but I'm guessing she has publicists to the eyeballs and that they'll be dragons about what events she'll agree to.

And I can't pay her.

The money I would have used for Wyatt I'm now going to have to use to pay back the debts I already have, not to mention the cost of changing all the marketing.

I reach the shelves, turn around and pace back to the front window.

My brain is falling over itself, trying to find alternative authors who would work, and not coming up with any. They're either too famous to cold call, or they're not famous enough to generate the kind of ticket sales I need.

Lisa Underwood is our best bet. But how can we get her to come? For nothing. What does Wychtree and Blackwood Books have to offer that she couldn't get at a book fair? Or any of the other literary festivals going on around the country at the moment?

I'm mid-pace when I notice something sitting on the top of my counter.

It's a book.

I go over and glance down at it.

Science fiction. Martha Wells.

I've been meaning to order her latest SF, because I read the last Murderbot book and enjoyed it immensely. But what with the festival organisation, I haven't got around to placing the order.

Where did it come from, though? I don't have any science fiction in the shop, and it's not from Dan because I didn't see him put anything down and he doesn't like SF anyway.

Was it a customer from yesterday?

I pick the book up and turn it over. There's a price sticker on the bottom of the cover with 'Portable Magic' printed in a jaunty font, complete with magic wand.

Instinctively I glance out of the front window and there she is, Miss Kate Jones. She's standing in her own shopfront window and looking at me, looking at the book.

She mouths, 'For you.'

Then she smiles. And waves.

Chapter Seven

*I wish I didn't feel this way about you. Life would be so
much easier if I didn't. But, if I said I felt nothing,
that would be a lie. And I can lie to anyone but you.*

C

KATE

That night, I sit cross-legged on my little sofa with my laptop
on my knees and compose an email to Lisa Underwood.

We haven't corresponded for a while and I don't want to
immediately barge in with a request for a favour, so I keep it
short, more of a 'Hi, how are you, what are you doing?' kind
of thing. When she emails me back I'll ask about visiting
Wychtree, and would she like to come to our festival.

I feel a bit awkward about asking her for a favour, a little
bit like I'm cashing in, which is exactly what I'm doing, of
course. And she gets those requests all the time, and I know,

because I used to chat to her publicist at lunch back when I worked in publishing.

Requests for panels and talks and interviews from every tiny, two-bit literary festival all over the world. Lisa is generous and attended quite a few, but in the end she decided she didn't have the energy for all of them, so, nowadays, she only attends the big-deal festivals.

I'm hoping she'll decide to come here because of our personal connection. I'm also hoping that the money Sebastian was going to use to pay James Wyatt will be enough to entice her. It might not, but that's where the personal connection will come in. Hopefully.

I stare at the screen and the email I've half written, wondering if I've made a mistake. Wondering if I shouldn't have blurted my great idea straight out to Sebastian without checking if Lisa was even interested first.

He'd been so angry, and for some reason I'd wanted to help him, and . . . okay, yes, I admit it: I kind of wanted to impress him too. Show him that I had literary connections, that I wasn't just romance novels and fluff and dogs.

Jasper used to say that about my editing job. He'd poke gentle fun at the books I used to edit, tease me about the 'girlie books' and 'mummy porn'. And when I'd protest, he'd tell me he was just joking and that I needed to stop being so sensitive.

I suppose that's why I've been so aggravated by Sebastian's disdain. Then again, he's never poured actual scorn on the books I stock or teased me about my shop. In fact, when I mentioned Lisa, the look in his eyes flared as soon as I suggested her and . . . ugh. It's galling to have to confess, but I liked the way he looked at me. As if he was truly seeing me for the first time.

I scowl at the laptop screen in response, irritated with the shiver that passes over my skin. Okay, he's hot, and when he looks at me that way, he's even hotter, but he's still snobby and rude. And I didn't appreciate the way he got all bristly when Doctor Dan said hello to me. As if Dan was encroaching on his territory or something.

God, men are stupid.

Not that I'm any better, to be fair, since I did get a petty sort of satisfaction at Sebastian's face when he'd realised Dan had signed up to the Portable Magic newsletter. Mean of me, considering it's clear that the two of them are friends. Still, that's their problem, not mine, and I'm definitely not going to tell Sebastian that Dan has ordered quite a few thrillers from me over the past couple of months already.

Dan's a nice guy. I haven't had much to do with him since coming here, but he's always very pleasant. Which makes it weird that Sebastian seems to be his friend. I can't imagine Sebastian having friends, if I'm honest.

I finish up the email and send it, shut the laptop, then pick up my phone, ready to text Sebastian to tell him that I've sent the email to Lisa, when I realise I don't have his number. Damn. I thought I had it. And I'm going to need it if I'm going to be part of his festival.

It could wait until tomorrow, I guess, but as you might have noticed, I'm impatient. Also, I remember that he and Doctor Dan arranged to meet for a pint tonight. I could quickly pop along to the Arms, tell him about Lisa and grab his number off him.

I don't want to know what he thought of the gift I left on his counter. I really don't. And I wasn't watching through my front window to see his reaction. I definitely didn't feel a single thing when I mouthed 'for you' at him, and he stared at me as if I'd done something extraordinary. Even when he nodded back in silent thanks, I wasn't actively *thrilled*. No thrills happening for this girl, nope.

So me wanting to go to the pub right this minute has definitely got nothing whatsoever to do with any of that.

Still, I can't resist a quick glance in the mirror to make sure my hair – loose again today – looks good, and the flouncy, pretty blue dress I'm wearing (another favourite of mine) doesn't have too many wrinkles in it.

Stupid to care about my appearance when there's no one I'm trying to impress, but, you know, a girl's got her pride. Also, I'm secretly pleased with how *un*polished I look, since Jasper was not a fan of OTT femininity. He thought it looked vapid.

Well, I wasn't a fan of his laid-back, friendly-verging-on-unctuous manner. I thought it bordered on sleazy, so I guess we're even.

I slip out into the warm evening and make my way to the Arms.

It's Friday night, which means it's darts night and there's a good crowd of people all clustered around the dartboard and cheering. Mrs Bennet is up and she's the darts champion of Wychtree, eyeing up the bullseye as she gets ready to throw.

I'm not here for darts, though, so I take a look around, trying to spot Sebastian and Dan, and I see them in the snug by the fire. They both have pints in front of them and Sebastian is doing his usual glower, sitting back in his seat with his arms folded across his broad chest.

I suddenly realise that he's wearing jeans tonight, and a plain black T-shirt, instead of his usual trousers and business shirt, and I'm abruptly gripped by the most intense wave of . . .

No. No. It's definitely not hunger. It can't be.

I've seen a man in jeans before, plenty of times. Jeans are great, big fan. But I never feel as though I've been punched in the gut at the sight of them the way I do now.

The cotton of his T-shirt is pulled over his muscled chest, making it clear that there isn't an ounce of fat on him, while the denim of his worn jeans clings to his powerful thighs . . .

My face flames. I look away, fussing with the strap of my bag, trying to get control of myself.

Good God, he's just a man and I don't like him, even if I respect his commitment to books. Really, it's only been a few months since I left Jasper, and then I swore to myself that I was going man-free for life. My heart was already cracked after Mum died, and when I realised how stupid I'd been to let such a bastard as him into my life, it shattered completely. These past two months, in the healing space of my bookshop, it's been slowly mending, but I want to limit all the ways it could break or crack again. Most especially when Sebastian Blackwood has heartbreak written all over him.

Fully in command of myself again, I turn back to the two men and make my way over to where they're sitting.

Dan sees me first and smiles, then darts a glance at his friend, who tenses the moment he spots me. His blue gaze narrows, but he doesn't move.

'Hello again,' I say to Dan. 'Sorry to interrupt.'

Dan grins hugely, as if something about my presence is amusing. 'Oh no, not at all, Kate. It's a *pleasure* to see you again. In fact, I was wanting to ask if you'll have dinner—'

'Yes, Miss Jones?' Sebastian barks, sending Dan a vicious glance. 'What is it?'

Dan leans back in his chair, looking smug.

Clearly some kind of guy thing is happening, so I ignore it.

'I've emailed Lisa,' I say to Sebastian. 'Thought you should know. Also, I don't have your mobile number and I'll probably need it. You know, for the festival.'

'It couldn't wait till tomorrow?'

I give him a look. He's still *very* grumpy and I get it: not having James Wyatt is a blow. But I've got my idea, one that'll be even better if we manage to pull it off, and while I know Lisa isn't exactly the literary star of his dreams, she's not no one either. Also, he said my idea was brilliant, so what is his problem?

'No.' I give him a saccharine smile. 'It couldn't.'

'Fine,' he says irritably. 'What's your number? I'll send you a text.'

I tell him and my phone duly chirps with a notification.

'Oh, look,' Dan says suddenly. 'There's Gerry. I need to speak with him about . . . um . . . Arsenal in the semis.' He gets up from his seat. 'Here, Kate. Why don't you sit and keep Heathcliff company?'

'Don't you dare,' Sebastian growls, whether to Dan or me, I'm not sure.

Dan doesn't seem to hear, striding off towards Gerry, who owns the butcher's and who apparently supports Arsenal, which is weird because I thought he was a Spurs fan.

Still, I plonk myself down in his seat, regardless of the hostile expression on Sebastian's face. 'Also,' I say, before Sebastian can get a word in, 'I saw you pick up the Martha Wells. Have you read her? I thought you might like it.'

'I've read her,' Sebastian says in clipped tones. 'Not the new one, though.'

'You like the Murderbot books?'

His hard mouth twitches slightly.

'You do,' I go on, because I'm sure that's what that twitch signifies. He *does* like them and he doesn't want to admit that to me. Silly man. 'In that case you'll love the new one. It's great.'

There's a moment of silence and I watch the visible effort it takes him to dredge some politeness up from somewhere.

'Thank you,' he says, as stiff as he was this morning in his shop. 'I'll try it.'

'There,' I say, twinkling at him. 'That wasn't so hard, was it?'

The politeness is instantly gone, leaving behind it that

blue-eyed glower. It shouldn't look so good on him, but it does, and I'm the most basic of women that I find it as sexy as hell.

'So, what did you say to her?' Sebastian asks, blunt as the end of a spade. 'To Lisa. In your email.'

'Oh, I didn't ask her about the festival straight away. It was a more "Hi, how are you?" kind of thing. When she responds, I'll ask.'

'And how are you going to get her to come?' He pauses a moment and that fascinating muscle in his jaw leaps. 'I don't have any money to pay her.'

'What? But I thought James—'

'I was going to pay him. But now he's pulling out, the marketing will have to change and his fee will have to pay for that, and for the other debts I've already got.'

My heart sinks, not going to lie. 'I didn't know you were that cash strapped.'

'Festivals are expensive, Miss Jones.'

That I *did* know.

'Well,' I say brightly, because he's starting to look like he should be haunting the battlements of some castle somewhere, given the amount of brood pouring off him. 'I'll ask her if she'll come as a favour.'

'Oh? Is she that much of a good friend that she'll come to this tiny village festival for absolutely zero payment?'

'Take it down a notch, Hamlet. It's not that bad. Maybe we can think of other things that would make her come here. Writers like inspiration and Wychtree's got a lot of character, a lot of history.'

Sebastian stares at me a second then leans forward, his gaze pinning me. 'What's she like?'

I'm taken aback by his sudden intensity and I'm aware my heart is beating a little too fast for comfort. I try to ignore it. 'You mean as a person?'

'Yes.'

'I know she *does* like history and she's an incurable romantic. I think she'd like Wychtree quite a bit if she came.'

Sebastian is still staring at me, but I have the feeling that this time he's not seeing me. Whatever is going on in his beautiful head, I can virtually see his brain ticking over.

'You have an idea?' I ask him.

'I do. But I'm not sure if it'll be enough to tempt her.'

'What is it?' I realise only belatedly that I have leaned in too, my elbows on the table top.

'I read *Colours*,' he says. 'She wrote it after finding a bunch of old letters in an antique shop. Love letters.'

'Yes, that's right. She had to get them translated because they were all in French. Hence her setting it in Paris.'

He nods. 'I have a box of letters in the attic of the shop. They're my great-grandfather's. I wonder if there might be something in there that might be used to . . .'

'Encourage her?' I finish.

His gaze glitters and I catch a hint of his aftershave. Warm spice and something else I can't identify, something musky and male and utterly delicious.

Oh dear. This is bad. This is very bad.

'I'll need to go through them,' he says. 'I don't think

anyone's looked at them since he died, so there might not be anything useful. But . . .' He pauses again. 'There were rumours that he was having an affair with someone.'

Well, this is fascinating.

I lean in closer, drawn by the glitter in his eyes. He's not grumpy now and he's not glowering. He's intense and as interested in this as I am.

'An affair? With whom?'

'It was only a rumour. No one knows for sure.'

'But you think there might be . . . what? Letters or something?'

'Could be. Nothing's certain. After he died, my grandfather refused to talk about him. I tried asking him what he was like a couple of times, but he wouldn't say a word. Dad wouldn't either, I don't know why.'

Wow. I'm even more intrigued. There's nothing like rumours of a forbidden romance and a hint at a tragic, possibly dark past.

Like his, really. Losing his mother so young. And now he's got hints of family secrets . . .

Steady, Kate. Steady.

'Was he horrible?' I sound almost breathless. 'Did he do something awful?'

Sebastian shakes his head. 'No. At least not as far as I know. Village gossip doesn't indicate he was a terrible person. I asked a couple of people, actually, who might have known him when they were kids, and they said he was just a quiet bookseller. Kept to himself. Then again, those are recollections of kids. All the adults who might have known him have passed on now.'

'What about your dad?' I ask. 'Does he really not know anything?'

This is clearly the wrong thing to ask, because Sebastian's expression abruptly closes down. 'No,' he says shortly. 'Dad doesn't live in Wychtree. He's in Bournemouth.'

This is a touchy subject judging from his expression, and, inevitably, now I'm curious. I want to know what's going on with his dad and why he's so angry about it, but I don't know him well enough to push. Also, we seem to have a détente and I like it. I don't want to ruin it.

'Okay.' I let the subject of his father go. 'So, what about these rumours of an affair, then? Are they true, do you think? Was it . . . illicit or something?'

'I'm not sure. I'll need to check through those papers and see what's there.'

Instantly, I straighten and get to my feet, because there's no point in wasting time. 'Well, don't just sit there. Let's go and have a look at them, then.'

Chapter Eight

I don't have a facility with words, unlike the great poets. So this might sound trite, but . . . you captured me from the moment I saw you.

H

SEBASTIAN

I blink as Miss Jones looks down at me, her grey eyes full of glimmer and sparkle.

'What?' I am unable to hide my surprise. 'Now?'

'Of course now.' She gives me a smirk. 'Unless you have something better to do?'

Clearly implying that I do, in fact, have nothing better to do than go straight back to my flat and unearth my great-grandfather's personal papers.

Naturally, now I want to give her a list of all the ten

million other things I absolutely have to do instead, but that would be petty.

I'm not above a little pettiness, but looking through those papers is in my interest too, and, after all, it *was* my idea. And I did very much like the glow in her eyes when I suggested it. That instant spark of curiosity.

I like her curious, though I shouldn't. I shouldn't like the thought of taking her to my flat, of her being in my space, in my territory, either, but I do.

I'm the biggest cliché known to man.

I'm a Neanderthal.

I flick a glance towards Dan, but he's deep in conversation with Gerry. The traitor. I shouldn't have risen to his obvious bait with his half-spoken dinner invitation, yet I did. I couldn't help myself. Now he's going to see us leave together and he'll be assuming all kinds of things.

Prick.

I can't pretend I'm not attracted to her now, not to him. And definitely not now I've given myself away so blatantly. But at least I haven't acted on it yet. Which I won't. I'll still be able to tell him with a straight face that I'm having nothing to do with her.

Honesty is important.

Ironic when I've been lying to myself for the past two months, but still. Admitting an attraction is one thing, acting on it is quite another, and I haven't committed that sin yet. And I won't.

I'm thirty-two. I'm a bloody man, for God's sake. I'm not fifteen. I'm not going into uncontrollable throes of ecstasy at the glimpse of a pert breast or a hint of thigh. Miss Jones, in her pretty blue dress that reveals no skin and yet is somehow sexy as hell, will not get the better of me.

'Where's the rush?' I won't allow myself to be hurried. 'Can't this wait?'

'Why wait?' Her smile is a delicate ray of sunshine. 'If there's a legitimate secret romance in your great-grandfather's papers, then we need to find out, because that's something that Lisa is going to *love*. I mean, seriously. A secret historic romance is kind of her jam. Especially if it's forbidden.'

'What about privacy issues?'

She lifts a golden eyebrow. 'Hey, you were the one who mentioned it as something that might entice her. You can't get cold privacy feet now. And if we look and there's nothing of interest there, then we can go on thinking of other things.'

She's not wrong, dammit.

I got carried away with finding a solution to our little problem of how to get Lisa here. Miss Jones was glittering away across the table from me and all I was able to think about was how to keep her glittering. I didn't fully think through the implications.

We're a private family, the Blackwoods, and I'm not thrilled with the idea of other people picking over those letters. Great-grandfather Sebastian stuffed them into a box and kept them shoved to the rear of his closet for a reason. I only know they're there because, after Dad moved to Bournemouth, I was clearing out the closet and found them.

Still, we need something to get Lisa Underwood here and if that something is in those papers then we must find it.

'Fine,' I say, rising to my feet. 'I suppose we do need to solve this dilemma quickly.'

She twinkles directly at me like a tiny star. 'Great.'

I stride from the pub, ignoring Dan as he raises a pint in my direction, as well as the sideways looks from everyone else. Miss Jones follows in my wake. She doesn't see all the looks because she hasn't yet comprehended what living in a village is actually like.

She'll learn.

'This is a fantastic idea,' she says, tripping along at my side. She has to trot since her legs are much shorter than mine and I'm not walking slowly. She doesn't seem to mind, though, keeping up with me effortlessly. 'Like, really great.'

'You don't need to flatter me, Miss Jones.' My tone is terse. 'There may not be any romantic letters there at all and the rest may be of no use to us.'

'Maybe not, but it's better than the nothing we had before.'

'I suppose so.'

There's a silence as we walk through the warm, summer-scented village twilight. It's one of my favourite times, when all the shops have shut and everyone has gone home and the high street is empty. It's very quiet and, in summer, you can smell the lavender from Mrs Bennet's window boxes next to the post office.

My mother used to love village evenings.

There's a small garden to the back of Blackwood Books, where the flat is, and she and I used to sit out there with a bowl of ice cream each, enjoying the warmth and silence, and the scent of lavender, and the roses she loved to grow.

The roses have gone now and so has my mother, but I still like a village twilight.

Except now Miss Jones keeps up a running stream of commentary as we make our way to Blackwood Books. Telling me all about Lisa Underwood and how she knows her and what a great writer she is, a consummate professional, and that Miss Jones didn't edit *Colours*, but was her point person and also edited some of her later work, though she had a senior editor's oversight, and on and on.

Part of me wants to tell her to be quiet, that she's ruining my peaceful silence. Yet another part of me likes the sound of her voice. It's light, but not shrill, and full of expression, and the things she's telling me are . . . interesting. I know the bookshop trade inside out, but not so much publishing.

I like my quiet. However, I'm also aware that maybe I've had too much quiet over the years. That maybe I could stand some chatter.

I'm torn.

I seem to be always torn with Miss Jones.

We come to Blackwood Books and I unlock the door, proceeding through the shop to the back-door entrance to my flat. I know a moment's tension when I push that door open – I want her to see my living space and yet I don't want her to see it. I feel absurdly like a boy finally deciding to show a girl his precious Matchbox car collection in the hope of impressing her.

The ignominy of it.

Ignoring the feeling, I usher Miss Jones inside.

The flat isn't big. It's got two upstairs bedrooms with a tiny bathroom between them, and a kitchen and living/dining area down below. There's a minuscule bathroom downstairs too, plus the garden to the back.

There's nothing in that garden now. I came home from school one day when I was ten to find that Dad had pulled everything out of it. All the plants and bushes, and the little herb garden that Mum had tended. Her roses. We'd ended up having a screaming match – the first of many – and I'd sworn to myself that I'd replant it when I had the chance.

I haven't, though. I don't know anything about gardening and the shop takes up most of my time.

Miss Jones comes through into the kitchen and then down a couple of stairs into the living/dining area, which is slightly lower than the rest of the house. I had some French doors put in so I could look out into the garden, and I had plans of sitting out there in summer, but I never do.

I spend my time in the shop.

'This is lovely,' she exclaims, going over to the French doors and looking out. 'And you've got a garden too.'

I don't want her obvious pleasure in my living space to matter, yet it does. I wouldn't have thought it would appeal, since it's very minimalist and she's definitely not a minimalist kind of woman.

I've made it a little like the shop, with floors of polished wood and Persian carpets. The walls are white, with some of my mother's favourite pictures hanging here and there. I have a large modular couch in dark linen that takes up most of the living area and faces a flat-screen TV on the wall.

Everything is geared to tasks rather than aesthetics, and I rarely have people over. Only Dan comes with any regularity.

Like the shop, it's my private oasis.

'Would you like a drink?' I offer, dredging up my hostly manners from somewhere.

She turns from the windows. 'Oh, yes, please.'

'I have scotch.' I like a single malt. Islay distilleries for preference. Lowland malts are too sweet for me. I like my whisky rougher and a touch salty. 'And if not scotch, then coffee or tea.'

'It's too late for coffee for me, and I don't think tea is quite the vibe.' She looks around my living area with wide eyes, as if she's never been in the living area of a house in her entire life. 'Scotch is definitely the vibe.'

I've never heard scotch be described as a 'vibe' and somehow the word scrapes across my already wired nerves.

She's here. In my house. In her pretty blue dress, her long golden hair lying loose across her shoulders, and she's talking about 'vibes'.

Fuck's sake. What am I doing? I'm offering her drinks and being pleased with her calling my interior decorating non-effort 'lovely'.

I should have made her wait in the shop while I got the letters from my study and then brought them down, given them to her and shoved her back out into the street, leaving me to my quiet twilight.

But no, here I am offering her whisky and no doubt a seat on my couch, and then I'll get the letters and we'll pore over them together . . .

Tension crawls through me.

I need to calm down. I need to get a fucking grip.

Grabbing two tumblers and the scotch from a cupboard, I take them over to the living area and put them on the coffee table in front of the couch.

'Sit,' I say, gesturing to the couch. 'Please.'

She does so, putting her battered leather bag down beside her and smoothing the flounces of her dress. It leaves her knees bare.

'Do you want water?' I ask, definitely not staring at her knees.

'Water? No, I said I'd have the whisky.'

'Do you want water with the whisky?' I explain patiently.

'Why would I want that?'

'It releases the flavours.'

'Oh . . . well, do you have water with it?'

'Sometimes.'

'A book snob and a whisky snob,' she says, grinning up at me.

She's teasing and I don't know if I like that or not. No, I'm sure I don't like it. Definitely sure.

'I prefer to think of myself as a purist.' I hear the insufferable note in my voice and feel suddenly trapped and restless. Itching for some reason I can't explain. It's a terrible combination. I usually go for a run when I feel that way, but I can't now, because she's here.

'Well, Mr Purist,' she says. 'I'll have it whichever way you're having it.'

Silently cursing this ridiculous conversation, I pour the

scotch into the tumblers, not bothering with the water. Then I put the bottle down. 'Wait here,' I say tersely.

The letters are in my upstairs study, which used to be Dad's room when I was a child, in a big box in the closet. Dad had had them for years, and when he moved to Bournemouth he didn't take anything with him. He just left the box here. I haven't looked at the contents. I'd actually forgotten all about it until Miss Jones started talking about Lisa Underwood and *Colours*, and then the story of the letters she'd bought reminded me.

I grab the box from the closet and take it downstairs.

Miss Jones is glaring down at her tumbler suspiciously and a flicker of amusement passes through me.

'What's the matter?' I ask, as I put the box down on the coffee table and sit, making sure there is a good amount of space between her and me. 'You don't like it?'

She makes a face. 'It's . . . interesting.'

'It's an Islay malt. They're a little more intense taste-wise than other single malts.'

'Intense and you like it, huh? What a surprise.' She takes another sip and pulls another face. 'Delicious.'

More amusement flickers through me and it feels strange. Almost . . . foreign. I know the village finds me aloof and reserved, and that's a Blackwood trait. But I have been known to smile on occasion, so I'm not sure why this amusement feels so odd.

Maybe it's simply because Miss Jones is the cause and that's a novelty. Especially since all she's made me feel so far is angry and hungry.

'Are you sure you don't want water?' I ask.

'I think I have all the flavours I can handle right now. I don't need the water to release any more.' She puts the tumbler down on the coffee table and looks at me expectantly. 'Also, I'm impatient. Are you going to open that box, or shall I?'

I'm very tempted to pick up my scotch, swirl it around for a good long time, take a sip and chew on it, really tasting it, and only then will I open the box. But that's being needlessly passive-aggressive and I've already decided I'm not going to behave like that. She won't make me stoop to that level.

So I say nothing, turn to the box and take the lid off it.

It's full of papers. Old accounts, postcards, Christmas cards, ticket stubs and pamphlets from various places. Ancient bills. Bank statements . . .

I carefully go through them all while Miss Jones vibrates with excitement right next to me, and as each paper is taken out and it's not a letter, I try to ignore the disappointment sitting inside me.

I want us to find something and not just because of Lisa Underwood. I want to find something for her. For Kate Jones. I want her to be pleased with me, which is humiliating in the extreme, yet it's all I want.

Then, just as I'm despairing of finding anything, my fingers close around a bundle of papers. I draw the bundle out and it's a stack of envelopes held together with an ancient rubber band.

Miss Jones's eyes have gone very wide. 'Oh,' she breathes softly.

The rubber of the band has perished and snaps when I take

it off. I discard the pieces then look at the stack in my hand. Small envelopes. Unaddressed. No stamps.

Miss Jones says nothing, but I can feel the pressure of her will, urging me to pick up one of the envelopes and look inside. That she hasn't snatched them out of my hands to look at them herself is a minor miracle, and also a point in her favour.

I take one of the envelopes, which is open already, and slide out the piece of paper inside. It's thin, lined, cracked a little with age. There's writing on it, in red ink, flowing cursive, and I take my glasses from my pocket and put them on so I can read it.

I am sorry about tonight. I wanted to meet you so much, but he's being particularly ruthless about me going out in the evenings. Perhaps in a couple of days, things will have died down and I can slip away.

I miss you.
C

It's not my great-grandfather's handwriting, I know that much. It's also definitely a love letter.

'What does it say?' Miss Jones demands. 'Let me read it.'

Wordlessly I hand it over and she looks at it, her pretty eyes getting wider and wider.

'Wow,' she murmurs, and glances up from the letter. 'Is this what I think it is?'

'Possibly.' I pick up another envelope and take out the piece of paper inside. Again, it's written in red ink, in a flowing cursive.

I loved Wuthering Heights. *Thank you. It was wonderful. It's very female of me to like it, but I cannot see what is so wrong about a love like that. It's trite, I know, but I think you are my Heathcliff. You said not to put down our names and I agree, but I cannot call you nothing. You are my own darling Heathcliff.*

Again, I hand it over and again Miss Jones reads it.

'Wow,' she says again. 'Your great-grandfather was courting hard. *Wuthering Heights* is a power move.'

I snatch the letter back off her.

'Hey,' she says, making a grab for it, but I hold it away, staring down at the initial at the end of the letter.

And I will be your Catherine.

Forever, C

So . . . the gossip was right. He *did* have an affair with someone. And he kept all the letters she wrote to him, because, surely, those are her letters in red ink. Unless they're from my great-grandmother . . . But no. By all accounts Grace Blackwood wasn't one for reading, and had hated the bookshop. She definitely wouldn't have loved *Wuthering Heights*.

'C,' Miss Jones says. 'Who could that be?'

'It's not my great-grandmother, I can tell you that.' I stare at the note, though what I'm trying to find, I'm not sure.

'Why not?' Miss Jones shifts on the couch, getting closer. She's reading over my shoulder, I can feel the warmth of her right next to me. I can smell her scent. It's sweet, vanilla maybe. 'Can you tell by the handwriting?'

My mouth waters. The red ink on the page I'm holding blurs and I struggle to remember what question she asked.

Something about my great-grandmother.

'Grace didn't like the bookshop,' I say, every inch of me aware of every inch of Miss Jones right beside me. 'She wanted my great-grandfather to get a better job and she didn't like the village. She didn't like him spending so much time in the shop. At least that's what my grandfather said.'

Miss Jones leans forward a little more, her breath against the side of my neck. 'Open another one. Go on, let's see what they all say.'

I grit my teeth. 'Personal space, Miss Jones. You've heard of it, I presume?'

Take off your clothes, Miss Jones. Let me see how pretty you are.

'What?' She sounds startled. 'Why?'

It's too much. I turn before I can stop myself and meet her grey eyes staring back. 'Because if you don't move away, God help me but I won't be responsible for what I might do.'

Chapter Nine

I would never have imagined that a kiss could change the world.
But yours did.

C

KATE

I don't realise how close I am to him until he turns his head and his gaze finds mine. Through the lenses of his glasses, his eyes are electric. He's all essence, this man, and I have the strangest thought: he's all passion or he's all ice, there's no in-between. Does he know there's a middle ground? Does he know how to be in it?

It must be exhausting being him, with no place to rest.

It's instinct that has me raising a hand to touch his cheek, for what reason I don't know. Maybe in comfort or reassurance, I'm not sure which. Not that he lets me touch him, because his own hand comes up, so fast, and his fingers close around my wrist, stopping me.

His grip is strong and warm. Not too hard to hurt, but enough to know I couldn't break it if I tried. His eyes are blazing.

Aisling told me that he looked at me like a wolf looks at a rabbit and I can see what she means now. He *is* a wolf. And he's hungry.

A hot shock passes through me. I've made a mistake, a bad one, but the letters got me carried away and I wanted to look at them. I hadn't known how close I was to him until it was too late. Until he turned and looked at me and I'm trapped now. Not by his grip, I know he'd let me go if I asked. No, I'm trapped by his gaze. By the lightning crackling in his eyes.

I can't remember the last time a man looked at me like that. I don't think Jasper ever did.

'What are you doing?' he growls. 'Touching me, Miss Jones, is a very bad idea.'

I know it's a bad idea. I know very well, and yet still I ask, 'Why?' It's a goad and my heart is beating far too hard and far too fast. But I want to see. I want to know what he would do if I pushed him.

He does not disappoint.

'This is why,' he says.

He discards his glasses, leans forward, and his mouth covers mine.

Somehow I always knew this would happen and I don't avoid him.

He lets go of my wrist and lifts his hands, his fingers sliding into my hair, curling into fists, holding me still. Not that I'm going anywhere, because my God . . .

This man can *kiss*. If kissing was an Olympic sport, he'd win a gold medal. He'd win *all* the bloody medals.

His mouth is so hot and he is demanding, nipping at my bottom lip, teasing it, coaxing me to open for him and before I'm even conscious of it, that's what I do. He doesn't hesitate, taking advantage of my invitation, deepening the kiss.

My heart races even faster and I'm hot all over, my skin tight. He smells good, the heat of his body inches from mine and all I can think about is getting even closer to him than I am already.

God, if he kisses like this, what else can he do? I want to find out. I'm desperate to find out.

I lift my own hands, touching the wall of his chest, testing the muscles beneath the warm cotton of his T-shirt. He feels strong and hard, and I want to press myself against him, relieve the sudden, nagging ache between my thighs.

Our kiss gets hotter, becoming feverish. He tastes good, too, the flavour of the scotch giving it a kick, though I really don't need the extra alcohol. Not when I'm half drunk on him already.

Then, just as I'm melting against him, my fingers curling into the cotton of his shirt, he releases me abruptly and pulls away.

I stare at him, open-mouthed, as he pushes himself off the couch and takes a couple of steps towards the windows, his back to me. His tall figure is rigid with tension and I can hear the harsh rush of his breath, his hands in fists at his sides.

My heartbeat thuds and I have difficulty finding air. It's as if I've been diving down very deep and have suddenly rushed to the surface, and all my addled brain can think is *Can you get the bends from a mind-blowing kiss?*

'That was a mistake,' Sebastian says, in a voice I don't recognise. 'You should leave.'

I blink and what's actually happening takes a minute to penetrate.

That kiss, that *astonishing* kiss, was a mistake. And now he wants me to leave.

I'm still breathing hard, my nipples feeling tight and sensitive against the lacy cotton cups of my bra, and the ache between my legs won't let up.

I don't know what happened. I mean, part of me knew that he was attracted to me, even if it was only on a subconscious level and, yes, I found him unbelievably hot, much to my annoyance.

But *he* was the one who crossed the line here, not me. He was the one who brought it out into the open, and if he's not going to do anything about it, then he'll have to do better than 'It was a mistake. You should leave'.

We're doing this festival together. We'll have to be in each other's company. We still have to go through these letters and, I'm sorry, but I'm not going to turn tail and run from the room like a sixteen-year-old virgin. I ran away from Jasper without telling him where I was going, it's true, but that was different.

He would have followed me and I was afraid he'd manipulate me into staying.

But I'm not afraid of Sebastian. We have to talk about this and like hell is he going to send me away.

'No,' I say. 'I'm not going anywhere. Tell me what that was all about.'

He gets even more tense, his shoulders just about around his ears, his knuckles white. 'If you know what's good for you—'

'Don't be such a drama king, Sebastian,' I snap, saying his name for the first time and getting some satisfaction from the way he twitches when I say it. 'We have to work together on this festival and, before you even say a word, no, I'm not going to pretend it never happened.'

He's silent a moment longer, then turns around. Again, he's blazing, his jaw tight, his eyes all fire. As if he's at the end of the rope he's hanging himself with and can't decide whether to kick the chair away or climb down.

'What do you think just happened?' His deep voice is full of anger, though I don't understand why. 'I kissed you.'

'Yes,' I say. 'You did.'

'I shouldn't have.'

'Why not?'

'Because I don't even like you.'

I ignore this, because I'm starting to see what the problem is and maybe I should have known it all along, but I didn't. The tension between us. Those sparks in his eyes sometimes when he looks at me.

I raise a brow. 'Is this why my existence is a problem? You're attracted to me and you don't like it?'

The muscle in his jaw leaps. 'Yes,' he forces out through gritted teeth.

Something turns over inside me. Satisfaction.

Yes, girl, you still got it.

I can't deny I like that. It feels healing, especially after Jasper with his petty slights and snide comments. His small criticisms that steadily eroded me away until I was listing on my foundations. I was too loud. Too quiet. I could be selfish. I needed to be less uptight. I gave out mixed signals. I needed to respect his time, and on and on.

I'd thought that *I* was the problem. That I was boring and not pretty enough, not experienced enough, too inhibited, or any one of the thousand things that women beat themselves up for not being. Even after the truth of him and our relationship was revealed, there was a part of me that still blamed myself.

Now, after kissing Sebastian, that part has gone silent. Because now, even though Sebastian obviously thinks I'm a problem too, it's not because I'm lacking in anything. It's because I've got *too much* of what he wants, and even though he's angry, he's not trying to make me feel less. He's not criticising me or slighting me, or manipulating me into thinking I've done something wrong.

He's angry for wanting me and is honest about it.

In fact, honest is all he's been since I met him.

God, that's refreshing.

Then something else occurs to me.

If one kiss from Sebastian can rock my world, then sex with him will destroy me. Literally.

Shit. Maybe he's right after all. Maybe this *was* a mistake.

'So,' I say eventually. 'What do you want to do about it?'

'Nothing.' There is finality in the word. He means it. 'I never date women in the village and I'm not changing the habit of years just for you.'

My stomach drops at that, but I ignore it. Sure, I like honesty, but sometimes it sucks.

'Okay.' I try to sound casual, like I don't care a bit, and I think I'm successful. Mostly. 'I hear you.'

He glares as if I'm arguing with him. 'If I want sex, I find it elsewhere. I don't sleep with women who live here, it's too close to home. And as you say, we're working together. This festival is too important to get derailed by an inconvenient sexual attraction.'

I lift my hands. 'Hey, I'm not arguing with you.'

He continues to glower. 'You're a problem, Miss Jones.'

'Miss Jones? Seriously? After you kissed me senseless? Surely I deserve a Kate?'

'Like I said, you're a problem, *Miss Jones*.'

My God. The man is so rigidly intense and dramatic, he's impossible. It's starting to annoy me. He may be more straight up than Jasper, but I'm really over being a problem.

'Actually,' I snap, '*I'm* not the problem. You're the problem, *Mr Blackwood*. I can't do anything about the fact that I exist, but if you're going to continue being a grumpy bastard just because of your own silly little rules, then may I suggest investing in a chastity belt? Now.' I lean forward and start gathering up the pieces of paper that are scattered on the floor. 'I'm going to look at these letters because we need to see if they're something Lisa Underwood is going to be interested in.'

'Take them.' He bites out each word. 'Take them home and have a look at them there.'

I glance up at him in surprise. 'You don't want to—'

'No.' He's still standing there, rigid, white around the mouth. Then he adds, 'Please, Miss Jones.'

He looks almost . . . tortured, and my annoyance fades. I had no idea I have such an effect on him. I'd be even more flattered if it hadn't appeared to actively hurt him, and I don't want to hurt him.

But then, of course it would. He's not a man comfortable with the halfway point, with the in-between, the shades of grey. It's all or nothing for him, and right now, all he can do is nothing.

It wouldn't be fair to push myself on him and it wouldn't be fair to argue. If the shoe was on the other foot, I wouldn't want him here either, and arguing will only make me look like a dick.

'Okay.' I clutch the envelopes in my hand as I get slowly to my feet. 'Thanks for the whisky.' I turn and go to the door, then pause before it and turn back. 'It wasn't a mistake, Sebastian,' I say. 'And I'm not sorry you kissed me. I'll text you tomorrow.'

I don't wait for him to reply. I leave.

It's only a few steps across the high street and then I'm back in my little flat above my shop.

I sit on my own couch and force the kiss from my head, giving my attention to the envelopes in my hand.

They're all love notes from C to H, none of them addressed or stamped. Which means they weren't posted. But if they weren't, how did they get to him? Were they put into a letter-box? Then again, that would mean that anyone could potentially have picked one up and opened it, and if they were afraid of being discovered, which I think they were, surely they wouldn't have risked that? So, not letterboxes then. They must have been slipped directly to him somehow.

I take a note from its envelope and sit back, unfolding the crackling paper, staring at the red ink. It's faded with time, the handwriting old-fashioned and flowing, but I can still read it.

I can't sleep now. Every night, when I close my eyes, all I see is you. I like it. It feels as if you are visiting me. I don't mind being so tired during the day when you visit me every night, even if it is only in my dreams.

C

I pull out another and this time it's different. This time the ink on the page is black, the handwriting forceful, with slash-ing capitals and hasty punctuation.

Three days and I miss you. I can't bear not seeing you. Can you think of an excuse to get away? Even for an hour. Even half that and I would be happy.

H

There is longing in the words, I can feel it, and it makes my chest ache.

I pull out another one.

We don't need anyone's permission. And he won't stop us. He doesn't have the guts. We could go north or even across to Europe. I can't stand being apart from you, not a second longer.

H

I swallow, the ache in my chest tightening. Who is 'he' that could stop them? And were they stopped? Is that why they didn't end up together? What happened?

I pull out more.

It's hard for me to get away in the evenings. I know you know. Perhaps tomorrow? After lunch? He'll be out for most of the day. As for

Mrs Dalloway, well, it's an interesting book. We
should discuss face to face, I think.

C

So, I was right when I read about *Wuthering Heights* over
Sebastian's shoulder: his great-grandfather had been giving her
books. The romanticism of it thrills me beyond measure and
the eventual tragedy of it makes my throat ache along with my
chest.

Perhaps she died and her family returned the letters to
him, and that's why he has all hers. Or maybe he did something awful and she returned them. Whatever happened, their
affair didn't last.

I open another one.

We can't go to Europe now, love. It's too dan-
gerous. I think war is going to come whether
we like it or not. Can you meet me tonight?
Same time, the usual place. I won't keep you
long, but we need to discuss this.

H

I stare down at the note, frowning. The war he mentions
would have to be the Second World War, which dates these
notes to before 1939.

Was that what happened in the end? Was it the war that interrupted their affair?

I reach for my phone, bite my lip a second, then text Sebastian quickly. It's a terse note, no mention of what happened between us earlier.

> Did your great-grandfather fight in WW2?

I probably shouldn't have bothered him again tonight, but this can't wait. Or at least, *I* can't wait. Also, I'll be damned if I let one kiss get in the way of something that could save this festival.

He replies immediately, his text as terse as mine.

> Yes. He was away for the duration.

Okay, interesting. I type out another question.

> When did he marry?

Again, Sebastian responds quickly.

> The year after he returned. 1946.

Right. But he didn't marry his C. He married someone else, Sebastian's great-grandmother. I wonder who C was and what happened to her. Because something *must* have. If Sebastian Blackwood the First was as intense as his great-grandson is now, then I couldn't imagine him letting any kind of obstacle get in his way.

Except, of course, if the obstacle was himself.

I let out a breath, not seeing the paper for a minute, only Sebastian's taut expression and the blaze of his eyes.

'I never date women in the village . . .'

I was brought up in London, not a small village, though even the largest of cities are just collections of villages if you really think about it. Certainly, London, as big as it is, could seem like a village sometimes.

So, I can see why he wouldn't want to have a relationship with someone who lived here. If it all went bad, there'd be no escape. You'd have to see them every day and that would be difficult, especially if they then went out with someone else. Also, it's a pretty small pool here and finding someone eligible that you like must be a challenge.

Even so, you could bend your own self-imposed rules for someone if you wanted them enough. Especially if you found yourself trapped by those same rules.

Except I can't see Sebastian bending his. He doesn't have any give in him and maybe his great-grandfather was the same. Maybe Sebastian the First got in his own way and wouldn't bend for the woman he loved. Maybe that's why he married someone else, because he had some stupid rule of his own that he wouldn't break.

In fact, maybe that's why the Blackwood men were supposedly cursed. Maybe they were all too rigid and, instead of bending, they broke.

I sigh. I shouldn't think about Sebastian. It's not like I'm going to have a relationship with him. In fact, I'm not going to have a relationship with any man for the foreseeable future, because men suck.

They all want you to be someone you're not and then get pissed off when you don't fit their vision of you. Jasper wanted someone more polished and contained than I was. Someone sleek to have on his arm, to parade around at his endless corporate dos. He thought having a girlfriend in publishing made him look intellectual, so he'd tell me not to mention the kinds of books I edited, because it reflected badly on him. He'd say it with a smile and put in an eye-roll, suggesting it was his bosses and colleagues who were uptight about it, never him. But it *was* him.

He had rules too, and I never saw the cage he was constructing around me until he'd almost locked the door. It was on the second anniversary of Mum's death and he had dinner with his new boss planned, and he wanted me to come. I told him that I wasn't feeling up to it because of Mum, and his response was: 'Bloody hell, Kate. This dinner is important to me. Your mum's been dead two years. Get over it.'

I sat on the couch that night, grieving my mother, desperately scrolling through my phone so I could ring one of my friends for a chat. But I couldn't find their numbers. Jasper had gone through my contacts a couple of months earlier on the pretext of helping me weed out 'contacts you don't need', and it was only then, when I could have badly used a friend, that I realised he'd deleted them all. I hadn't noticed because all my time was taken up with my job and him.

That's when I knew. That's when I saw the bars of my cage.

He only cared how he looked to his new boss. He hadn't cared that my mother was dead or that I was still grieving.

He didn't care about me. He'd *never* cared about me.

He took my love for him and twisted it subtly to centre himself in everything we did. Everything became about him. Nothing was about me.

The four years of our relationship hadn't been a relationship at all. It had been a pot of water on the stove slowly coming to a boil, and I was the frog sitting in it. I was the frog who didn't know she was being boiled alive.

He didn't speak to me for a week after that night, but that week was enough for me to realise that I had to leave.

That's why I walked out on him, and it's a mistake I won't make again.

I open another envelope.

Yesterday you told me that you had never read Dickens, so here is David Copperfield *to try. It is my own personal copy. If you like it, send the book back with anything you want to say to me in between the pages. Do not sign the note or write anything that could identify us. That way, we can say whatever we want to each other.*

There is no signature on this one, but I know it's from H, Sebastian's namesake, and that it's clearly the first note.

Is that how it started? With a note in a book?

A shiver of excitement goes through me. Because if this is true and he brought her books with notes between the pages, then this is the most romantic thing I've ever seen. It also makes me desperate to know the answer to the other question: who was the woman?

I pick up my phone again and text what I've discovered so far to Sebastian.

> We need to meet up to discuss

I add.

He's typing a response and I watch my screen as the typing bubble appears then disappears. Appears then disappears. As if he can't think what to say to me.

Finally, he settles on:

> Later.

I stare at it. 'Later.' What does that mean? When the bloody hell is 'later'? Does he not want to talk to me? Is that the problem? But even as I think that, I know. Of course that's the problem.

Irritated, I toss my phone back down on the couch, trying to tell myself I'm not disappointed that he doesn't want to meet. It's late and I'm starting to second-guess myself. Did he really like that kiss? Or was it awful? Perhaps it was awful and that's why he broke it off. That's why he wanted me to leave. He couldn't look me in the eye, couldn't be straight with me and tell me I'm a terrible kisser. He didn't know how to say it.

No, no. It can't be that. He's honest, I know it, and that kiss wasn't terrible. He wouldn't have continued to say that I was a problem if it was. Besides, those kinds of self-loathing thoughts are Jasper's voice in my head, and I promised myself I'd stop thinking them.

I swallow and my head falls back against the couch. I close my eyes.

I feel his mouth on mine. Hot. The fever I tasted in that kiss now in my blood. My fingertips brush over my lips and it almost startles me because I hadn't realised I'd even lifted my hand. My lips feel sensitised and raw.

What a bastard for doing that, for making me feel this.

I don't know whether I hate him or whether I'm half in love with him.

I really hope it's the former. Love is something I don't want to tangle with again, and definitely not with him.

Later, after I drag myself to bed, I'm just on the verge of sleep when the phone at my bedside vibrates. I pick it up. It's a text. From Sebastian.

I'm not sorry either.

Just like that, I'm wide awake.

Something tight in me releases. I know exactly what he's referring to.

I stare at the phone a moment, unsure of how to reply. A 'like' seems weird, a 'heart' too much. A thumbs-up strange. I could send a heart eyes emoji, then again . . . maybe not. A kiss seems a little passive-aggressive. I'm tempted to send a saluting emoji – that would annoy him – but in the end, what I send is a basic text.

Good.

There's another pause and then my phone vibrates again.

You taste like sunshine.

A wave of warmth goes through me, starting at my toes, flooding through my cheeks, a blazing heat.

I don't know what to say to that. I literally have no words.

I shouldn't respond, I really shouldn't . . .

You go straight to my head.

I send it.

Then I turn my phone off.

Then I try to sleep.

And don't.

Chapter Ten

You are in my thoughts again. I cannot get rid of you. I am constantly angry that you are not mine.

H

SEBASTIAN

I'm trying very hard not to pay any attention to the shop across the road today. I need to ring various people about James Wyatt's exit from the festival, but I want to confirm Lisa Underwood first. I can't do that until I hear from Miss Jones.

I stand behind the counter, staring hard at my laptop screen, ostensibly checking my emails for anything festival-related. But in reality my attention is focused on the front window, which calls like a siren on a rock. Urging me to look through it to Portable Magic, see what Miss Jones is doing.

I resist. I have to resist. But the memory of how she tasted has caught in my head and I can't forget it.

Sending her that text last night was a mistake, but I couldn't sleep and I was angry. Angry with myself and my own weakness. Angry with her for being beautiful and sexy as hell, and taking up so much space in my head.

Angry that I don't know what to do with myself except resist and keep on resisting.

Which, as it turns out, I am shit at.

Fuck the text. I shouldn't have kissed her, that's what I shouldn't have done, but . . . She was looking at me with smoky eyes, her cheeks pink, knowing full well why she shouldn't have been sitting that close to me. Knowing, yet not moving away. Instead she raised a hand to touch me and I knew if she did that would be it. So I caught her wrist before she could, her skin warm beneath my fingertips.

My Achilles heel. My kryptonite.

I should *not* have leaned forward and taken her face between my hands and kissed her. That was a mistake and I told her so. Because now the taste of her is in my head and it's there for good. Like sunshine. Summer days full of heat, and sweetness, and languorous, lazy desire. Strawberries and champagne. Ice cream at the end of a day at the beach.

I'm not sure how I managed to dredge up the will to pull away, yet somehow I did. But pulling away hasn't made things any easier. I want more. I want everything. I want her naked on my bed, reaching for me with that smoky-eyed look on her face.

The bell above the door chimes, announcing a customer, and I realise that, despite my good intentions, I'm standing there, staring through the front window at Portable Magic. Watching Miss Jones's figure move through the shop, shelving books.

Jesus. What's happening to me?

I force myself to turn, to greet my customer, and it's Gillian Marshall, another of my regulars. She's in her seventies and a large woman in every way. Tall. Wide. With a certain . . . presence.

She and her banker husband bought a mouldering stately home just up the road from Wychtree, and she strides about the village, all very lady-of-the-manor, though she's more oblivious than condescending.

I don't mind Gillian. She's mostly harmless. But she buys a lot of books for show and never reads any of them, and is always trying to badger me into stocking her self-published memoirs. She also always brings her wretched dog, which is the most ill-behaved golden Labrador I've ever had the misfortune to meet. There's a reason, after all, why I told Miss Jones no dogs in the bookshop.

'Aloysius!' Gillian bellows at the dog, who has followed her inside, because God forbid it should spend ten seconds out in the street alone. 'Come!'

Aloysius doesn't come. He's gone off to the shelf of Art History books, sniffing at the place where he peed the last time he came in.

By Christ, if he pees again—

'Sebastian!' Gillian continues to bellow, ignoring the dog, who's also ignoring her. 'I hear you're having a festival!'

I force a tight smile. 'Mrs Marshall, good morning. Yes, that's correct.'

She smiles at me, red-faced in her yellow mac, despite the fact that there's nothing but blue sky outside. Gillian may be bluff and blunt, but there's not one bad bone in her body. 'Good show, good show.' She puts one large hand on the counter. 'Are you giving workshops by any chance?'

Oh God. I hope she isn't going to say what I think she's going to say.

'Workshops?' I ask carefully. 'What kind of workshops?'

'For writing, you know.'

Sadly, I do. 'Why do you ask?'

'Well, I was thinking I could offer a memoir-writing workshop. I've written my own, as you know, and it was a fantastic learning experience.'

She's retired, Mrs Marshall. An ex-teacher, though I'm sure no one ever spots that.

I'm jesting, of course. It's one of the first things you'd spot about her.

'It's a readers' festival,' I say, with manufactured regret. 'So, I'm sorry. We're not offering any writing workshops.'

She frowns. 'Really? Oh, what a shame.' She turns abruptly. 'Aloysius! Come away!'

The dog is behaving suspiciously.

'Mrs Marshall,' I begin. 'Perhaps Aloysius might be more comfortable outside?'

'Eh? Oh, right you are.' She goes over to her dog and ushers him away from his potential desecration of a volume on Italian architecture.

As she's in the process of herding him outside, she asks, 'Have you got a programme for the festival, then?'

My smile is fixed, thinking of all the marketing I had to pull because of James *fucking* Wyatt. 'Very soon.'

'You might want to get cracking with that,' she points out unnecessarily, not helping my already pissed-off mood. 'Give people some time to decide what sessions they want to go to.'

'Yes, I'm waiting on confirmation from a special guest,' I say, probably unwisely, since we haven't had confirmation from said special guest, but what the hell.

Instantly Gillian gets a very intent look on her face. She loves gossip more than anything and loves being the first to know even more than that.

'I shouldn't tell you since she hasn't confirmed yet,' I say casually, which might end up being a mistake: this will all go to hell in a handbasket if Lisa Underwood doesn't want to come. Then again, I need to gauge interest somehow, and a rumour might very well be the only way.

Gillian couldn't write an engaging memoir if her life depended on it (yes, I read some of her manuscript, because she asked me to and I couldn't say no), but she's truly excellent at inadvertently letting slip secrets. Especially secrets she's not allowed to tell anyone.

'Oh, go on,' she says. 'You can tell me. I'm the soul of discretion.'

'Fine. But . . .' I fix her with a gimlet eye. 'If you could keep this to yourself, I'd be grateful.'

Her face lights up. 'Of course, dear boy. You can count on me.'

She will love this news, I know she will, because while she's got a whole shelf-ful of classics she's never read, she did read *Colours*. And she loved it. She couldn't stop raving about it.

'Well, as I said, we don't have confirmation yet, but . . .' I draw the moment out. 'Word is Lisa Underwood might be interested in coming.'

'Oh? What?' She's looking at me like a child on Christmas morning looks at their presents. 'Is that really a possibility?'

I give her a solemn nod. I'm not lying. It *is* a possibility.

'Oh, dear boy, that would be amazing,' she says and I know she truly means it. 'That would be wonderful. I've never met an actual author and to meet her . . .' She stops and presses her lips together as Aloysius disappears off to bother some other poor shopkeeper. 'Well, mum's the word. I'll be first in line for a ticket, that's for certain.'

'I'll let you know,' I assure her, and as she disappears through the door after her dog, I can't decide whether I've made a mistake and tempted the gods, or made an excellent marketing decision and tempted a great many of Gillian's well-heeled friends. The people who pretend they only read the classics, while secretly devouring James Patterson under the blankets.

Feeling more like I've dug my own grave than I care to, I

get my phone out of my pocket and glance at the screen. There are no more texts from Miss Jones and I can't stop myself from checking again the one she sent me last night.

You go straight to my head.

I didn't respond. The satisfaction her message prompted wasn't something I could allow or indulge. Yet it sweeps over me again as I look at her text and remember the look in her eyes as I pulled away. The grey deepening to charcoal, her cheeks flushed, that pulse at the base of her throat racing.

She'd liked it. She'd liked that kiss.

I shouldn't be thinking about this. I should be thinking about my great-grandfather's notes and how Miss Jones also texted that it seems likely my ancestor slipped them into books that he'd then given to this 'C'. That there was definitely a secret affair happening and that it was something Lisa Underwood would probably be interested in.

I need to see these notes, read them for myself, but the thought of being in Miss Jones's presence right now is too tempting and I have to resist.

Resistance has never been a problem for me before. My father's relationship with the bottle was the same as my grandfather's with the racetrack, and both addictions were enough for me to know that I don't want to head down the same path. But I've never felt the pull of addiction before and so I'd ignorantly assumed I've escaped it somehow.

I haven't, though, and I know it now, because the pull in

me to cross the road and go into Miss Jones's shop is almost
irresistible. I can think of a thousand different excuses to go
and all of them are completely plausible, and I'm sure that's
how it starts, the addiction.

I've had a taste of her and now all I want is more.

Then again, I *do* need to know what's happening about
Lisa Underwood, so I quickly type out a text.

Did you email Lisa U?

I start to put my phone away, because I don't want to stand
around waiting for her to reply, but she's replying already
before I can.

I got a response from her this morning and so
I emailed back re the letters and also re the festival.

That's good. In fact, that's excellent.

You think she'll accept?

I text back.
Miss Jones responds.

I think so. Those letters are so interesting.
I really need to talk to you about them.

I shake my head.

Later. I told you.

When?

There is a pause and then she adds,

Scared?

I give a low laugh.

What would I be scared of?

Me. That kiss.

I grit my teeth.

Forget the kiss.

There is a long pause.

Was it really that bad?

I stare at my phone for a long time as something tightens inside me. Does she think that's why I stopped? Because it was a bad kiss? I thought I'd been clear about why. I can't start something with her, not when she lives here. Not while we have competing businesses and the festival to plan.

And definitely not considering the Blackwoods' terrible

history when it comes to women. We always let them down in some way, shape or form, and since I know I haven't escaped the same genetic weakness that undermined my grandfather and father, I have to assume I'll also be a terrible partner.

Miss Jones surely deserves better than that.

Still, while it would be easier to let her think that the kiss was a terrible one, I can't do that to her. I'm an arsehole but I'm not *that* much of an arsehole. Also, I don't want to lie about a kiss that good.

> It wasn't bad, Miss Jones.

I text back.

> It was extraordinary.

There is no response to this.

My muscles tighten. I prefer honesty – everyone knows where they stand – but there is such a thing as being too honest. Perhaps I revealed far too much and now she doesn't know what to say.

Too bad. I can't stand around wasting my day texting her, not when I have so much to do.

I thrust my phone back into my pocket and return my attention to the laptop on the counter, just as the bell above the door chimes again and someone else comes in.

I look up.

It's Miss Jones.

Today, she's wearing a silky-looking dress of delicate pink that wraps around her body lovingly, swirling at her hips and thighs. She has silver bracelets on one wrist and silver feather earrings that swing amongst the fall of her golden hair.

She looks like a rose in full bloom and her grey eyes are full of determination, and I wish I was anywhere else but here.

She strides to the counter, dumps the stack of envelopes on it, then folds her arms and fixes me with a glare. 'Later isn't going to work for me, Sebastian. Let's talk now.'

An electric shock arrows down my spine at the way she says my name.

God help me, but I love it.

'Now doesn't work for me,' I say with cold precision, fighting the urge to reach over the counter and pull her close, taste her sunshine again. 'Thank you for the letters. I'll go over them tonight. Now, if you'll excuse me . . .'

'No, you're not excused.' Her chin lifts. 'You can't text me about the kiss, tell me that it was extraordinary, then expect me to just ignore it. Also, "later" is not a time frame.'

Yes. It was a mistake to text her. I should have known she wouldn't leave it alone. Now I'm well and truly fucked.

I fix her with my own glare. 'That's exactly what I expect you to do, Miss Jones. I expect you to ignore it. To pretend it didn't happen. That it was a mistake. Because the alternative is you taking all your clothes off and climbing into my bed and I'm not sure you want that.'

Her cheeks have gone as pink as her dress. 'What if I did?' she flings back. 'What if that's exactly what I do want?'

Chapter Eleven

Come tonight. He is away. I need you.

C

KATE

My mouth is dry and my heart is on its way to Athens from Marathon to tell the Greeks the Persians are coming. Okay, so that's a reach of a metaphor, but seriously . . . telling me to take my clothes off and climb into his bed?

There was no hesitation in my response. I didn't second-guess. I only saw him, with that burning look in his eyes, and all I thought was 'yes'.

Yes. That's exactly what I want. And if it destroys me, then so what? My life already destructed when Mum died and then when I left Jasper, and for six months things have been drama-free, and, quite frankly, it's getting boring. I could use a little more destruction.

'You did not just say that,' Sebastian says.

'I think you'll find I did.'

'Why? Why do you want that?'

'Why do you think? You said the kiss was extraordinary and I agree. I want more. I want you and I think you want me too.'

He scowls. 'It's not going to happen.'

'Why not? Maybe we'd get on better if we didn't have this ridiculous sexual tension getting in the way.'

'No.' The word is flat and hard, and it's the most profoundly irritating thing I've ever heard him say.

I step closer to the counter and lean in. 'Give me one good reason. And not the stupidity about not sleeping with women who live in the village.'

'I do not owe you an explanation.'

'Actually, you do. *You* kissed me, don't forget. What do you think is going to happen? That one night with you and I'm going to fall at your feet and beg you to marry me? That I'm going to demand you be my boyfriend? That I'm going to fall hopelessly in love with you?'

He says nothing, his mouth a hard line, his hands thrust in the pockets of his tailored black trousers. The shirt he's wearing today is black and he's so insufferably handsome I can't bear it.

I lean in even further. 'I'm not a virgin, you know. I've just come out of a long-term relationship and I'm not looking for another one.'

His eyes seem even bluer and darker somehow, the colour

of the sky just before it breaks into the stratosphere. He's like a high-tension wire, a tautly drawn bow. He could snap at any moment and I want him to.

I want to see him lose control again.

The air around us is so thick you could cut it with a knife and spread it on your toast for breakfast.

Anything could happen . . .

Then the bell above the door chimes, shattering the seething tension, and Mr Parsons, the ultimate book snob, who has never once darkened the door of Portable Magic, comes in.

I'd have thought he'd be oblivious to the atmosphere, but he's not. He glances at Sebastian then me, then at Sebastian again. 'Am I . . . interrupting?'

That muscle in Sebastian's jaw is leaping, fury in every line of him. Though I don't know whether it's at Mr Parsons for interrupting, or at me, presumably for existing, or at himself for being utterly ridiculous.

I'm hoping he's annoyed at himself for being ridiculous, because he is. Though Mr Parsons' interruption has given me a moment to think, and now I'm aware that I'm furious myself.

That's why I charged over here. Because of Sebastian's text about the kiss – extraordinary, he said – and my own impatience with his 'later' response to the letters. Mainly, though, it was about the kiss, and how I didn't sleep well last night because I was thinking about it. How my dreams were full of heat and desire, and how when I woke up this morning, I was in a foul temper.

So much for good thoughts.

His kiss has woken up something inside me and I'm angry about it. I want him to do something about it.

'Not at all,' Sebastian says, his cool tone utterly at odds with the look in his eyes. 'What can I do for you, Mr Parsons?'

Mr Parsons approaches the counter. He gives me a nod, but keeps a wide berth, as if I'm going to infect him with my horrible genre germs or something.

'I read *The Bay at Midnight* on your recommendation,' he says to Sebastian. 'And, look, I have to say, it was really very good. You said the author was coming to the festival, if I recall correctly?'

Sebastian opens his mouth, but I get in first. I'm feeling petty and thwarted and, again, as if I'm the problem. But I'm not. I know what I'm talking about, dammit, and both of these men need a lesson in that.

'Have you ever read *Colours*, Mr Parsons?' I ask.

Mr Parsons blinks and reluctantly looks at me. '*Colours*?'

'Yes. By Lisa Underwood.'

'Er . . . no. Should I have?'

'You should.' I stride unerringly to Sebastian's contemporary fiction section, take the book off the shelf, and stride back over to Mr Parsons, who is gazing at me suspiciously.

I hold the book out to him. 'Try it.'

Mr Parsons glances at the book as if he's never seen one before in his life, and then he glances at Sebastian. Clearly for guidance.

Of course. Ask the man. He is infinitely wiser than me, a mere woman. I let him have his moment, though, because regardless of anything else, Mr Parsons knows Sebastian and he doesn't know me.

Sebastian's gaze is opaque. I can't tell what he's thinking. Then he says in the same cool, measured tone, 'It really is excellent, Mr Parsons. Easy reading, naturally, but with some bite to it.'

I shouldn't feel pleased that he's backing me up, but I do.

Mr Parsons looks down at the book I'm holding as if I'm handing him a dead rat. 'Two pages,' he says to me. 'That's my rule. If it doesn't engage me in two pages then I won't read on.'

'Fine.' I wave the book at him. 'Read two pages. I'll wait.'

Again, he glances at Sebastian, probably wondering what on earth this madwoman is doing trying to force books on him.

But I don't care. I'm trying to prove a point, that I know what I'm doing. That I'm good at this. That I'm not just fluffy blonde hair, and dogs, and costumes and events. It's the books, it's always been the books, and I know what I'm talking about. No matter what Jasper said about me.

Sebastian nods, then gestures at the leather armchair positioned in a nook by the old fireplace, where the fiction section is. 'Please.' He smiles slightly. 'I think it will surprise you.'

Mr Parsons has a dubious expression on his face, but he takes the book, goes over to the chair and sits down. Opens it up.

'What is this in aid of?' Sebastian asks me, *sotto voce*.

'He's your most snobbish of customers, yes?' I reply.

'Nothing wrong with appreciating good writing.'

'He's a book snob,' I insist. 'I want to see if Lisa Underwood would be a drawcard for him too.'

'The two-page rule has been the downfall of many an author . . . I want you, Miss Jones. But you might prove to be an addiction I cannot quit, so it's preferable if I do not even try.'

He says the whole thing in the same tone of voice and it takes me a moment to realise exactly what he's said.

I might be an addiction. An addiction he cannot quit. I have never been an addiction for anyone and now I feel hot all over.

'Would that be so bad?' I whisper.

'Yes.' He is gazing steadily at Mr Parsons, not me. 'Yes, it would. The Blackwood men cannot be trusted with women, Miss Jones. We do not treat them well and . . . you deserve much better than that.'

I feel even hotter. Again Jasper enters my thoughts, the bastard. He never talked to me about what I deserved. Only about what he did.

'It's just sex, Sebastian,' I say, trying to minimise the moment for both of us.

Only then does he deign to look at me. 'It will never be just sex with you, Miss Jones.'

I can see it then, in his eyes. Conviction. Certainty. As if he knows already what it will be like and that it will destroy not only me, but him too.

I want to tell him he's being dramatic, but I know deep in my heart that he's not. He's right. It will never be just sex between us. It will be incendiary and that's a door we should keep firmly closed.

I don't even like him, yet I can sense, just beyond the

borders of that, something more. Potential. Possibilities. What if I dig beneath the surface of this attraction between us? What if I dig beneath the surface of him? What will I find if I do?

Something amazing, I just know it.

But I know, too, that I'll be committing myself if I do. That I won't be able to change track or course. I'll have to follow my curiosity wherever it leads, even to heartbreak.

Deep thoughts for a sunny morning in early summer.

Too deep.

'Look at those letters,' I say, because I can't think of anything else. 'I think Lisa will love the mystery of it. Especially when we don't know who Sebastian was writing to.' I look up at him. His eyes are so blue it's almost painful. 'Keep me posted about Mr Parsons.'

Then I turn around and leave the shop before I say something or do something I regret.

Back inside the haven of Portable Magic, the shelves full of books that normally give me such calm and happiness, now make me feel flat.

It's stupid to be so disappointed, and about sex of all things.

Sure, Sebastian's hot, but there are plenty of hot men in the world. If it's sex I want, I can find another guy. It doesn't have to be with him.

The morning proves to be a quiet one, so I go over the draft of my programme for the festival. I don't have the money to pay anyone to come, so I have to rely on goodwill and the promise of exposure, but the few feelers I've put out to various local authors have been successful. I've also used some of my publishing contacts to invite a few other authors: not big names, but well-loved in their genres, including a guy who does some very popular graphic novels. Some have refused, but enough have accepted to make my programme look enticing. I've got a romance book-club session planned, and one for the cosy mystery fans. With dogs. Naturally, there'll be a cosplay cocktail evening. I haven't run that past Sebastian yet, but it's one of my most popular nights, so I'm sure I can talk him into it.

It's exciting seeing it all take shape and yet . . .

I can't shake off the flat feeling.

Maybe it's not all Sebastian. Maybe part of it is the letters and the history they contain. They're part of his history and they're making me think of my own. Or rather, my lack of history.

He's lucky in many ways, to have a sense of place, of belonging. Mum and I moved around a lot when I was a kid, and she never spoke of Wychtree. Of her mother or her grandmother. She never spoke of my father either, and now whatever she knew has been lost. It didn't bother me before – I had too many other things to deal with – but it's bothering me now.

There's a history there that I'll never know because of her choice not to speak and that would be fine if I didn't care. But . . . I do care. When I lost her, I lost my only connection to the past, to any family I had, and now it doesn't take a psychologist to understand that what I'm trying to do here is to replace that lost family.

I'm gathering people to me, trying to reconnect those old connections.

Sebastian is one of those connections. He's the one that, despite our differences, I feel the most kinship with, even if it's only because of the books.

Anyway, it's romance book club tonight, and, for the first time, I'm not looking forward to it. I can't seem to muster up my usual enthusiasm as our regulars pour through the doors. Aisling attends and she comes in with the others, carrying her usual platter of food. It's all items she hasn't been able to sell that day that must be eaten, but no one cares about that.

We never look a gift éclair in the mouth. Even if it is a vegan one.

I've arranged the chairs in a circle and Mrs Abbot – who is our convener – sits down and gets out the book we're discussing. We're going old-school with *The Shadow and the Star* by Laura Kinsale, so cue the complaints about rapey heroes. Which is Mrs Abbot's favourite topic and on which she has a lot to say about the nature of female desire and how society has changed since the early nineties when the book was written.

The conversation then devolves into what's sexy in a love scene and we're just debating the merits of the word 'cock' when Sebastian walks in.

At the sight of a man in our hallowed romance space, everyone falls immediately silent.

A normal man might have been intimidated by the relentlessness of the female gaze turned upon him, but Sebastian isn't. He's impervious to the sudden silence, his attention skimming over the circle of romance fans and stopping on me where I sit near the counter.

Aisling gives me a surreptitious thumbs-up, while Mrs Abbot, a rebel deep in her heart, says, 'Sebastian, what are your thoughts on the word "cock"?'

Sebastian's blue gaze doesn't budge from mine. 'I think it's a perfectly adequate word, Mrs Abbot. And speaking of words, Miss Jones, can I speak to you for a moment?'

Everyone's collective breath holds and I can feel myself blushing, which is hugely annoying.

I don't know what he's doing here, given our discussion this morning. I was expecting more terse-sounding texts, not his presence in my bookshop, a dark, brooding cloud of masculinity that every woman here is suddenly mesmerised by.

'Well,' Mrs Abbot says briskly to the room at large. 'Let's all reconvene at my house. I'll get out the sherry.'

No one moves.

Mrs Abbot frowns. 'Come on now. Chop, chop. Let's give them some privacy.'

Finally there's a scraping of chairs as everyone gets to their feet, grabbing coats and bags, and eyeing Sebastian and me.

I want to tell them they don't have to leave, but before I can get a word out, Sebastian says, 'Thank you, Mrs Abbot. Yes, privacy is exactly what we need.'

He's not even blushing, the bastard. Not like I am. How infuriating.

The romance book club begins to file out the door, grinning at me as they leave and throwing approving glances in Sebastian's direction. He's a famous bachelor in the village, but most of the single ladies don't bother with him because, as he's already made very clear, he prefers to find his partners elsewhere.

He doesn't look at all the women filing out, though.

He only looks at me.

As the last person leaves, shutting the door behind them, I say, 'Come upstairs, Sebastian.'

It sounds like an invitation to something more and it's not.

But I try not to think about that as I turn and guide him up to my flat.

Chapter Twelve

Tonight then. Keep your window open.

H

SEBASTIAN

I follow Miss Jones up the narrow set of stairs, ignoring the part of me that's busily screaming that this is a very stupid decision.

It's not a stupid decision. Not at all.

I've merely come to get my great-grandfather's letters. I need to see them and I thought it was pointless waiting for Miss Jones to deliver them back to me.

I thought about it all afternoon and eventually decided that I was attaching far too much importance to what essentially is mere physical attraction. So what that she's beautiful and I want her? And, yes, I told her this. So what? Yes, the kiss was a slip-up, but today will be different, because today I'm *not* going to stay.

I'm going to get the letters from her and then I'll leave.

I didn't expect to walk in on a book-club session, but all I could think when all those eyes turned in my direction was that I'd never seen so many people inside a bookshop before. I never have that many in mine, not even on busy days.

They were all laughing too, all smiling, all enjoying themselves.

In the space of two months she's created a little community of book lovers right here in her shop, and while part of me is annoyed about it, I also can't help but respect it.

She knows her market and she knows her books, and I had first-hand experience of that today after Mr Parsons finally moved from the chair having read half of *Colours*. He didn't say a word. He merely handed me his credit card and, after I'd rung it up, walked out holding the book, still reading.

I couldn't have predicted that and it makes me wonder if what I've been doing all these years has been wrong. Oh, I still sell books, but it's getting harder and harder to make those sales as the demands on people's time keep growing and become ever more varied. I don't have a newsletter, for example, and I don't do social media. I don't have 'event evenings'. I've always thought those kinds of things were stunts, that they weren't really about the books in the end. Because that's what it's all about, after all. Books. They should sell themselves – or at least, they used to.

Not now. Hence me reviving the festival.

I walk up the stairs behind Miss Jones and she opens the door to her flat.

I'm not sure what I'm expecting, but when I take a step inside, I find myself in a small space filled with clutter. A little couch with some patterned throws over it. A battered wooden coffee table covered in papers and rugs on the wooden floor. A galley kitchen painted turquoise, with bright tiling and colourful mugs and mismatched plates stacked haphazardly on the draining board.

A little lamp on a side table near the couch has a pink scarf over the top of it and glows with muted warm light. It's a fire hazard, obviously, but I can't deny it makes the whole place feel . . . warm and homey.

Miss Jones fusses around collecting mugs from the coffee table and other dishes, her cheeks pink. Muttering apologies for the dreadful 'mess'.

Yes, it is a mess. But I don't mind it. Somehow it feels right for her.

She dumps the mugs on the kitchen counter and turns, folding her arms. 'So, what did you want to talk to me about?'

There's a wary look on her face and I don't like it. I want her to smile at me instead. Then again, I haven't earned the right to a smile and I know it, not after that murmured conversation back in my shop.

I keep making mistakes with her, and I should know better. I should have known, for example, that she'd push back about the sex. She's a stubborn woman and it turns out she's not shy about what she wants. Me.

It's tempting, so tempting to give her what she wants, what

we *both* want, but I can't. I can't start down that path, even knowing she doesn't want a relationship. Even knowing that she's okay with one night.

Resistance and control are all that separates me from the addictive tendencies of my father and grandfather, and I can't compromise on that.

Because what I told her was true.

It would never be just sex with us and I can't have it be anything more.

'I came for the letters,' I say. 'I need to look at them.'

'Of course.' She turns away without another word and vanishes through a door. A few seconds later she's back, carrying the stack of envelopes. She hands them to me, her face a mask of politeness. 'Here they are. But . . . are you sure you gave me all of them? I feel like some are missing.'

I take the stack and frown down at them. 'How can you tell? None of them are dated.'

'It's just . . . some of the notes refer to earlier ones and I was trying to find one of them and it was missing, so I just wondered.'

'Not that I know of,' I say. 'But I'll see if there are any more in that box.'

'I wonder how he got them all. I mean, he has not only her notes, but his own as well. Which means she must have returned them to him.'

'Good question. Perhaps she was angry with him?'

She lifts a shoulder. 'It could be. Something must have happened, I suppose, because, as you told me, he went to war and there are no notes mentioning him leaving, so he must have stopped sending them before he left.'

'That makes sense. He married not long after he returned.'

'And your great-grandmother definitely isn't C?'

There's a wistful note in her voice, as if she hopes my great-grandmother was the other correspondent, but I know it's not the case. Dad told me that Sebastian's marriage was unsuccessful and that my great-grandmother, Grace, did not like the village *or* the bookshop, which rules her out as a candidate for C.

'No,' I say. 'Definitely not.'

'Well, there goes that idea.' She sighs. 'I was really hoping she was and that they ended up together.'

She's a romantic at heart; I can see it in her face, hear it in her voice. Which makes my decision about not repeating the mistake of the kiss a good one.

'Sadly they didn't.' I am not a romantic. At all. 'Will that put Lisa off?'

'No. In fact, it's probably better that they don't. Lisa loves a tragedy.' Miss Jones is looking dreamily off into space. 'Perhaps she was married. "He" gets mentioned a lot, and how she couldn't sneak out to meet your great-grandfather in case "he" found out. Could be her husband.'

'Or her father,' I point out. 'Parental authority still mattered back then.'

'True,' she admits. 'Would your great-grandfather go after a married woman?'

I want to tell her that of course he wouldn't, but sadly I don't know that. 'My grandfather didn't say much about him, but apparently he kept very much to himself after the war. There are a few village rumours that he returned from where he was stationed in North Africa a changed man. That he used to be wilder. His father wanted him to give up the bookshop and study law, but he refused.'

As I speak, I'm conscious of the similarities between my great-grandfather and me. I too refused my father's edict to study. I too preferred working in a bookshop. And, if I'm honest, I too have an interest in a woman off limits to me.

At least Miss Jones isn't married, though she did mention earlier today that she'd just come out of a long-term relationship.

I'm not interested in that, though. Not in the slightest.

'Sounds like someone I know.' She gives me a pointed look.

'My father wanted me to study medicine,' I say, for some completely unknown reason. 'But I refused, so I suppose, yes, there are some similarities.'

Her eyes widen. 'Medicine?'

'Dan and I both applied to get into medical school. Me because my father wanted me to and Dan because he couldn't think of anything better to do. We both got in, but I didn't go.'

She's staring at me in surprise. 'Why not?'

It's the same response most people give me. As if it's unheard of to refuse a place in medical school. As if doing that in favour of owning a bookshop is the height of stupidity.

'Because I wasn't interested. Like I said, Dad pressured me into applying, but I wanted to work in the bookshop instead.'

She's giving me an intent look. 'Why was medical school important? Oh. It was because of your mother, wasn't it?'

I haven't told her about my mother, so some other kind soul, aka a fucking busybody, has let it slip. It's not a state secret or anything, I just can't stand the 'oh, you poor thing' looks I get when people find out.

'Yes,' I say tersely. 'Cancer. It was a long time ago.'

She opens her mouth and I expect the usual platitudes, but all she says is: 'I'm sorry. I lost my mother a couple of years ago. That was cancer as well.'

I'd heard. The relationship breakup was news, but not her mother's death.

I'm not sure what to say. Grief shadows her eyes, echoes of an incalculable loss. A loss that echoes inside me too. But my grief is older, the edges filed away and not so sharp these days. Hers is still raw. It still has teeth.

Words can't encompass it, but words are all we have in the end, so I say, 'I'm sorry too.' And then, 'You don't get over it. But you do learn to live with it. It's not what people want to hear, but it's the truth.'

The moment sits between us, heavy with the weight of our losses. But it's not uncomfortable for a change. It feels as if we're sharing something.

Her mouth curves and, finally, there is the smile. Bittersweet but there, and, yes, it's mine. She gave it to me. 'I'd prefer the truth any day of the week.'

And just like that I can't stand the distance between us. I can't stand that she's just across from me with the little breakfast bar in between us, preventing me from reaching her and pulling her into my arms.

Her dress would be so easy to get rid of. I'd only have to pull the tie that holds it closed and it would open. It would fall off and then she'd be in nothing but her underwear.

I bet she is beautiful.

I bet she is to die for.

Would she smell as sweet as she did last night, sitting on the couch next to me? Would she melt like warming candle wax against me, all soft and pliant? Would she sigh again? As if she'd been waiting her whole life to kiss me?

This is a disaster of epic proportions and only now do I see how much I've been lying to myself the whole time.

The envelopes are just an excuse.

I didn't come here for them, I came here for her. And this . . . obsession, or whatever it is that I have with her, won't end until I have what I want.

Which is her. All of her. In bed. All night.

Taste her sunshine. Wrap it around me, cover myself in it.

And maybe if I do, then I'll be able to think.

A silence falls, thick and heavy and full of the buzzing tension that is always between us.

She flushes. 'Would you . . . um . . . Would you like a drink? I don't have any scotch, I'm afraid, but I have some white wine.' She smiles again and there's a faint, wistful hope in her gaze. 'Or maybe some tea?'

Every muscle in my body is tense. 'I don't think that's a good idea, Miss Jones.'

'Why?'

'I would have thought the reasons would be obvious.'

She blushes deeper and, as with every expression I've seen on her face so far, it suits her. Makes her eyes glow. She really is a rose in that delicate pink dress. 'You can't even have one drink?'

I shouldn't reply. I shouldn't.

'I think you're underestimating your considerable charms,' I say, like the idiot I am. Then again, it's not as if I haven't told her how I feel already. 'And my susceptibility to them.'

She doesn't look away. 'Susceptible? You? I could be dancing naked in front of you and you probably wouldn't even blink.'

My throat is tight all of a sudden and so are my trousers. If that isn't a direct challenge, I don't know what is, and of course my inner Neanderthal wants to rise to it (double-entendre *absolutely* intended).

Her. Naked. Dancing.

'Care to test that theory?' I say, before I can stop myself.

Her eyes widen, then turn smoky, and her full mouth hardens. 'Oh no, I'm not testing anything. We already did that and not only did you push me away, you told me it would never happen again. You want me dancing naked, you'll have to beg for it.'

This is wrong. This is very wrong, and yet the words come out of my mouth all the same.

'Come here, Miss Jones,' I order.

She hears the change in my tone and her eyes darken even further. 'No,' she says. 'You want me, you'll have to come and get me.'

So many reasons why this is a bad idea.

So many reasons I've told myself I can't do this with her.

But they're all excuses.

Like I told her, sex won't be just sex with us.

It will be a cataclysm.

Perhaps that's why I start walking. Not out the door, but towards her.

Perhaps I need a cataclysm in my life. That's why my heart stopped the moment I first saw her. Why my world shifted on its axis. Why I've been nothing but restless since the moment she arrived.

My life has felt suffocating, pressing in on me, and I never saw that until she appeared. Bringing with her the endless joy she has for books, the respect and care she has for readers. Building communities, making connections. Doing things differently while all I'm doing is the same.

I'm trapped in the past.

Trapped by my life. Suffocated by my history.

She makes me want to blow it apart and why not?

Perhaps it's time.

And perhaps I'll start with her.

I move around the breakfast bar and stalk up to her. She watches me and I can't read the expression in her eyes now. But she doesn't move away as I come closer. She leans back against the kitchen bench and looks up at me from beneath golden lashes.

There are only inches between us. I can feel her warmth,

smell the scent of her body, vanilla and musk and summer sunshine. The pulse at the base of her throat is racing.

This moment, just before I touch her, is precious. Aching with tension. Infinite with possibilities. I want to make it last, because I have no idea what will happen after I take this step. One thing I do know, though, is that things will change, and change is something I do not care for.

Yet I think it is also something I need.

I take her hands in mine. They are small and her fingers are slender. She is trembling slightly, but it's not fear I see in her eyes.

I guide her hands to my chest and hold them there, pressing her palms flat so I can feel her touch bleed through the cotton of my shirt. Into my skin.

Into my blood.

Into the cells of my being.

Suddenly, I feel as if I've been suffocating for years and never noticed, and only now, with her hands on me, can I take a full breath.

I look down into her eyes, see the flames of desire flickering high. And I allow myself this one indulgence. Her name. 'Kate,' I murmur.

Her lush mouth opens and her hands are pressing hard to my chest, fingers curling into the cotton of my shirt as she rises on her toes.

And presses her lips to mine.

Chapter Thirteen

You changed me. You made me different.
My life will never be the same, and I don't know whether
I love you or hate you for that.

C

KATE

I don't know what I'm doing. I don't know if this is a good idea or the worst one I've ever had. I don't know if this will make my life even more difficult or not change it one iota, and which is worse out of the two . . .

Well, I don't know that either.

I only know that I'll die if I don't kiss him.

He came to me. He crossed the space between us and touched me first. That's what I wanted. I wasn't going to force myself on him if he really didn't want me to. I wanted him to make the choice.

And he did.

His chest is hard and I can feel his heartbeat. Strong. Fast. His mouth is hot and at first he doesn't move as I kiss him, as if he's waiting for something.

I touch my tongue to his lips, tracing their shape and he opens his mouth and fire consumes us. His kiss is as demanding as it was the night before and his hands are in my hair. He closes his fingers into fists and he's holding me still as he devours me, stepping in closer and pushing me up against the kitchen bench. He's tall, muscular and very strong.

I'm not afraid of him. I'm exhilarated, the blood roaring in my ears, a nagging ache between my thighs. I feel as if I'm in a sleek, powerful sports car, travelling far too fast, taking corners wildly, recklessly, and I don't care. All I want is to go faster.

I smell his skin, musk and spice, and my mouth is watering. I claw at his shirt, wanting to get it open so I can taste the salty hollow at the base of his throat, but his fingers leave my hair to close around my wrists and he holds me tight. He lifts his mouth from mine.

I can still hear his voice saying my name and it echoes inside me like a prayer.

'What?' I ask, looking up at him, my voice husky. 'If you're changing your mind I might just have to kill you.'

His eyes have gone dark, that blue just before the blackness of space again, and there's a feral glint in them that thrills me down to the bone.

'I'm not changing my mind,' he says roughly. 'But I've

been dreaming of this moment for six fucking months and you're going to have to do it my way if you don't want me to embarrass myself.'

A shiver goes through me. Six months? He's been dreaming of . . . this? Me? For six months?

I swallow. 'But . . . I've only been here for six months.'

'Yes.' His eyes glow. 'Exactly.'

'I thought you hated me,' I say, staring at him in shock.

'I never hated you.' He lets one of my wrists go as his hand drops to the tie of my wraparound dress. 'It was wanting you I hated.'

He pulls the tie and the little knot unravels and my dress falls open.

I don't stop it.

His gaze drops to my body and he lets out a breath. His expression is almost reverent as he stares at me, taking in all of me, from my throat, down over my breasts, to my hips and thighs. I don't feel self-conscious, not the way I did with Jasper, because Sebastian looks at me as if he's seeing something precious, something holy.

Jasper didn't look at me at all.

'I knew it,' he breathes. 'I knew you'd be beautiful.'

I *do* feel beautiful in this moment. I feel precious, and holy, and when he lifts a hand and touches my throat, his fingertips brushing over my skin, over my breasts and my stomach, tracing the line of my hips and thighs, I shiver.

I don't want to admit it to myself, because admitting it means Jasper's been in my head for longer than I wanted him to be, but . . . it's been a long time since I've felt beautiful or precious or holy. Mostly it's been *'Time to lay off the crisps, love'* or *'Would it kill you to use a razor sometimes?'* Or *'Can you not make that weird sound?'*

Little comments, but in a constant stream, like water torture, until every drop is painful. And you can't move in case another falls, and you think keeping still will help.

I've been keeping still for a long time.

But Sebastian makes me want to move. His touch is gentle and I want more so much and so badly it's agony.

I take a shuddering breath. 'Sebastian . . . please . . .'

The expression on his face tightens, intensifies and he pushes the dress off me so that it slides onto the floor. Then he reaches around and unhooks my bra, pushing the straps off my shoulders and letting the lace fall away.

He sighs and his hands cup my breasts, testing the weight of them, and I sigh too. His palms on my skin are so hot and I'm trembling. I can't help it.

He leans down and presses his mouth to my throat, tasting my racing pulse, making everything inside me get tight and restless. I arch my back, leaning into his hands, leaning into his mouth as it trails down from my throat, and down further. My nipples are hard and so sensitive, and I gasp as he teases them lightly with his thumbs. Then when he bends and flicks his tongue over one, I groan.

Pleasure crackles like lightning over my skin and I'm a slave to it. All those small voices in my head, the ones I hadn't realised were there, that had Jasper's voice, are gone now.

Stripped away. I want his mouth on me, his hands. I want him next to me, on me, inside me, nothing between us. He makes me feel so good I can hardly stand it.

'Oh my God,' I whisper, as he shifts one hand between my shoulder blades, bending me further back, his mouth on my breasts, nipping, teasing, sucking. Then he slips his free hand down over my stomach and beneath the waistband of my lacy knickers, his fingers sliding over my slick sex.

I feel as if I've been plugged into a power socket and he's flicked the switch, lighting me up from the inside with the most extraordinary physical pleasure. He touches me with so much gentleness and explores me with such delicate precision. He could do whatever he wanted with me and I wouldn't protest. I'd let him do anything at all.

My hips lift against his hand and he growls, his mouth against my skin, and then I'm being lifted up and placed on top of my kitchen bench. He spreads my thighs and moves between them, then reaches into the back pocket of his trousers and gets out his wallet.

A condom. Of course. What guy doesn't have one in his wallet?

I'm not complaining, though. In fact, I want him to go faster. Clearly picking up on my impatience, he takes out the condom, drops the wallet onto the floor and reaches for his fly.

'Let me,' I whisper, reaching for him too.

But he gives one definitive shake of his head, and given how much my hands are trembling, that's probably a good thing. His movements are fast and deft as he undoes his fly and gets out his cock, dealing with the protection.

Then he's pulling aside my knickers and I feel him push against me, then thrust deep inside.

The breath goes out of both of us in an explosive rush, and then we're still, staring at each other. He's big and hard and he feels utterly perfect inside me.

His blue eyes are like stars and there is wonder in them. And awe. He's looking at me as if he can't believe I'm real, as if there's nothing wrong with me, nothing that needs fixing. As if I'm perfect just as I am and I . . . I feel the same about him.

The sense of connection we have in this moment is amazing.

He grips one of my hips and cups the side of my face with the other, his thumb tracing my mouth. 'Are you okay?' His voice is so deep and rough it's almost unrecognisable. I can also hear the tension in it. I can feel the tension in him too. He's holding himself back.

My heart aches at the question. Such a simple thing, to ask if I'm okay. As if it matters to him. As if my pleasure is of the most vital importance.

'I'm more than okay,' I murmur, unable to be anything but honest with him. 'I'm fantastic. And you feel . . . incredible.'

A flicker of male satisfaction crosses his face and he lowers his head and kisses me. At the same time he begins to move and the electricity of the sensation expands outwards and tightens, catching me in a fine net of pleasure.

I lift my hands and take his face between them, glorying

in the prickle of stubble against my palms. And I kiss him back, devouring him as he devours me, and the pleasure we're generating between us devours us too.

I knew this would destroy me and it will. And I don't care.

I want to feel this for ever. Have his mouth on mine and him inside me, moving, making me feel so good. Better than Jasper ever did. Sebastian makes me feel beautiful. Sebastian makes me feel strong.

He moves faster and it gets wilder, hotter, more desperate. I wind my legs around his hips, trying to get closer, frantic for more of him, and he gives it to me.

We're both as lost as each other, our hands touching, stroking, grasping, clinging. Then his fingers find their way between my thighs, giving me more friction, and the orgasm rushes over me, far too fast and intense, and I'm crying out, clinging to him as it takes me.

I'm still shaking when he moves harder and faster, and then it takes him too, his mouth turned against my throat, the sharp edge of his teeth on my skin. He growls my name again, '*Kate*,' and I close my eyes, holding on to him as he shudders against me.

Neither of us move for a long time afterwards.

It's as if I've had an out-of-body experience and I'm trying to find my way back to myself again. I almost don't want to. I want to stay where I am, play amongst the stars he threw me up into.

But then I feel him move, pulling away from me, and I hate the cold of the air against my heated skin. I'd much rather have him there instead.

He deals with the condom and, as he does so, I feel suddenly self-conscious and weird. I'm sitting on my kitchen bench in only my knickers, while he's still fully dressed. All he had to do was zip up his fly.

Perhaps it was terrible. Perhaps this perfection was all in my head. He probably didn't think I was beautiful at all, and those things he said were just—

He turns back to me and all my thoughts scatter as his hands slide possessively up my bare thighs. The expression on his face is as intense as it has ever been.

'You wanted me to come and get you,' he says. 'And I did. Now you need to ask me to stay.'

I swallow, searching his face. Does he really mean it or is this something he says to every woman he sleeps with? 'Do you . . . want to?'

'What do you think? I want a night, Miss Jones, and a night I'm going to have.'

He means it, I can see it in his eyes, and I should know that about him by now. That he's always straight up. He always says what he means.

The band that has tightened around my heart eases. Yet his dark brows twitch and he lifts a hand to cup my jaw. 'What is it?'

Somehow he's picked up on my doubt, which is annoying, because I don't want to talk about Jasper and everything he did to me, not here. Not with him. So instead I say, 'Miss Jones? Really? Still?'

His hands stroke my sides, a tender touch that makes me

want to arch my back and purr like a cat. 'Kate, then,' he says. 'Miss Jones when you're bad.'

I shiver. I like that idea very much. 'What if I don't want a night?'

'If I thought you meant it, I'd walk away, and you know that.' His fingertips gently trace the curves of my breasts. 'But you don't mean it.'

There's a smug, male note in his voice and I can't help smiling. 'No, you're right. I don't.'

'Good,' he murmurs. 'One night and that's all.'

Somewhere in my heart I can feel something twist, as if part of me is disappointed. As if part of me wants more.

But that's why it can only be one night.

He doesn't want more and neither do I, and I'm fine with it.

I ignore my doubts, wrap my arms around his neck, and when he asks me where my bedroom is, I give him directions.

He carries me there and, even though I protest, I don't make any effort to leave his arms. I like it there. I like it too much. Lying here against his warm chest, looking up at him and his taut profile. His Roman nose. His mouth that doesn't smile as much as it should. That doesn't smile at all.

I'm going to get a smile, I vow to myself silently, as he carries me through into my little bedroom. I'm going to make this man smile come hell or high water.

He doesn't look around as he steps into my bedroom. He keeps his attention on me and me only as he deposits me on the edge of my bed. Then he falls to his knees in front of me, kissing my throat and then going down further, between my breasts and over my stomach. I sigh as he pushes me back and grips the waistband of my knickers, pulling them down and off until I'm finally naked.

He kisses his way up my thighs and between, and yet although I'm loving his mouth on me, I want to touch him. I want him as naked as I am.

'No,' I whisper, and push him away, sitting up and meeting his shadowed blue eyes. 'Take off your clothes, Mr Blackwood.'

And there it is, at last. The corner of his mouth lifts. It's not a smile so much as a smirk, but I love it. There is arrogance in it and also knowledge. He knows he's beautiful to me and he's going to milk this moment for all it's worth.

Good.

I want him to.

I want to sit back and worship him in all his glory.

He stands, his blue gaze pinned to mine, and he unbuttons the shirt I've already clawed at, exposing his broad chest and going down further to his muscled stomach. He shrugs out of it and discards it on the floor. Shoes next, then his hands go to his belt, undoing it and the buttons of his trousers.

It's unspeakably erotic.

He shoves his trousers down, taking his boxers with them, and steps out of the fabric. Naked.

He's so gorgeous I can't breathe.

Hard everywhere. Muscled and strong. Crisp hair on his chest, and shoulders to carry the world. Narrow hips and powerful thighs.

My God. This man isn't a bookseller. He's a god.

I reach for him, but he's already pushing me down on the mattress, his warm skin sliding over mine, his weight settling on me. I make a sound and push at him, and we roll over so I'm on top.

I sit up, liking this for now, and look down at him, my palms on his bare chest. His skin is golden and velvety and I love touching it. I stroke him and he stares at me, his gaze dark.

'Kiss me,' he says, low and intense. 'Now.'

'So demanding,' I murmur. 'Not yet. It's my turn.'

His fingers close around my hips and he holds me down on him, moving beneath me in a way that makes me gasp. 'Not yet,' he echoes.

Then he reaches one hand up and closes it in my hair and pulls my mouth down on his.

I love his demands. I love his intensity.

What seems too much in the bookstore is perfect here, and I feel myself change to meet him.

I grab his wrists and put them down on either side of his head and hold them on the pillows. I bite his lower lip and move on him, making him growl. 'My turn,' I whisper. 'Deal with it.'

'Then touch me, damn you.'

I do. I stroke him, caress him. I taste him. He tastes of salt and heat and musk and he's delicious. I can't get enough of him. Despite his demands and his growls, he lets me play, lets me do what I want and, at the end, when I grab another condom from his wallet and straddle him and ride, he grips my hips hard.

'Fucking beautiful,' he says roughly, looking up at me. 'You're fucking beautiful, Miss Jones.'

He's the anti-Jasper. The antivenom to my ex's venom. He gives me back what Jasper took away, and I love him for that.

I smile, then lean down and kiss him. 'So are you, Mr Blackwood,' I murmur against his mouth. 'So are you.'

He makes another growling sound and then he turns us, pins me beneath him and he moves, slow and deep, and I'm lost.

I don't think I'm ever going to recover from this.

And maybe I don't want to.

Chapter Fourteen

'You have bewitched me body and soul'.
Forgive me for using another's words,
but sometimes only Austen will do.

H

SEBASTIAN

A warm, muted light presses against my closed lids and I open them, for a moment content to do nothing but lie, warm and sated, in sheets that smell of . . . sex. Of . . . vanilla. Of . . . her.

I blink. And turn my head.

There she is, lying next to me, her hair golden on the pillow and all spread out. She has her hands tucked beneath her chin like a child, and her golden eyelashes rest softly on her satiny cheeks.

She's beautiful.

She's fast asleep and I must leave her.

I don't want to. Even now, I can feel my body hardening, wanting more of her heat, of the feeling of being inside her. Of her breath in my ear and the sound of my name in her mouth as she comes.

I had no idea that pretty Miss Jones, with her fluffy golden hair and her pretty little dresses, hides the most passionate of souls. She's as fierce in bed as she is stubborn out of it, and I was right about what I'd thought the night before. It *was* a cataclysm and she wrecked me.

She's changed me and I'm not sure what to do about it.

I should leave, slip out before she wakes up, but . . . I can't bring myself to do so. That would be a coward's way out and she deserves better than that, especially after last night.

So I lie there and watch her and, eventually, her golden lashes flutter and they open, her grey eyes meeting mine.

There's no shock in her face, no surprise. She smiles slowly, like the sun coming up, as if finding me beside her is the best thing that's ever happened to her.

My chest aches for reasons I can't explain, yet despite that, I find myself smiling back. It feels like we're sharing a wonderful secret.

'Did you read the book I gave you?' Her voice is soft and husky with sleep.

I turn on my side to face her. 'Yes. I read it in one sitting. I stayed up until three a.m., thank you very much.'

Her eyes sparkle. 'I knew you'd like it. I'd never have picked you for a science fiction reader, though.'

It feels easy to talk to her like this, without the relentless tension of physical chemistry between us. Though the chemistry hasn't gone. I can still feel it crackling in the air. It doesn't bother me now, though, not like it did before. Not when every muscle in my body is relaxed and I feel sated and lazy with the after-effects of magnificent sex. Not when I can reach out and pull her close if it gets too much.

'I've always read it. Since I was a kid.'

'Don't tell me, you were a space geek.'

I don't deny it. 'I also liked the ideas, and the escapism factor.'

'So, what was your favourite book as a kid?'

'*The Hobbit*,' I say, without hesitation. 'And *The Lord of the Rings*.'

'Oh my God, you were an *LOTR* nerd too.' She looks delighted, her face glowing, and I feel insufferably smug for having so delighted her.

'Guilty,' I say. 'What about you? What was your favourite childhood read?'

'*I Capture the Castle*. Dodie Smith.'

I haven't read it, but I know the title. 'About the girl who lives in the castle with her disaster of a family?'

'That's the one.'

'That's an old book.'

'I know.' The sparkle in her eyes fades. 'It was my mother's favourite.'

Her mother, whom she lost two years ago. I know how that feels.

I reach out and tuck a curl behind her ear, touching her gently. 'You were close?'

'Yeah. She brought me up on her own. We had no money, so she used to take me to the library for some free entertainment. Then there was that one birthday where she took me into a bookshop and told me I could choose any book I wanted.'

I can see how much that meant to her. 'What book did you choose?'

'I can't remember the title now. But I was a little girl, so it had fairies in it.'

I smile, thinking of her as that little girl, walking wide-eyed into a bookshop. 'Is that where your dream of being a bookshop owner came from?'

She nods. 'We used to live next door to one when I was ten. Mum was out a lot, working, and she knew the bookseller and would ask her to keep an eye on me. She never minded. She'd let me sit there for hours, reading.'

Another feeling I know all too well, that escape from reality into another one. A better one.

'But you got a job in publishing first?' I ask.

'Yeah. Mum lived paycheque to paycheque, and she didn't like owning things or having "stuff". She was kind of a free spirit, which is fine when you don't have kids. But when you do . . .'

I don't miss the bitter note in her voice. 'Was your childhood difficult?'

'In some ways. I was alone a lot, and moving around constantly was tough. But I did love the bookshops and libraries I went to. Anyway, I wanted something more stable and secure for myself, so I went to uni, then finally managed to get an editorial assistant job at a publishing house.'

'Did you like it?'

'I did.' She smiles at what is obviously a pleasant memory. 'It was great. But . . .'

She's reeling me in with these little glimpses into her past, and I'm helpless to resist. I want to know. I want to know everything. 'But?' I prompt.

Her smile vanishes, the sun going down. 'But then Mum died, and a couple of years after that, my relationship broke up, and then I didn't want to be in London.'

'And so you came here.'

'And so I came here,' she echoes. 'It took me a while to decide what I wanted to do with the property, but once I realised I wanted to get away from the big city, it seemed like fate was trying to tell me something. Then I got here and took one look at the building and it just . . . was a bookshop to me. That's how it started.'

I can't help staring at her. She has lost a lot and that must have been difficult. Her mother, her relationship, her job. Her life in London. It takes strength and resilience to come back from that, to create a new life in a different place, yet that's exactly what she's done.

She is remarkable.

'That must have been very hard,' I say, my fingertips brushing her cheek.

She turns her face against my hand, her eyelashes lowering,

veiling her gaze. 'It was. I loved the job, but Mum got sick very suddenly. She hadn't told me about the cancer, so that was a shock. She only lasted a couple of months, which was a blessing, really. I hated to see her in pain.'

I know that thought. I know it intimately. My father kept most of my own mother's last weeks from me, but even as a kid I knew that lingering on, in pain, was in no one's best interests.

I stroke her skin, the weight of everything that I want to say all at once too much for me. Words aren't enough, sometimes.

'I am very sorry about your mother,' I say at last, the emptiest of empty statements. 'Cancer is a terrible disease.'

'It is. Sometimes, though, you have to take what you can from an awful situation. You know, find the silver lining. And I suppose my silver lining was realising that, if I didn't open my own bookshop now, I never would. I needed to come back to my roots, too, even though I knew nothing about those roots.' She fixes me with a direct look all at once. 'I think I want to find out. Those letters of your great-grandfather's make me want to know more about my own family.' A shadow flickers through her eyes. 'Because, now, I'm the only one left.'

The Blackwoods have always been here in Wychtree and I have always known where I come from. Sometimes that's a millstone and sometimes it's reassuring. Either way, I can understand why she would want to know about her origins too.

'I could help you,' I say. 'There are bound to be people around who knew your grandmother, and maybe even your mother, too. I don't remember them, but someone else must do.'

Her smile this time makes my chest ache. 'Would you?'

'Yes, of course,' I promise, even though there are doubts inside me at the wisdom of such a promise. 'You helped me with Lisa Underwood, so it's the least I can do.'

'We don't know if she's coming yet, though.'

'No, that's true.' She's too far away, I realise, and I want her nearer. I reach out and pull her close, the warmth of her naked body sliding over mine making me instantly hard. 'I'll help you regardless.'

She folds her hands on my chest. 'Thank you,' she says. 'You're not half bad, really, are you?'

I sift my fingers through her hair. It feels like raw silk. 'I can be all bad if you prefer.'

'You know I do.' She studies me as if she's looking for something, but I can't tell what it is. 'What about you? Tell me about the Blackwoods.'

I'm relaxed and the uncoiling desire inside me is lazy, and with the softness of her hair between my fingers, I don't mind telling her. 'Not much to say. My great-grandfather, as you know, was a bookseller. He married after coming back from the war and they had my grandfather. His wife left him when my grandfather was little so he had to bring him up by himself. He died when my grandfather was eighteen.'

'He died young, then.'

'Comparatively, yes. It's thought that he drowned. His clothes were discovered on the riverbank near Wychtree, but his body was never found. My grandfather once said that he drowned himself because he never got over my great-grandmother leaving, but now . . . I'm not so sure.'

'How awful.' There's sympathy in her eyes. 'Do you think it might have something to do with C?'

'Judging from those notes, possibly. Anyway, my grandfather took over the bookshop afterwards, but his successful running of it was stymied by a gambling addiction that only got worse after my grandmother left him.'

Her brow creases. 'Oh dear. How did that happen? Your grandmother leaving, I mean?'

'Oh, she met my grandfather when they were both very young. Too young. She was one of those sixties hippies who lived an itinerant lifestyle. There was some music festival happening near Wychtree and she was staying in the village, and wandered into the bookshop one day. Love at first sight, apparently. Anyway, she was a free spirit, and didn't like the village any more than my great-grandmother did. My grandfather had to marry her because she got pregnant, and that was what you did back then. Not long after having Dad, she left my grandfather and went back to London.' I sift yet more strands of her hair through my fingers, relishing the feel of it. 'I don't remember her – she didn't have much contact with Dad after she left, or so Dad said – but it broke my grandfather's heart. He gambled a lot afterwards and my father had to take steps to protect the bookshop as he got older and could take over. My grandfather then died about nine years ago of a stroke.'

The crease between her brows deepens. 'Oh, that's tragic.'

'The Blackwoods are famous for falling for and marrying unsuitable women far too young,' I say. 'My father was the same.'

She puts her chin on her folded hands. 'How?'

An old grief grips me, but I'm the one who's introduced the subject, so I go on. 'Dad met Mum in a café when he was in London for a book fair. She was studying law, was bright and ambitious, and they hit it off talking about books.' Memories play through my head, of sitting in the garden with Mum as she tells me about the day she met Dad. How she loved his intelligence and his quick wit. I remember her smiling and shooting me a glance. *And his blue eyes,* she added. 'She loved the bookshop, unlike the other Blackwood wives. And she loved the village. She studied law through the Open University and wanted to start her own practice here. But . . . my father preferred the bottle to her. She was actually going to leave him, I think, but then she found out she had cancer.'

An old anger twists in my gut. At Dad and how he let his addiction get in the way of being a good husband. How he let it control him and eventually how he disappeared into it and into his grief. How he stopped being a husband to my mother and a father to me.

But I don't want to talk about Dad. We're talking about my mother and she's more important.

'I'm so sorry,' Kate says. 'That must have been really awful.'

'It was,' I say simply. Because that's exactly what it was. Awful. 'It was a long time ago, but I was very close to her.' I hesitate a moment, then add, 'I started reading fantasy books and science fiction when she was sick. Because it was an escape. I could lose myself for a few hours in a totally different world.'

She nods. 'That makes sense. But . . . why did you never expand what you carry in the bookshop? You don't include genre fiction at all and I can't help but wonder, if you like it, why you don't?'

It's a fair question and one I've never put much thought into, because I've never had to. Not until she came along. 'Because that's the way it's always been done,' I say, thinking. 'My grandfather didn't want to stock what he thought were "cheap" books, so we never did. And Dad . . . lost interest in the bookshop after Mum died.' I wind one of her curls around my finger. 'A good thing, since if I had, your bookshop may not have got off the ground.'

She smiles. 'Oh, you think so?'

I'm only partly teasing her. 'Of course. I am a very good bookseller, Miss Jones.'

She shifts on me, the press of her body against mine rousing me, and the lazy desire coursing through my veins becomes less lazy. 'You are, Sebastian. But you could have some amazing events at Blackwood Books. Different from mine, but along the same lines.' There's excitement in her eyes now. 'You could have talks on art history or architecture or photography or something.' Her face is beautifully flushed. 'Oh, what about a chess evening? Or a poetry reading? Do you have a book club?' She gives me a sudden and very direct stare. 'Why do you not have a book club, Sebastian?'

I let go of her hair and shift, turning us both over and

pinning her beneath me. 'Because I never knew I needed one,' I say, as I settle myself between her thighs.

She puts her palms flat to my chest, stroking my skin with her thumbs. It feels good. More than good. It feels fantastic. 'Well, you do. As much as we'd like them to, books don't just sell themselves these days. You have to get out there and sell them. Tell people why they should be reading instead of watching Netflix or playing World of Warcraft or whatever else they're doing. Ask people what they like to read, tell them about new releases . . . There's lots you can be doing.' She reaches one hand to my face, touching my cheekbone. Her fingers are gentle and it's been so long since I've been touched this way, I can hardly stand it. 'You have so much experience and so much knowledge about what you do, Sebastian. But more than that, you have passion. And I think there are a lot of people who'd love to share that with you.'

I lean into her hand the way she leaned into mine, then I turn and press a kiss to her palm. 'I don't take kindly to people telling me how to do my job. But I'll make an exception for you.' Again, I'm only partly teasing.

'It's a good idea,' she says earnestly. 'You know I'm right.'

I move on her, pressing myself against the sensitive place between her thighs, making her gasp. 'You are. You're an incredibly intelligent woman, Kate Jones. In fact, I'd go so far as to say you're brilliant.'

Colour flushes her face, her hair spread and tangled on the pillow like sea-drenched kelp. A mermaid I've caught and am taking my pleasure with. 'Tell me something I don't know,' she says, smiling. 'If you help me with my history, I could help you with getting events started at Blackwood Books, or even a newsletter.'

I shouldn't agree, not when being in her company constantly is such a test. Then again, I've already agreed to too much and what she's suggested will help the bookshop. As to having her around all the time . . . well, that will be the future's problem. Right now, there's only one issue that's concerning me.

'I would love your help,' I say. 'And I could also use your help with this other little problem of mine.' I shift again, making her groan. 'It appears some beautiful witch has got me hard and I really don't know what to do about it.'

She's breathing faster now. 'You really don't? Do you need some instruction?'

I take her wrists in my hands and press them down on the pillow beside her head. 'Oh, I think I can work it out.'

I bend and kiss her.

And lose us both in the never-ending moment.

Chapter Fifteen

I can't come tonight. I'm so sorry. I miss you so much it hurts

C

KATE

I unlock the bookshop's front door and turn the sign over to 'Open'. Then I stand a minute, staring through the glass to Blackwood Books across the road.

He's finally changed his front window. A large map hangs as a background and, if I'm not much mistaken, it's a map of Middle Earth. Stacks of books are arranged artistically in front of it – multiple editions of *The Lord of the Rings*, *The Silmarillion* and *The Hobbit*, as well as books about the making of the movies, including a guidebook to Hobbiton in New Zealand.

It's a wonderful window and it makes me want to do a companion piece. I'm already thinking of a sign I can put up.

'If you loved *The Lord of the Rings*, you'll love these fabulous fantasy reads too!'

I can see his tall figure moving around in the shop and my breath catches.

It's been two days since our night together and, while I knew it would destroy me, I'm still trying not to let it. He didn't linger that morning, even though I offered to make him breakfast. He only shook his head, kissed me hard, then left without another word.

We didn't need to repeat what we'd already said to each other. We both knew it was only going to be for one night.

Yet ever since then I've felt . . . flat. I'm annoyed about it. I should have known that I'd feel shitty after he left and I do, and it's galling. I hate being right sometimes.

He hasn't contacted me, not for two days, and that's making me feel crappy too. I haven't texted him, it's true, but I want to give him space. And I need space for me, since mooning around after him like a lovesick teenager isn't working for me either.

I'm not a teenager and I'm *not* lovesick.

That night with him was the best sex I'd ever had in my entire life. It was healing after the awfulness of Jasper. But good sex doesn't mean love. I'm not that stupid.

I turn away from the door, ignoring the complicated mix of feelings sitting inside me, and go back to the counter. I start up the computer and check my email. There's a message from Lisa, so I open it, my heart racing.

She loves the notes. She loves the thought of Wychtree.

She's between books and has been looking for some inspiration and this might be it. She'd love to attend the festival and, no, she won't require a fee!

A surge of adrenaline hits me and I give the air a quick punch. This is wonderful news. This is brilliant. We have our headliner.

I make for the door again, all set to dash across the road to tell Sebastian. But as I reach for the door handle, I stop.

And take a breath.

And think.

Is it really a good idea to be in his presence again? And so soon? Should I text him instead? Respect the distance he's putting between us?

I hate these questions. I hate how uncertain I feel. I've felt more in charge of my life since coming to Wychtree than I ever have, yet I'm not in charge of this and I don't like it.

I was right, he *has* destroyed me. Like Jasper destroyed me, but in a different way.

Jasper was sneaky and sly: he took little pieces of me away, bit by bit. Pieces I hadn't even known I was missing until the night he wanted me to put my grieving aside for him and I realised he'd effectively deleted all my friends from my life.

Like that picture of Dorian Gray, I finally saw him for who he really was. Not the handsome, successful man I'd been living with and loving for four years, but a petulant narcissist.

Sebastian is handsome too, but he isn't a narcissist. He's intense and full-on, but he doesn't lie, and not everything is about him. He doesn't take things away from me, either; he gives them back. Calling me brilliant, calling me beautiful.

However, I can't let my feelings about him dictate my behaviour. The festival is something external that we're organising and it has nothing to do with any relationship we may or may not have. It's separate.

This life I've built here, too, is separate. It's mine, in a way the past four years with Jasper weren't, and if I want any chance at staying in charge of it, I have to keep it separate.

I can't let what happened between Sebastian and me affect the festival or our businesses, and there will always be things that we need to discuss. So to hell with a text. He should know about Lisa and I need to tell him personally.

I pull open the door and walk with determination over to Blackwood Books. The bell chimes as I go in.

Sebastian is at a shelf, talking to Lucy, one of the local estate agents. She's tall and sleek in her white suit, her black hair perfectly coiffed. Aisling told me once that she had a crush on Sebastian and I see it in action now. The delicate blush in her cheeks. The smile. Her attention focusing on him.

Jealousy slides a needle beneath my skin, but I try to ignore it. I don't care if she flirts with him. We had our one night together and it's over. I have no claim on him and he doesn't have one on me. It's fine.

She laughs and it's like sandpaper scraping over my skin.

I should leave and come back when she's gone, but I'm stubborn now. What do I care if she's here or not? She's a customer anyway, so he won't be that long.

As he goes to the counter and rings up the book, Lucy chats away. His gaze shifts to mine and the air crackles around us. With heat and with knowledge. With the memory of our night together. His hands on my skin. His mouth on mine. Him inside me, moving . . .

I tear my gaze away and study the spines on the bookcase nearby. I study them really, *really* hard.

Lucy is in no hurry, still talking.

My God, I think, *leave the man alone!*

Finally, after what seems like a full two hours, she leaves and I approach the counter. He watches me. His shirt today is dark blue and it makes the colour of his eyes even more intense.

My face is hot, my skin tight, and my fingers itch with the need to reach for the top button of that shirt to flick it open.

'Miss Jones,' he says, aggravatingly formal. 'What can I do for you?'

'Sebastian,' I say, hating the awkwardness in my voice. 'I heard from Lisa today. The letters were a hit. She says she's between books and has been looking for some inspiration and would love to come to Wychtree. She won't require a fee.'

His face lights up and his mouth curves, and that smile hits me right in the centre of my chest, making it difficult to breathe. 'That's fantastic,' he says. 'Amazing news. I'll get in touch with the printer for the programme this morning.'

Another smile in the space of two days. It's a bloody miracle and even more pleasing that he smiled because of me.

'I know,' I say, smiling back, because I just can't help myself. 'Isn't it great? It's extremely late notice and everything, but I think having her name as the headliner is going to make a huge difference.'

For a second there is no awkwardness between us. Nothing but a shared triumph and delight that this festival might just work out after all, and maybe not just work out, but be a success.

'Yes, given that, we might need a bigger venue.' Sebastian looks around, his black brows twitching together. 'This place and Portable Magic are quite small.'

'Let's see what tickets we sell,' I say. 'There's the village hall if an event gets out of hand, but we should have the majority of events here and at my shop. This place is so beautiful. People will love being in here, and for the out-of-towners, they'll want to come back.'

He glances at me, that smile on his face, and I feel my heart turn over in my chest. 'They're going to come back for Portable Magic too. You're good with people.'

I love his praise, which is pretty stupid of me, but I can't help it. Jasper's compliments always held hidden barbs, and he certainly never admired anything I did, not like Sebastian does. It really means a lot coming from him, because I've only been in the bookselling game for a scant couple of months, while he's been at it for at least a decade.

My face gets even hotter, which is annoying. 'Thank you,' I say, flustered. Then, changing the subject, 'We should go over our schedule for the festival again. I can also help you with that newsletter, if you'd like.'

Slowly the light fades from his eyes and from his face,

the warmth of his own excitement cooling. Like lava, he hardens back into stone. 'Yes, we should do that.' His voice is formal once again. 'How about tomorrow evening after closing?'

The loss of his smile is upsetting, but I decide I'm not going to let it matter. We're going to be colleagues now, which is much better than enemies, so, really, any meeting where we're not arguing is a win.

I keep my own smile pasted on. 'That sounds great.'

He looks away. 'If you'll forgive me, I have some stock I have to order.'

It's a dismissal loud and clear, and, yes, it hurts. But I can't let it. This was not what I promised myself. I'm not going to let a man hurt me, not again.

So I swallow down my hurt, keeping my smile as a shield between him and me. Good thoughts. Good thoughts.

'No problem. I've got a few things to do myself. See you tomorrow, then.' I turn and head to the front door.

I'm reaching to push it open when he says, 'Miss Jones.'

I stop and glance at him, my heart racing. 'Yes?'

'Mrs Bennet in Wychtree Crafts might have known your grandmother. They're of an age, I think. Why don't we go there before closing tomorrow? We can look at the festival stuff afterwards.'

I'd thought he'd forgotten the offer he'd made, while in my bed, to help me investigate some of my own lost history. Apparently not.

My chest feels tight. 'We?'

'Mrs Bennet is a little . . . standoffish. You might find me being there will help things.'

He's not wrong. Mrs Bennet *is* very standoffish, though I'm not sure how him being there will help, considering how standoffish he is. Maybe Mrs Bennet has a soft spot for him. I want to tease him about it, but we're both still doing this hideous formality thing, so I only say, 'That would be great, then. Thank you.'

He shrugs a shoulder. 'It's nothing. There're a couple of other people who might know more too. I'll conduct further investigations.'

'You don't have to.'

'I know I don't.' His gaze is very direct and intense. 'But I made you a promise and I intend to keep it.'

He made more promises to me that night. He promised me he'd make me feel better than I ever had in my entire life, that I'd come so hard I'd scream his name. He kept those promises too.

Perhaps he's thinking about that as well, because fire ignites in his eyes, leaping and burning, and it's back, our physical chemistry. Burning twice as high and twice as hot. Because we know now what it's like between us and it's . . . amazing. Fantastic. Phenomenal.

But it's not happening again.

I realise now the truth of that, settling down inside me like a weight.

My eyes prickle, which is ridiculous. I will not cry over him. I will not.

I will never let a man make me cry again.

I blink and turn on my brightest and bestest smile ever. 'Thank you, Sebastian. I'll see you tomorrow.'

Back in Portable Magic, I distract myself from the ache in my chest with an effusive email to Lisa. Then I contact her publicist and send her the details of the festival. I'll no doubt need to find her a place to stay, so I make some suggestions, including the Wychtree Arms, where all the rooms have recently had an update. Not five star by any stretch of the imagination, but they're homey and comfortable, and I can afford to pay her accommodation expenses there at least.

I'm finishing up when Aisling comes in, her little girl Beth on her hip. I have a box of toys near the kids' shelves for toddlers, and Aisling goes right there and gets them out for Beth. 'Hey,' she says, as she gets Beth sorted with a cloth book and some blocks. 'How are you? I need you to give me an update on Tall, Dark and Brooding.'

I try to keep my face in some semblance of pleasant. 'Update? What kind of update?'

Aisling shakes back her red hair and comes over to the counter as Beth happily paws through the cloth book. 'Last I saw of you was you waiting to talk to him "privately".'

'We were only talking about the festival.'

Aisling eyes me. 'Is that why you're blushing?'

I don't know what to say. Sebastian and I didn't have a conversation about whether we should tell people we'd slept together, but . . . I've been here over two months now and I know there's a village rumour mill. If people knew, the gossip would be rife, I'm certain. I'm also certain Sebastian would hate that.

Then again, I don't have anyone else to talk to about him, not a single person, and I could use an understanding ear.

I give Aisling a meaningful look. 'I don't want anyone else to know, okay?'

She raises a brow. 'Oh, so it's like that, is it?'

'Please, Ash.'

'Hey, no problem. I'm not a gossip and I know gossips say that all the time, but I honestly mean it.'

I know she does, so I nod. 'Okay. So . . . we slept together.'

She does not look surprised. 'About time.'

'It's not like that. It was only a one-off.'

'I have to say, that's not what I was hoping.' She puts her elbows on the counter and looks at me. 'Was he that bad? I've never heard anything about his skills in the bedroom, to be clear. But . . . well.' She smirks. 'He looks like he knows his way around a woman.'

I glare. 'It wasn't bad. It was the opposite. It was . . . I don't have the words to describe it, to be honest. But neither of us is looking for a relationship and so . . .'

'So, what? One and done?' She frowns slightly. 'His decision or yours?'

'Both of ours.' I'm trying to sound certain.

She looks sceptical. 'I hear wistfulness.'

'No. No wistfulness is happening.' I bite my lip, trying not to say the thing I really want to say, the thing I really want to ask. But it's a battle I lose, because the next thing I know, I'm asking, 'You knew him, right? As a kid? What was he like at school?'

'Oh dear,' Aisling mutters. 'That's not a good sign.'

'Ash.'

'Fine. He was serious and very reserved. A lot of girls had the hots for him, but he kept to himself. Which, quite frankly, made the general hysteria over him even worse. His father was a drunk and his grandfather almost lost the bookshop due to gambling debts. You know, the whole tragic backstory nine yards.'

Yes, so I heard. And as backstories go, it's rough. I think again about what he said regarding his grandfather and his father, about the gambling addiction and the alcoholism that nearly lost him the bookshop. About what he said about unsuitable women.

I think of his intensity and his passion and the way he looked at me. The hunger in his eyes when I touched him. Of how reserved and aloof he seems.

He's lonely, I think. He's desperately, horribly lonely, and he doesn't know what to do about it.

'Does he have any friends here?' I ask. 'Apart from Dan, I mean?'

Aisling screws her face up in thought. 'Hmm. Good question. No, I don't think he does. He's really reserved, like I said. He doesn't let people get close.'

I almost ask her why, but I think I know already.

When he lost his mother, he escaped into the pages of a book. And when his father was busy drinking, he escaped into the bookshop and never came out again.

He doesn't share himself with people, he cuts himself off. He's been hurt and he's protecting himself, I think.

Then it occurs to me that his shop is the only common ground he has with people. It's how he communicates. Through the pages of the books he sells.

It's what I do too, except my shop isn't there to protect me. I invite people in, I want them to be there. I want to share myself and my love of books. I want connections. But he doesn't.

Even his predilection for taking his pleasures elsewhere is him cutting himself off. So he can have sex without strings. Without commitment.

As I've already discovered, he's an all or nothing man and, right now, he's decided to have nothing. No wonder he's lonely.

We're the same in some ways and yet so different in others.

'I wouldn't go there if I were you,' Aisling advises. 'The sex might be great, but the Blackwoods . . . Well, they're not exactly great when it comes to relationships.'

'Don't worry,' I say. 'I wasn't thinking of going there. I was just curious.'

But I'm lying.

Of course I'm thinking of going there.

Maybe it's compounding error after error, but still. I hate the thought of Sebastian Blackwood being lonely.

I hate it with all my heart.

Chapter Sixteen

You looked so pale today.
There were shadows under your eyes.
Are you well, darling C?

H

SEBASTIAN

I sit in my living room with the letters from Sebastian Black-wood the First scattered on my coffee table. I'm trying to make sense of them. They're not dated, which is an issue, but it's possible to work out a vague sort of timeline based on the content.

It's very obvious that Kate – *Miss Jones* – was right about H passing them to C through books he lent her, with the notes hidden in the pages. And then C replying with her own note when she gave the book back.

What's also obvious is that they're love notes and that C

was unavailable. However, it's not clear who the man controlling her life was. A husband? Father? Someone else? He's only referred to as 'he' in the notes.

I study them. Kate – *Miss Jones* – was also correct when she said there were some missing. That does seem to be the case. There are notes that indicate they spent the night together, but afterwards they seem to peter out. One or two of the notes reference a reply that isn't in the stack my great-grandfather left behind, so either some really are missing or the notes stopped.

I pick up the one that I think might be the last one. It's from H, my great-grandfather.

> *You looked so pale today. There were shadows under your eyes. Are you well, darling C? Are you not sleeping? Perhaps* Ash Wednesday *will help. Not that it is boring! Far from it. There is some wonderful imagery in Eliot's poetry that I think you will enjoy. I prefer it to* The Waste Land.

> *H*

> *P.S. The shadow under your right eye looks more like a bruise, now that I think of it. What happened?*

I stare at it, frowning. It's clear he was worried about C, and now I'm wondering the same thing. What happened?

There's no answering note in the pile and none of the other notes seem to indicate anything was wrong.

A glass of scotch sits beside the notes on the table and I pick it up and take a sip, relishing the burn as it slides down. I'm parsimonious with my drinking because of Dad, and even though I probably shouldn't be drinking anything at all, I enjoy testing myself on the odd occasion.

The way I'm going to test myself tomorrow when I take Kate – *Miss Fucking Jones* – to see Mrs Bennet.

I allowed us both a couple of days of space and, though I was surprised when she came charging into the bookshop today to deliver the news about Lisa Underwood, I was pleased with my response.

I was cool, calm. Lucy Coulter from Coulter's First Real Estate didn't know that inside me a Neanderthal was roaring to close the space between me and *Miss Fucking Jones*. Take her in my arms. Have her on the floor.

But, no, I continued to sell her the latest Martin Amis with nary a blink.

Only when she'd gone, when there was no one but me and Miss Jones, wearing a long, white, oversized linen shirt and leggings, her hair braided down her back, standing there, did I blink.

Of course, what I wanted was to rip that shirt apart and get my mouth on her skin, my hands on her breasts, and—

Well. I didn't. Instead, I calmly agreed to help her find out more about her family, which means I passed that first test just fine.

Enough to know that tomorrow I'll also be fine.

I take another sip of my scotch, shoving the memories of what happened between me and Miss Jones completely out of my head. It's over, just as we both agreed it would be, and there is no need for me to think about it again.

The most important thing is now we can progress with the festival, since Lisa Underwood has confirmed.

I gaze at the love notes on the coffee table. Lisa obviously liked the idea of them, plus the mystery element must have appealed too. Actually, if I'm honest, the mystery element appeals to me as well.

I want to know who C was. I want to know why she and H didn't end up together. This is my history and it's *my* great-grandfather, Sebastian. The one whom I relate to the most out of all the men in my family. He was the one who first opened Blackwood Books, way back in the thirties. Unfortunately, I don't know all that much about him, because my grandfather died when I was eighteen and I didn't even think to ask him about his father. I wasn't interested in our history back then. The only thing I was interested in was the bookshop.

The Blackwood men, though, are all flawed. They all have their obsessions, their addictions, and they all left behind them a legacy of heartbreak.

I don't want to end up like them. My legacy will be Blackwood Books, and hopefully it'll be going a long time, even in these difficult times. Because the one thing about books is that they never let you down. They never argue back. They offer solace and comfort, and knowledge and beauty. They offer an escape, even if it is only for a couple of hours.

They're not as fickle as people, and if maybe some of them are flawed, too, you can put those ones down and pick up another. There's always a new book and a new discovery within its pages.

Of all the Blackwoods, it feels as if my great-grandfather was the only one who felt that way about books. Until, it seems, he fell in love and wrecked himself in the process.

I was wrong about that, by the way. Regarding me.

Kate – *Miss Jones* – hasn't wrecked me. I'm back at work and everything's the same as it was, and, really, I don't know why I was worried.

Her face flashes in my head, the way it lit up this morning as she told me about Lisa Underwood, her grey eyes full of that special sparkle. I smiled too, and for a moment we understood each other perfectly.

Something inside me aches, an echo of pain, but I ignore it completely.

Instead, I drain my glass, then head upstairs to see if I can't unearth some more of my great-grandfather's papers, maybe find the missing notes, if there are indeed any missing notes.

In my study, I go through the box again, taking everything out, but there's nothing left at the bottom except the confetti scatter of torn-up paper. I turn the box over to shake out the pieces to bin them, then see a familiar flash of red ink on one of the small pieces.

I can't read the word, but that's her ink and her writing. It's C.

Shit, what is this?

Painstakingly, I sort through multiple tiny pieces of paper, and gather up all the ones with red ink on them. Then, back downstairs on the coffee table, I try to fit them together, a kind of paper jigsaw. Because it's clear she sent him a note that he then tore to shreds for some reason.

It takes me a while, but at last I manage to piece it together.

There is nothing wrong. I am perfectly fine. Please do not worry about me. C

I frown over it. Why would he have ripped that up? She was saying she was fine.

At that moment, my phone buzzes and my heart jolts. Perhaps it's Kate – *Miss Jones, for fuck's sake!*

But it isn't. It's Dan.

Come for a pint at the Arms? Need to talk to you.

I wouldn't mind the distraction, so I text back a quick yes. Then I frown at the ripped-up note for a moment more before grabbing my keys and heading out the door.

The Arms is busy tonight and usually I get a few nods and a few 'all right?'s. But this evening I get some stares, side-eyes, and a few knowing smiles. It's disturbing.

Dan's in our usual place in the snug beside the fireplace and he's already got a pint for me on the table. Good man.

I slide in opposite and give him a nod. 'Cheers,' I say, and reach for my pint, a Guinness chaser to the scotch I've already had. Perfect.

'I heard Lisa Underwood said yes to the festival,' Dan says.

Interesting. He must have heard it from someone connected to Gillian, since no one else knew. Unless Miss Jones has been telling people. Not that it matters, not when we have confirmation.

'She did,' I say.

'I thought you didn't have the money for her?'

'We don't. But we have some other . . . inducements.'

'Such as?'

'Great-grandfather Sebastian had a whole lot of letters in a box. Love letters. And Ka— . . . Miss Jones thought Lisa would be interested in looking at them, since apparently she's between books, and *Colours* was based on some letters too. Turns out she is very interested.'

'I see,' Dan says slowly, then gives me a look. 'Ka . . .?'

My jaw tightens. 'Got something to say to me, Dan?'

'Yes.' He puts his pint down on the table and leans forward. 'That's what I wanted to talk to you about. You were seen coming out of Portable Magic at a very early hour a couple of days ago.' He raises his brows. 'Do you have a walk of shame you need to confess?'

My jaw tightens still further. Of course I was spotted. God forbid there's a secret in the village that stays a secret. Can't

have people going about their own private business uncom-
mented on.

'Who saw me?' I bark, a little too sharply for plausible
deniability.

'Kevin.'

Kevin Roundtree. Local plumber. He goes running at
arsehole o'clock every morning and of course he'd be running right when I'm coming out of Portable Magic. He's
another who's partial to gossip too, which means everyone
must know by now. Prick. That explains the sidelong looks I
was getting.

There's no point pretending it didn't happen, though, not
with Dan, and anyway, it's hardly as if I'm ashamed of it, so I
shrug. 'And?'

'You spent the night there? With Kate?'

'No, I spent it with her non-existent cat. Of course with
Ka—Miss Jones.'

Dan grins. 'You sly dog.'

'Don't,' I say sharply, and mean it. 'It's no one's business
but ours.'

Dan is unbothered. 'I'm not implying anything. It's
just . . . well, Bas. You don't sleep with anyone in the village,
so it's . . . notable.'

Which is why I'm wary of people knowing. Most villagers
know I don't go out with people here. And now they will know
that I made an exception for Miss Jones, and there is nothing
exceptional about Miss Jones. Nothing at all.

Her hair. Her smile. The warmth of her skin. The way she

sounded when I pushed inside her. Her hand on my back, stroking me. The way she gasped my name as I—

Nothing. Fuck.

'It was a one-time thing,' I say flatly. 'Not happening again.'

Dan's expression is doubtful, but he only holds up a hand. 'Okay, I hear you. She good with that too?'

'Yes, of course she is. I wouldn't have done it if I thought she wasn't.'

Dan eyes me. 'And here was I thinking getting laid would make you less of a prick.'

I grit my teeth. 'Did you come to harangue me or to talk?'

'Both?' He takes a long sip of his pint. 'You like her, don't you?'

'Yes, of course. She's perfectly pleasant.'

Dan says nothing.

'She's a nice woman.'

Dan continues to say nothing.

I am tense. Even tenser than I was before my night with her. I was hoping it would make things easier, but it hasn't. All I can think about is her in my shop today and the expression on her face as she saw Lucy standing there. And I swore I could see the glint of jealousy, of possessiveness in her eyes, and the satisfaction that gave me in that moment . . .

Dan is waiting for me to confess to something he already knows. That he can see, but I'm not willing to admit to, and, yes, it's putting me in a vile temper. I've never been openly rude to people, though I admit to being somewhat cool and reserved. And I've never thought this before, or at least, not been conscious of this before, but there is a certain . . . reluctance in me at the thought of being rude to Dan.

He's been my friend for a long time and he's put up with a lot. I'm not an easy person to be with.

It's hard for me to be open with people, to talk to people about personal things. I prefer to talk about books and the characters in them and the subjects they discuss. Books are one step removed. They're my escape and that's what I prefer to do.

Yet . . . Miss Jones . . . *Kate*.

She's stuck in my head and I can't get her out, and I need to somehow. Perhaps talking to Dan about her will help.

'Yes, I . . . like her,' I say haltingly.

Dan sips at his pint. He is silent.

'I . . . can't stop thinking about her.'

Dan nods. Says nothing.

'There must be a Bechdel test for men or something,' I say in frustration. 'Our conversation should *not* revolve around women.'

'You're being a tosser, Bas,' Dan says succinctly. 'Stop it.'

That's one reason I'm friends with Dan. Not only does he put up with my idiosyncrasies, he also calls me out when I need to be called out. Not that it's pleasant when he does, but it keeps me on the straight and narrow.

Now, I take what he says on the chin, even if I do slump in my seat and gulp at my pint. I'll probably be drunk soon and that's not a state I ever want to get into, not after watching Dad reach for the bottle the second the sun was past the yard-arm, and sometimes even before that.

But I can't seem to control myself at this point.

'Sorry,' I mutter. 'I . . . don't know what I'm doing. I don't know what's happening.'

'Well,' Dan says calmly. 'I can tell you. You're falling for her, Bas.'

I scowl, even if something inside me relaxes, as if it's given up fighting. 'No. I am not.'

'You are, and you don't know what to do about it, because you've never met anyone who makes you feel this way. And you're emotionally constipated because of your upbringing and you have no idea how to handle it.'

'Yes, thank you, Dr Freud.'

Dan shrugs. 'Just a few things I learned from counselling.'

Dan sees a therapist once a month to discuss things to do with doctoring because he's not good at compartmentalising.

That, however, is something I'm fantastic at. Maybe I should have done medicine after all?

'I would rather not feel this way,' I say at last. 'I don't like it.'

'Have you ever thought . . . I don't know . . . about giving it a go?'

'Giving what a go?'

'A relationship, Bas. Have you ever thought about . . .'

'Being her boyfriend, you mean?' I say the word 'boyfriend' with the contempt it deserves.

Dan rolls his eyes. 'Fine, if you don't want to listen to good sense then ignore me.'

I let out a silent breath and try to marshal my thoughts. 'I can't,' I say. 'I can't be with her. We're too different.'

'Are you seriously kidding me right now?' Dan looks at me with utter amazement. 'Different? You're the same, you cretin. You both love books, you both are intelligent, passionate, and utterly—'

'The Blackwoods have a terrible track record,' I interrupt, because I have to stop him somehow. 'Every one of us has hurt the women we're supposed to love. We're drunks, gamblers, we cause nothing but harm, and Kate deserves better than that.'

Dan shakes his head. 'Just because your father and grand-father were like that, doesn't mean you have to be. Change the ending, Bas. You can do that, you know.'

'Life isn't a book, Dan,' I say bitterly, because I know that all too well. 'And some endings are shit.'

He looks at me for a long time, then holds up his hands. 'Fine. If that's the story you want to tell, you tell it like that. But don't include Kate in your shitty endings, because you're right, she doesn't deserve that.'

'No,' I say. 'She doesn't. Which is why it was one night and that's it.'

Though, of course, now I'm wondering if that night should have happened at all.

Chapter Seventeen

J am sorry, darling H. J cannot come tomorrow.
Perhaps another day?

C

KATE

Sebastian is waiting for me outside the door of Wychtree Crafts the next day. I've been successfully not thinking of him all day and his presence makes my traitorous little heart leap inside my chest.

I feel as if I'm always cataloguing what he's wearing, but I can't help it. I notice these things. Today he's in a plain white shirt and plain black trousers. He should look like a waiter or something, but he doesn't. He's ascetic as a monk and it suits him. There's nothing to distract from his perfect bone structure and the white makes his eyes glow blue as cornflowers.

My God. I'm sixteen again and mooning over the captain of the school rugby team. It's ridiculous and I need to stop.

I smile at him, bright and unbothered. 'Hi,' I say.

He nods. 'Miss Jones.'

Miss Jones. What crap. I want to tell him he can call me Kate, the world won't blow up or anything, but I can't be bothered having that discussion today. Not when I'm about to meet someone who might have known my grandmother, so all I do is gesture at the door. 'Shall we?'

He pushes it open for me and I step inside.

It's a homey, cosy little shop. Full of hand-knitted jumpers, baby blankets, quilts of all shapes and sizes, pottery, carvings, rugs, assorted souvenirs and a small case of locally made jewellery.

Mrs Bennet presides behind the counter and she's chatting to a customer as Sebastian follows me inside and the door closes. This current awkwardness in front of someone else from the village is too much for me, so I ignore him and wander amongst the shelves while we wait for her customer to leave.

It's *especially* awkward after Aisling texted me this morning, informing me that Sebastian had been seen leaving my shop in the early hours of the morning a few days earlier and that now the village is rife with rumour.

In fact, I thought I caught a gleam in Mrs Abbot's eye this morning when she came in to view the latest romance titles, not to mention some significant side-eye from the mums' morning tea group this morning.

Gossip doesn't bother me, as a rule, and I don't particularly care that someone saw Sebastian – they can think what they like. But Sebastian *will* care, I already know that. It's not fair, since he was the one who started it with that kiss, but still. He's lived here his whole life and he's already done his utmost to distance himself from the village. Gossip will make him want to put even more distance between himself and everyone else now.

The customer leaves and Sebastian approaches the counter, so I gird my loins and follow him.

Mrs Bennet is in her late seventies, still sharp as a tack, and her eyesight's perfect – which is why she reigns supreme re the dartboard. Her iron-grey hair is cut in a severe bob, she wears bright red lipstick, and her nails have the most beautiful French manicure. She looks after herself, does Mrs Bennet.

She eyes us as we come to the counter. 'Sebastian,' she says, in measured tones. 'And . . . Kate.'

Sebastian gives her a cool smile. 'Mrs Bennet. You're looking well this afternoon. Is that a new lipstick I see?'

Much to my surprise, Mrs Bennet blushes like a schoolgirl. 'Why, yes, it is.'

'It looks fantastic on you.' He's not effusive, yet his attention is wholly on her, as if he can't think of anything else he'd rather be doing than talking to her, and, well, all I can think is that the man is downright charming when he wants to be.

I feel as if I'm watching a master flirt in action as stone-faced Mrs Bennet positively melts under his regard. I don't know her well, since Mrs Bennet doesn't read. She knits and sews and crochets instead, so I don't have that much to do with her. Though I have more than a few of her items in my kitchen cupboards; I love a pretty mug.

'Why thank you, Sebastian,' she says, fluttering a little. 'The girl in Boots said it flattered my complexion, but I wasn't sure.'

'Rest assured, Mrs Bennet, it is, indeed, very flattering.' He leans a hip against the counter. 'So, I'm here on a little mission and I wonder if you could possibly help us.'

'Oh yes?' She doesn't look at me, only him. 'What help do you need?'

'Miss Jones has been here in the village a couple of months now and she'd very much like to find out more about her family.'

'Oh, she does, does she?' Mrs Bennet finally looks at me, dark eyes sharp, then back at him. 'I heard a rumour about you two, you know.'

Sebastian raises an imperious brow while I try not to blush, as it's not as if I'm a simpering virgin. 'It was just one night,' I say, before he can stick his oar in, because there's no point in denying it. 'No big deal.'

'Hmm.' Mrs Jean Bennet is disapproving. 'So casual, you young people. We were more careful about it in our day.'

'Your day?' Sebastian asks. 'You mean the "swinging sixties"?'

Mrs Bennet's stern expression relaxes. 'I said we were careful, child. I never said we didn't have sex. We did. A lot.'

I don't quite know what to say to this, but Sebastian only shrugs. 'As I was saying, Miss Jones wants to find out about the Joneses. Her mother took her away from Wychtree when she was very young, and never returned.' He pauses and gives her another full blast of his total attention. 'I think you were friends with Rose Jones, weren't you?'

A rush of excitement goes through me. She was my grandmother's friend? I had no idea.

Mrs Bennet nods. 'Yes, I was. We went to school together. All that.'

'Mum never talked about her,' I say. 'So I never knew her.'

'No, well, she wouldn't,' Mrs Bennet says. 'Rose was a difficult woman. She was unfailingly loyal but she had her opinions, and woe betide anyone who got on the wrong side of her. Fierce, that one.'

'How interesting,' Sebastian murmurs, glancing at me. 'Seems that might run in the family.'

I ignore him and lean forward, fascinated. 'Do you know what happened between her and Mum? Mum would only say that she left Wychtree because we weren't welcome here.'

Mrs Bennet looks at me carefully. 'You've the look of her. Blonde hair and grey eyes. Pretty. Rose was like that too. Very suspicious of men. Didn't like them.'

'Oh? Why?'

'Her father was a bad 'un. Used to beat her mother.' She shakes her head. 'Terrible stuff. Rose was very protective of her mother. Was a stickler for propriety too. Though she wasn't above breaking the rules herself. That's how she fell pregnant with your mum.'

Shock pulses down my spine, and along with it comes a

sudden rush of anger. No wonder Rose didn't like men, not if her father was abusive. 'Mum never talked about my grandfather either. Or my dad.'

'Not surprised. No one knew who your grandfather was, though there was plenty of speculation. Rose tried to protect your mother from going down the same path she did, but Rebecca was a free spirit. Headstrong. Very much like Rose in her own way – that's why they butted heads so badly.'

'Hmm,' Sebastian says.

I try to ignore his tall figure next to me, but it's difficult because he's standing far too close and I'm all too aware of him. He also smells delicious, which doesn't help.

'Did Rose ever talk to you about my grandfather?' I ask.

Mrs Bennet shakes her head. 'Not one word. Was the big scandal in the village at the time.'

'What about my great-grandmother? What happened to her?'

'Kate,' Mrs Bennet says. 'Her name was Kate. Like you.'

I blink. I had no idea. None at all. 'Seriously?'

'Yes. Poor woman. She had a terrible husband and then her teashop closed not long after Rose was born.'

'She had a teashop?'

'Oh, yes. You inherited that building, didn't you?'

'I did. Mum left it to me. But . . . she never said anything about a teashop.'

'The shop was Kate's initially. That's where her teashop was.'

This is all news to me. Mum had said she'd inherited the building, but that was as much as she'd ever said about it. I'd assumed she'd inherited it from Rose, but I'd never imagined that it had actually been in our family for longer than that.

'What happened to her shop?' I ask. It's not lost on me that Kate the First had been a business owner, and now so am I.

Mrs Bennet sighs. 'I don't know much. I was only a little 'un. But there was a lot of talk at the time. Her husband made her close it down just before the war started. A woman running a business on her own was unusual back then and her husband didn't like it. He turned it into a newsagent's.'

Instantly, I'm outraged on Kate's behalf. 'What? That's appalling!'

Mrs Bennet shrugs with the kind of calm that people only get after living a long time and seeing everything. 'It was what it was. Anyway, her husband died in a car accident – good riddance to bad rubbish, I say – and she lived quietly here until Rose was around twenty-one. Then she – Kate – ran away.'

I blink, not sure if I've heard her correctly. 'She ran away?'

Beside me, Sebastian has gone very still.

'No one knows what happened to her,' Mrs Bennet says. 'Rose went to the police, and there was an investigation, but all the trails went cold. Kate was declared legally dead in the early seventies.'

'Oh my God,' I murmur. 'No trace was ever found?'

'No. But back in the sixties it was easier to disappear, not as easy now.' She glances at Sebastian. 'It wasn't like your great-granddad. It was very clear he drowned.'

Sebastian's expression is impossible to read. 'Yes,' he says. 'Of course.'

I'm more interested in Rose and Kate, though. Especially Rose, maybe because I identify with her situation too much. 'Poor Rose. She was left without her mum so young. That must have been terrible.'

Mrs Bennet nods. 'It traumatised her, I think. Then there was the palaver with her getting pregnant, and the village gossip when she made it clear she was going to keep the baby.'

I lean my elbows on the counter. 'Did you know who the father was? Did she tell you?'

'No. Rose wouldn't say a word. But she had plenty to say when Rebecca got pregnant with you. Some young Australian working at the Arms, apparently. Took off when he found out about you. Rose kept insisting that you should be given up for adoption, but Rebecca wouldn't hear of it.' She sighs. 'I told Rose that being so stubborn wasn't going to earn her any favours with Becca, but she wouldn't listen to me. When Becca left, I didn't want to say "I told you so", but . . .'

So, my father was some unknown man who took off. Then Rose wanted to give me up for adoption. I can understand her reasons for it – Mum was young and on her own, and then there were also Rose's own experiences as a single mum, especially in a time when such things were a terrible scandal – yet a dull pain aches inside me all the same.

Mum left Wychtree because of me. My father also left Wychtree because of me. My grandmother ruined her relationship with her daughter because of me. And Mum had a small, narrow life because of me.

It's you. You're the problem.

The voice in my head sounds like Jasper's, and conscious of Sebastian's gaze, I try to ignore both him and it as I force myself to give Mrs Bennet a smile. 'Well, thank you,' I say. 'That's extremely helpful.'

Mrs Bennet gives me a narrow look. 'When Rose died, she left me a box of her things. It's not much. She didn't keep a lot. But seems like you should have it.'

The dull ache vanishes at this news, and excitement fills me. 'Seriously? Oh, yes, absolutely! I'd love to have it.'

'Okay. Wait here.' She disappears into her back room, leaving Sebastian and me standing at the counter.

'I'm sorry,' he says quietly. He doesn't say anything else, so I'm not sure what he's sorry about, but it's clear he knows I'm upset. So maybe it's *everything* he's sorry about.

My great-grandmother disappearing.

My grandmother having my mother to an unknown man.

My mother also having me to an unknown man and then refusing to give me up.

The history of these women, their stories that are lost, all because there's no one left to tell them. No one except me, and I don't know anything, because no one told me.

I feel cheated in some way and I can't look at him, can't acknowledge he's even spoken, otherwise a dam might break in me and all the grief that I've been consciously pushing aside since I came to Wychtree might come rushing out and swamp me.

Luckily, at that moment Mrs Bennet comes back with a small cardboard shoe box and hands it to me. 'There you are. I should have given it to you weeks ago, but I forgot it was there until now.' Her habitually stern expression gives way into a smile. 'I think Rose would have liked you. She and your mother should have made up, let bygones be bygones. No point holding on to grudges, is my feeling.'

My throat is tight as I clutch the old box and I feel an uprush of warmth towards her. 'Yes, I *so* agree. Look, I'd love to sit down with you and talk some more about my grandmother. Would that be okay?'

'Of course, dear. That would be lovely. You let me know, hmm?'

I nod, thank her profusely, then without a further word turn and walk out of the shop. I can sense Sebastian behind me, so once we're out on the footpath, I turn to face him. I feel oddly protective of the box and I only want to open it in the safety of Portable Magic.

'Thank you,' I say. 'That was very kind of you to come with me.'

His blue gaze scans my face and I know my emotions are plastered all over it. It makes me feel vulnerable, so before he can answer, I turn away. 'I'd better get back to the shop,' I say.

'What about the festival?' he asks. 'We were going to look at the programme.'

'Tomorrow,' I say over my shoulder, and don't wait for a reply.

I don't look back as I carry my box into Portable Magic. I should have been more gracious to him than that, but I just don't have it in me.

The 'Back in ten minutes' sign is still up and I've been gone longer than ten minutes, but I don't take it down.

Instead, I carry the box over to the counter and put it down. Take a breath. My pulse is very fast and I'm nervous for reasons I can't pinpoint. This is some of my history in this box, a history I had no idea about, but I also know that, whatever is in here, it won't be enough.

I never thought I'd be angry at my mother, but I feel an ember of it now, flickering in my heart. I know she didn't want to give me up and I'm so grateful, yet her argument with Rose has meant here's a whole side of my family I will never know. I wonder if she ever thought about that. I wonder if she ever thought that I might want to have a part in it, to have them in my life. Still, it's not all her fault. I didn't push for answers, because I got so caught up in my own life that I stopped asking questions. And now I'm here, and I'm nothing but questions, but it's too late to ask them. Because she's gone.

The past is important, though. Especially since we are all of us the sum of that past. We are the consequences of the choices our parents made and the choices their parents made and so on.

It matters. It gives context. It can show us who we are.

I'm not just the past, I know that, but I'm a person who loves books, who loves stories, and the story of my own family is important to me. In fact, I never realised how important until now.

I take the top off the box.

Inside there are postcards. Letters. A broken necklace. A silver ring. A small Bible. A lipstick. Some old, beaded brace-lets. Newspaper clippings. A hospital tag with 'Baby of Rose Jones' on it.

I hold the tag, my throat tight. That baby was Mum, and Rose kept the tag all these years. The door that Mum had closed so firmly had been unlocked all this time and she'd just never opened it. Then again, neither had Rose.

Sighing, I pick up the newspaper clippings. They chronicle the disappearance of Kathryn Jones and how she vanished without a trace, and how long she'd been missing. Days. Weeks. Months. Years.

No wonder Rose was so difficult. That must have devastated her.

Finally, I pick up the letters and it's curious, because the paper they're written on is familiar, thin and crackling with age. Slowly, I open one and it's the red ink that stands out. Familiar red ink.

Rose, I'm sorry. I have to go. I can't explain why but know that your existence is the only thing that has made my life bearable. You were the best thing to come out of my marriage. The only good thing. I want you to be happy. I want you to find love. I had it once and I threw it away because I did not have the courage. I do now.

Know that I will be safe. Know that I will be loved.

Know that I will be happy.

Your loving mother.

The red ink has run in several places as if someone had cried over it, and of course someone *had* cried over it. Rose.

My own throat gets painful and the dull ache in my chest returns.

I pull another letter out.

I am sorry, darling H. But I cannot write to you. He watches me constantly. I think he knows.

C

My eyes prickle; shock echoes through me.
I pick up the next one.

I love you. I never thought I would find someone I would feel so passionately about. I thought I would always be alone, always be trapped. Then you appeared and none of it mattered any more. You freed me. I wish I had met you five years ago.

C

I pick up another.

I always seem to be saying I'm sorry, but you must know that I am. I am a coward. I want to be with you so badly, but now I have her to think of. He might let me go, but never her, and I cannot leave her. I cannot come with you, no matter how much I want to. Please understand.

C

Tears fall down my cheeks. I know who she's writing to. I know who C is now, and I probably should have guessed, but I didn't.

I know you won't ever see this note, not now, but I saw you leave. You were so handsome in your uniform. You were so much braver than I. Stay safe, Sebastian.
  I will love you till the day I die.

Kate

It was her. C was Kate Jones, my great-grandmother. And she had an affair with Sebastian's great-grandfather. And she wanted to leave her husband . . .

The tragedy of it hurts. I can almost feel the sorrow and the longing rise physically from the letters in my hand. He must have asked her to come away with him and she must have refused. That's why the letters stopped. Not because she stopped writing them, but because she stopped sending them.

He then went off to war and, when he came back, her teashop was closed and she had closed herself off from him.

There's one last note in the box. I pick it up. This time the script is in dark blue and in Sebastian the First's strong hand.

> *I am taking a risk doing this again and I know it. Send this back to me if you want to hear from me again. If not, I will never contact you again.*
>
> *I still love you. I always will.*
>
> *H*

But she didn't send it back. He never contacted her again.

I ache all over at the thought.

The missing notes are here and they're not missing, not really. Because hers were never sent. And she kept one of his and never returned it.

A tear drips slowly down my nose and onto the blue ink that has already been stained by over-seventy-year-old tears.

Chapter Eighteen

You are not well. Don't lie to me.
Is it him? Is he hurting you?

H

SEBASTIAN

I stand at my counter, trying to look busy with the laptop open. It's right on closing and I'm still thinking about Miss Jones at Mrs Bennet's not an hour earlier. Yes, she's firmly Miss Jones now, not Kate. I can't call her that, I can't cross that line. I have to hold fast to it because I don't want Dan to be right.

And he's not right. He's not. Of course I'm not falling for her, that would be preposterous. Ridiculous. Marriage and that whole domestic nightmare has never been something I've wanted for myself, and that hasn't changed just because a pretty ray of sunshine of a woman has come into my life.

I have my bookshop. I don't need anything or anyone else, nor do I want it.

This restlessness that's been eating away at me for the past few days, such that I'm unable to keep still, making me wander about my shelves like the minotaur lost in his own maze, is *only* sexual desire. Nothing more.

I need to get a handle on it, and the most obvious way to do that is to make a visit, as I so often promise myself I'll do, to London. Find a woman in a bar and take her back to my hotel room. Easy. Problem solved.

Yet I can't help but be aware that it's not sex that's making me restless now. It's not Miss Jones in my bed that I can't stop thinking about, but Miss Jones standing at the counter in Mrs Bennet's shop looking almost . . . devastated.

And my own urge to reach out and pull her close in response.

She didn't know any of the things Mrs Bennet had told her, I could see that, and if I'm not much mistaken, the thing that hit her the hardest was the knowledge that her mother and grandmother were at odds because of her existence.

It must have hurt. Doubly painful, too, knowing that, since Rose and Rebecca have gone, there will be no reconciliation. No way to make a connection to that past, either. A difficult thing to accept for a woman who is all about making connections with people.

I don't know why I can't stop thinking about it.

I don't know why it hurts me too.

The bell chimes and the door opens, and as I'm about to utter the immortal words 'We're closed', Miss Jones comes in.

Instantly, I tense. I'm not sure what she's doing here, since she told me we'd talk about the festival tomorrow.

She's wearing a loose, white, oversized T-shirt that falls off one shoulder, exposing the pale-blue strap of her lacy bra. Her jeans are loose too and low on her hips. She wears a wide belt of distressed brown leather and gold sandals on her feet. She has hoops in her ears and her hair is just the way I like it, falling down over her shoulders and—

I catch my wayward thoughts and haul them back into line as I notice something else. She's carrying the small cardboard box Mrs Bennet gave her and her pretty eyes are red, as if she's been crying.

The feelings I had in the craft shop all rush in on me again. My chest tightens and I have the most absurd impulse to go to her, gather her into my arms and hold her. Ask her what's wrong, why is she crying, and what can I do.

It's ridiculous. I've never cared overmuch about other people's feelings before, so I can't imagine why I should care about hers. Yet . . . I do.

'What's wrong?' I ask.

Her mouth tightens. 'I found something out. About H and C. In the box Mrs Bennet gave me.'

I tense even further. 'What?'

She deposits the box on the counter. 'Look.'

A pull of foreboding tugs inside me. I remember the note

from H about the shadow that looked like a bruise under C's eye and the expression on Mrs Bennet's face. *'He was a bad 'un . . .'*

Slowly, I take the lid off the box. Some letters are arranged on top, so I take them out.

The red ink in the first one gives it away and adrenaline pours through me as I read it. *Dear Rose . . .* Then another. *I'm sorry.* Then another. *I've been a coward.*

Bloody hell. C's missing letters. Except it's not just C now, is it? C is Kathryn, Miss Jones's great-grandmother.

It seems as if she was having an illicit affair with my great-grandfather.

'Fuck,' I murmur, as I put her last letter down. *You looked so handsome . . .* And I stare at Miss Jones as it begins to sink in.

'Kathryn and Sebastian,' I say. 'They were having an affair.'

She nods.

'And her husband . . .'

She nods again.

Yes. He hurt her.

Christ.

I'm still trying to process that when another thought hits me. 'We're not—'

'Related?' she finishes, clearly knowing exactly what I was going to say. 'No. Rose was born near the end of the war, I think. A long time after H left.'

'Thank God,' I mutter. 'But this is . . . incredible.'

She nods, but looks devastated.

I push the box away and try to resist the urge to step out

from behind my counter and go to her, offer her comfort. I can't do that, I can't touch her. I need something between me and her, otherwise I don't know what I'll do.

'You're upset,' I say, stating the fucking obvious in lieu of doing anything remotely useful. 'Why?'

'Why do you think?' Miss Jones's eyes are full of tears. 'She loved him and she was with a husband who beat her, and she couldn't leave. She used to own a teashop, but he made her close it just before the war started.' The tears slide down her face. 'She had to live with the love of her life being just across the road and she couldn't be with him. He sent her another note, but she never returned it, so he thought . . .'

I think of the ripped-up note upstairs. The anger in it. 'He didn't know,' I say quietly. 'But he suspected.'

'And she didn't tell him. All those notes are ones she never sent.'

'So, as far as he was concerned, she just . . . ghosted him.'

Miss Jones nods, her tears tugging at something inside me that feels unbearable. I don't want to care. I don't. Dan called me emotionally constipated and he's right. Emotions are the key to addiction, that's the problem, and emotions turned that key in my father and my grandfather, and probably in my great-grandfather too. Love turned them into beggars looking for something, anything, to fill the empty void inside them.

Who wants that? Not me.

'It's sad,' I say coolly. 'But it happened a long time ago.'

'I know,' she says. 'But Kate disappeared when Rose turned twenty-one. Her husband died and she just . . . vanished.

They never found out what happened to her.' More tears slide down her face. 'I want to know how Rose coped. I want to know if she knew Sebastian's son, if Kathryn knew him. I want to know so many things and, all those things, all those stories . . . They're just gone, Sebastian. That's why I'm crying. I'll never know what happened to them. All their joys and their sorrows, all their little moments of happiness are gone. Because Mum and my grandmother didn't talk to each other. Because of me.'

I understand now. I understand deeply. Lost stories are the worst, lost histories we'll never know, because no one ever told them. I have my own history, my own story here in this book-shop and I know the stories of my family – at least I thought I did. Until now. Until we discovered a connection we never knew we had.

It's worse for Kate, though. I have the bookshop and a sense of permanence, but Kate doesn't. All she has is a box of letters and a sense that maybe she's to blame for the loss of her history.

And, yes, that's devastating.

I'm round the corner of my counter before I can think and then I'm reaching for her, drawing her into my arms. She doesn't resist, turning her face into my chest, and weeping. Her arms creep around my waist and my hands are in her beautiful hair, stroking. Her scent winds around me, so sweet, and the warmth and softness of her body against mine is making me hard.

But she's grieving and now is not the time for my baser self to take over, so I ignore it. Instead I hear myself murmuring nonsense to her about how it will 'be all right', how 'it's not because of you', and whispering, 'Please don't cry, sweetheart.'

Sweetheart. I've never called anyone sweetheart in my entire life.

'I know,' she murmurs, her voice muffled by my shirt. 'I'm being way too dramatic, but I can't stop thinking about Kate. About how she must have felt, trapped in that terrible marriage. I know what it's like being with someone who hurts you, and how awful it is. Then not being able to be with the man she loved. Hurting him . . .' Her shoulders shake.

I go very still, bludgeoned over the head by the words *'I know what it's like being with someone who hurts you'* . . . What does she mean by that? Is she talking about her ex? The relationship that broke up before she came here? Did *he* hurt her?

My arms tighten around her as a sudden upwelling of rage fills me. I want to know everything about this ex of hers, everything. So I can strangle him with my bare hands. Then maybe go back in time and strangle the man who hurt her great-grandmother too.

It takes a conscious effort to pack my rage up into a tiny box and shove it away. Now is not the time for those kinds of questions and I don't have the right to ask them anyway.

This is about her grief, not my anger, so instead I gather her closer and kiss the top of her head. Her hair is soft against my mouth and she smells good, and naturally this is the moment that my body decides it wants some action.

'Kate,' I say, because it's getting so I'm going to have to say

something and it seems ludicrous now to call her Miss Jones.
'Please, ignore that.'

'Ignore what?' She sniffles and shifts her hips against mine.

The movement makes my breath catch. Audibly.

She goes still. 'Oh,' she murmurs. 'That.'

I grit my teeth. 'Yes, that.'

A sigh escapes her and she lifts her face from my chest. Her
eyes are red and her cheeks are shiny, and she is honestly the
most beautiful thing I've ever seen. 'I'm sorry,' she says huskily.
'I didn't mean to end up sobbing in your shirt.' She makes as
if to pull away, and I can't help myself, I tighten my grip.

'I didn't say I wanted you to leave,' I murmur.

And I don't, I realise. I don't want her to leave my shop. I
don't want her to leave my arms. Not yet. I haven't finished
with her yet.

It's physical, that's all it is. It's *not* because I care about her
feelings or how good it was to hold someone, to make them
feel better. It's *not* because I'm falling for her.

I want her, that's all, and one night doesn't feel like enough,
not any more.

The pulse at the base of her throat is beating hard and fast,
and she's looking up at me, searching my face. There's a fearful
kind of hope in her eyes.

One night wasn't enough for her either.

'What are you saying?' she asks.

'Kate.' Her name is a sweet bite of sound. 'Kathryn.'

She blushes, a tide of rose sweeping across her lovely face.
'Be clear, Sebastian.'

'Clear? Fine, I'll give you clear.' I let her go, but only so I can cup her face between my hands. 'I can't stop thinking about you, Miss Jones. And I've been thinking about you solidly ever since I walked out of your door. You're in my head, in my dreams, and I want you naked in my bed. I want you all night and in the morning I'll probably want you again.'

Her throat moves as she swallows and her eyes darken. 'Another night then?'

'Yes.' I hesitate, then add, 'Maybe more.'

She has questions. I can see them drift like shadows through her eyes, but they're questions I don't have answers for, because I don't know. This is new to me. Wanting someone the way I want her is new.

I let her go and step back, bracing myself and putting some distance between us. If she wants to leave, she can. I won't stop her.

She knows what I want. The next move is hers.

And she makes it.

She closes the distance between us and reaches for me, drawing my mouth down on hers. She tastes so sweet, her lips are soft and hot, and I feel the part of myself I show the world begin to dissolve, leaving me without a facade, without a veneer.

I am hungry for her and I am desperate for the sunshine she brings with her.

I don't hesitate. I push her up against the counter as I devour her, tasting her sunshine and sweetness, the flavour of warm summer days. I want it. I want all of it.

My hands are in her hair, holding on as I feast.

She kisses me back and I'm savage, because she's just as desperate as I am. Just as hungry. It makes me feel like a god.

I tear off her T-shirt and touch the warm skin beneath the fabric. She gasps and arches into my hands, her fingers threading through my hair, her head going back to grant me more access to her mouth.

I am so hard I ache.

Her hands drop to the button of my trousers and that's when I remember where we are.

In my shop. It's closed, but the lights are on and any passer-by can see through the front window.

Fuck.

I grip her wrist and hold her hand away. 'Let's take this out the back.'

'No, I can't wait that long.'

I know how she feels.

I can't seem to think, but there's one spot here where no one can see, a little space in the bookshelves, where History meets Poetry.

It's perfect.

I pull her away from the counter and down towards the back of the shop. There's my spot. I push her against the bookshelves and she makes a soft noise.

'Oh, yes,' she murmurs, rough and husky. 'Here, right here.'

Of course she loves it. This woman doesn't need a bed. A bookshelf is fine, surrounded by art and science and history and poetry. So perfect. She *is* poetry.

'Do you like this bra?' I ask.

She glances down and shrugs, excitement gleaming in her eyes. 'I could take it or leave it, to be honest.'

'Then let's leave it.' I rip it apart. It's surprisingly easy. But what's better are her breasts, full and pale and perfectly shaped to my hand. Her nipples are pink and delicious and when I bend to take them in my mouth, they harden.

She gasps and arches against the shelves, her fingers twisting my hair.

I slide a hand down into her jeans, into her knickers, and I can feel her heat, soft and slick and so sensitive.

Fucking delicious.

I want a taste.

I sink to my knees and rip open the denim, shove her knickers down.

'Sebastian,' she gasps, as I put my mouth on her.

I remember the taste of her, sweet and salty, and I familiarise myself again. My God, she's sensational. I can't get enough. I explore her tenderly and with reverence, paying attention to every part of her.

She moves restlessly against me, gasping out my name.

I want to draw this out, but I'm desperate myself and I don't think I can. So I tease her with my tongue, use my fingers to stroke and caress, and she cries out, shuddering between my hands as she comes.

So raw. So passionate.

My Kathryn.

She should never be Kate. Kate is pretty, but short and

bitten off. You need to take your time with her name, roll it around in your mouth and really taste it. Two syllables. A sensual flavour I can draw out, indulge in.

Kath*ryn*.

She's panting as I get to my feet and still shaking, and it's a good look for her. Flushed cheeks and soft mouth, post-orgasmic pleasure glowing in her darkened eyes.

My inner Neanderthal is satisfied.

I put that look on her face. That was *all* me.

Without hesitation I get rid of the rest of her clothes and leave them on the floor by the shelves. She doesn't stop me. She doesn't protest. Just looks at me with desire in her eyes.

Yes. I am fucked. Well and truly.

I should walk away now, tell her never to darken my door again, but I know they're empty threats. Words I will never utter.

The addiction is in me now, in my bones and cells.

It's got a hold of me and I'm never going to get rid of it.

I've replaced the condoms in my wallet since our last encounter, so I grab one and get it out. Undo my trousers, roll it down my cock. Then I step forward and grip her, lifting her up against the solid oak shelves before pressing against her. She winds her legs around my waist, her arms around my neck, her breasts pressed to my chest.

I push into her and the tight heat nearly makes me lose control then and there. And like we did before, I have to pause and take a breath. Appreciate this incredible moment once again. When she is mine, all mine.

I look down into her eyes and she looks back.

My God, she's beautiful.

I begin to move and she makes the most delicious sound. Half a moan, half a sigh. Her hips lift against mine, and she moves with me.

The pleasure begins to wind around and around us, pulling tight.

She gasps again as I move deeper, faster, and her hands grip the shelves. Books fall to the floor, but I don't see them. I don't hear them. All I see is her.

'Sebastian . . .' She groans, arching against me. 'Oh my God . . .'

The shelves shake as I move even faster, driving her on and myself along with her. The feel of her is incredible.

I bend and taste her neck, then her shoulder. My fingers dig into her hips, gripping her hard. I can't get enough of her. I never will.

She's going to haunt me for the rest of my life.

The orgasm comes like a freight train, barrelling down on me and I know I'm not going to last. I bite her breast, nip her, tease her nipple and pinch it. She gives a breathless cry and then I slip my hand between us, where she is sensitive and slick, and I give her a flick of my finger.

She screams as I thrust and then it's over for her, and she's shaking and shaking, and I'm shaking along with her as the orgasm hits me over the head and I go down.

We don't move. I'm physically unable to. She's panting in my ear and I can hear my own heartbeat, thudding, deafening. I feel the way I do after a long, hard run, when the endorphins kick in and you're on that physical high.

Christ. I've just screwed a woman in my bookshop, and what a woman she is . . . I'll never be the same again.

There's a circle of fallen books around us, which feels appropriate. But I don't bother picking them up. I deal with the necessities first, including locking the front door of the shop, then, when I'm done, I pick her up from where she's slumped against the shelves and gather her close.

She puts her arms around my neck, lying back against my chest, all sleepy and sated. Her gaze is dark as she looks up at me from beneath her lashes. 'Where are we going, Mr Blackwood?' she asks, husky and sensual.

I stride towards the entrance to my flat. 'You know very well where we're going, Miss Jones.'

'Miss Jones again. Hmmm. Have I been bad?'

'You've been excessively disobedient. I'm going to have to punish you.'

She smiles as I kick the door open. 'Oh, goody.'

Chapter Nineteen

I am fine. Nothing is wrong. I just didn't sleep well last night.

C

KATE

I lie naked on Sebastian's bed with my chin on my folded hands, watching him. We've just talked about what we need to do to get stock of *Colours* in for Lisa's book-signing and then discussed including Portable Magic as a venue for some of the festival events, and now I'm helping him set up Blackwood Books' first newsletter.

He's sitting beside me – also naked – apart from the absurd little glasses he wears on the end of his nose. It's quite the dichotomy, the glasses in contrast with his magnificent body.

And he is magnificent.

Really, the village doesn't know the half of what lies beneath this man's clothes and it's a damn shame they don't.

There should be a naked statue of him outside the bookshop so everyone can see and worship him.

Then again, I'm not sure I want them to. I want the sheer beauty of him to remain my little secret. The thing that only *I* know. And there are many things that only I know.

The growl he makes when I take him in my mouth.

The way his eyes glow fiercely when he thrusts inside me.

The sound of my name when he comes.

The women in the village don't know what they're missing out on and I'm glad. Because that makes him mine. All mine.

'Stop distracting me,' he says, without looking up from the laptop screen.

'I'm not.'

'You are.'

'How am I distracting you?'

That earns me a flash of intense blue as he glances at me. 'You exist, Miss Jones.' And smiles.

My heart turns over in my chest.

That's another thing the village doesn't know. What he looks like when he's naked and smiling, and desire is in his eyes.

Only I know that.

He glances back at his screen, taps a few more times, then pauses. Frowns slightly. 'I'm not sure what to say.'

I lean over him to peer at the screen. He's got a very formal introductory sentence, but that's it. 'Hmm. My newsletter is chatty, but I don't think that's your vibe.'

'Really? What makes you say that?' His tone is dry as dust.

I love it when he teases me. When you first see Sebastian

Blackwood, you'd think that a man that uptight couldn't possibly have a sense of humour. But he does. Just as underneath his cool reserve there's a volcano.

Another secret I get to keep.

'I don't know,' I say, grinning. 'Maybe it's got something to do with your complete inability to do small talk.'

There's a wicked gleam in his eyes. 'Small talk is overrated. Especially when there are other things we can do instead.'

'Settle down, Casanova. Your vibe is informational and intellectual. So, no, not chatty. You should have your new releases in various subjects, plus reviews, and I think you should have a regular column where you discuss what you're reading.'

He nods and types some more, then pauses again. 'What would you say to writing a paragraph or two for me. Include some of your new releases that you think might have some appeal to my readers.'

A little shiver of delight runs through me that he's thought of me. 'I would love to,' I say. 'You can write one for me too.'

'Excellent plan.' He types a little bit more.

'Don't forget to do something about important dates. You know, advertising upcoming events.'

'What upcoming events?'

I elbow him. 'The festival, duh.'

He gives me the most charming boyish grin. 'Oh, yes, I've almost forgotten about that.'

'You have not.'

'Nearly.'

'Lies.'

His eyes gleam yet again and my breath catches. His attention span is limited this morning, clearly. 'You haven't finished,' I say. 'You need to talk about the chess evening you're going to start running. And the poetry night. Not to mention the mainstream fiction book club.' I glance at his screen. 'Actually, start with the book club and see how much interest you get.'

He shuts the laptop with a snap, takes off his glasses, and turns to me, gripping my hips and hauling me up so I'm lying on top of him.

'You have the attention span of a goldfish,' I inform him.

'How am I expected to concentrate on anything when you're naked beside me?' he says plaintively. 'On second thoughts, don't answer that. It's a rhetorical question.' His hands stroke down my back, an idle, absent touch that is somehow even more erotic for being so. 'We're going to have to tell Lisa we solved the mystery of who my great-grandfather was writing to.'

I relax onto him. He makes a fine bed, his body hard and smooth and hot, like sun-warmed stone. 'We will. And I think she's going to find it even more romantic that Sebastian Blackwood the First was writing to Kathryn Jones the First. And slipping notes into books, no less. And now we're . . . well, we're kind of together, aren't we?'

I feel a ripple of tension go through him. We haven't talked about this yet, about where we go from here and what last night and this morning mean.

Last night it was all about physical demand, but he told me that he wanted 'maybe more'.

Well, it's morning now and I suppose we need to talk about what 'maybe more' constitutes.

Part of me is reluctant, because the atmosphere between us has been so easy, so sexy and tender. He woke me with a kiss, his hands stroking me, and then that turned into slow, sleepy, sensual sex.

Now, I don't want to disturb anything or rock the boat, but . . .

We do need to talk about it.

He lifts his hands and pushes my hair back from my face, his gaze shadowed. 'We're not together, Kate,' he says. 'We slept together and that's not the same thing.'

I appreciate his honesty, even as something twists in my chest. 'Then perhaps you'd better be clear about what exactly "maybe more" means.'

He lets out a breath, his gaze searching my face. 'Maybe more means maybe more sex. That's all.'

'I thought you said it would never be "just sex" between us?' I know I wasn't going to do anything to rock the boat, but I can't help myself. I'd like this thing between us to be about more than just sex, but I'm not clear on how much more I want either.

I didn't want another relationship; I knew that much when I came to Wychtree. In fact, I'd sworn off men for good. But then Sebastian appeared and threw a spanner in the works, and now everything feels uncertain.

I don't like uncertainty. I grew up with too much of it, moving from flat to flat around London, depending on how much money my mother had at the time. Then Jasper and the constant state of emotional uncertainty he kept me in.

So when I moved to Wychtree, I told myself that this was where I'd put down roots, make myself a home.

That did not include falling for a man who definitely does *not* want a relationship and yet is frustratingly unclear about what he *does* want.

And, yes, I probably am falling for him.

I felt it last night when he held me against the bookshelves. When he pushed inside me and his eyes went electric blue. When I thought to myself that I never wanted this to end. I wanted him to look at me like that for ever.

I'm an idiot.

A complete fucking idiot.

'That's true,' he says at last. 'And it wasn't just sex.'

'Can't we try this?' I make an attempt to not sound quite so desperate. 'It doesn't have to be a relationship per se. We could just be . . . I don't know . . . "friends with benefits" or something?'

He smiles at this and the tension in me releases. It's a warm, natural, genuinely amused smile. 'Friends with benefits,' he echoes. 'Is that what the kids are calling it these days?'

'Try to sound less like you're eighty years old.' I elbow him again. 'Actually, what we have is more like a "situationship".'

'That's even more ridiculous.'

He grips my hips and rolls over, pinning me beneath him, which I suspect is his favourite position. He's a bossy lover, but I like that, because he's also a hungry one, and that means

I get to be bossy as well. He allows me anything as long as I touch him.

'Casual, then.' He threads his fingers through mine and lifts my hands over my head. 'A casual relationship. No-strings sex.'

I like the idea of that. Casual. No strings. No emotional attachments.

My heart protests, but I tell that bitch to shut up. She knows nothing. She thought Jasper was a catch and look how that turned out.

'Fine,' I say, gasping a little as he settles between my thighs, his hard-on pressing against me and sending the most exquisite bolt of pleasure through me. 'I can do that.'

'What did he do to you?'

The question sounds so easy and natural that, for a moment, I don't quite know what he's talking about. Yet there is nothing easy or natural about the intent way he's staring at me.

Jasper. He wants to know about Jasper. Because, yesterday, in the heat of the moment, when I was so upset about my great-grandmother, I inadvertently let slip something I shouldn't.

My stomach hollows. I haven't talked to anyone about him, not since I left. Mum didn't think much of him, but I loved him. Or, at least, I thought I loved him. And I thought he loved me. I thought that all the little slights and criticisms and gaslighting lies he told me were genuine. I thought they were him being honest and I knew that honesty was important in a relationship. Putting the work into a relationship was also important and you put the work in when someone matters to you.

I just didn't see that I was the only one being honest, just as I didn't notice that I was the only one who put the work into our relationship.

It's embarrassing, and I don't want to talk to Sebastian about it. Jasper only used words to hurt me. He didn't hit me, he never raised his hand against me even once. I had no bruises, no marks on my body, and while I had scars, they weren't physical ones. Not like what some women have to deal with.

Not like Kate.

Smart women these days aren't supposed to let guys treat them that way. We're supposed to spot red flags. We're supposed to know what a 'good' relationship looks like, so that we're not complicit in our own abuse. But you know what they say about not seeing the wood for the trees? With Jasper it was all trees. That's all I saw and I felt stupid that I didn't see anything else.

I feel stupid even now.

'Kate,' Sebastian says softly, and I know I've been silent too long. Already this is becoming a bigger deal than it needs to be.

'Oh, he wasn't that bad,' I say eventually, trying to keep it light. 'He just used to say things that were a bit mean.'

'What things?'

'It's nothing, Sebastian. Honestly.'

'You don't like talking about it?'

I let out a breath, annoyed that he's pushing. 'Not really. He wasn't very nice in the end and let's leave it at that.'

Sebastian's blue gaze searches mine and he stays silent.

'I know I said that about knowing what it was like to be

with a man who hurt you,' I say, because it's clear he's not going to let this go. 'But Jasper never hit me or anything, okay? Not even once.'

Sebastian doesn't move, his fingers warm and strong, laced through mine. 'He did hurt you, though.'

It's not a question and suddenly the embarrassment and shame that rushes through me is almost choking. 'Do we have to talk about this?'

'No,' Sebastian says. 'But if you want to talk about it, you can. You can trust me with anything.'

The words get lodged in my heart and they stay there, vibrating, like an arrow shot into a target. He's not going to make me tell him. He's not going to insist. But if I want to, he's here, and I can trust him.

It's been a long time since I trusted anyone. A very long time. And as soon as I think that, all the words start spilling out, as if they've only been waiting for this opportunity, waiting for him all this time.

'Jasper was lovely initially,' I begin. 'He said all the right things, treated me like a queen, and then . . . after about six months, he'd compliment me but then follow it up with something I could do to make it "even better". I didn't mind that, I wanted to please him, but then those things turned into little criticisms about my appearance or my cooking or my job. It wasn't anything that awful and he never got angry or raised his voice, but . . .' I swallow, feeling a familiar acid sickness settle in my gut. The same sickness I felt whenever Jasper made those comments. 'It was a constant stream of criticism and commentary, making me feel as if nothing I did was right. He wanted my attention all the time, but only suggested going out if I'd made plans with friends. He'd tell me how much he liked being with me and wouldn't I rather spend time with him, that kind of thing.'

Sebastian's attention is all on me yet he's silent, leaving space for me to talk and I like that. It makes me brave.

'He never said outright when he was angry with me,' I continue. 'He'd joke about it instead, and when I didn't laugh or I'd call him out, he'd tell me I was being too sensitive. Of course, when I actually wanted to spend time with him, he'd tell me he was going out with "the lads". And if I protested, he'd tell me to stop being clingy.' I keep expecting the acid feeling inside me to get worse, but for some reason, it doesn't. As if the pressure of Sebastian's gaze drains it all away, taking the poison from it.

'I never realised how he'd manipulated me or how narcissistic he was until he wanted me to come to some work dinner on the second anniversary of Mum's death. I said I didn't feel up to it, and he got angry. Told me that Mum had been dead two years and I needed to get over it. Then I realised he'd gone through my contacts in my phone and deleted all my friends' numbers.' I take a breath. 'It took me four years to understand that he'd been steadily isolating me from my friends and making my entire life all about him. Stupid, huh?'

'Stupid?' Sebastian echoes mildly. 'Is that what you'd tell another woman in the same position? That she was stupid?'

A flicker of anger goes through me. 'No, of course not.'

'Is that what you would tell your great-grandmother?'

The anger abruptly dies, leaving me feeling cold as I'm brought face to face with the similarities in the first Kate's life and my own.

'But Jasper didn't hit me,' I say again, as if saying it a lot makes it okay. 'It's different.'

'He hurt you.' Sebastian's fingers tighten through mine. 'And just because you can't see the bruises doesn't mean he didn't. It doesn't make those wounds hurt any less.'

I swallow yet again, the acid inside me draining away until it's gone. Until there's nothing left but the ferocious blue of Sebastian's eyes, and only then do I see the fury in them. Fury for me.

'You're not stupid, Kate,' he goes on. 'And none of this is your fault. You went into the relationship in good faith and he betrayed you.' His voice deepens and I hear the same fury echoing in it. 'If he ever comes near you again, let me know, and I'll kick him all the way back to London.'

He's not joking, I can see it in his face. He means every word.

Intellectually, I know it's not my fault. Intellectually, I know Jasper was the one to blame. Yet that's the problem with abuse. It sits in your heart, hooks into your deepest fears about yourself and undermines you.

Right now, though, here in this bed, with Sebastian's weight on me, his fingers laced through mine, and the full force of his conviction in his eyes, I feel some of my own shame leave me. I don't need him to tell me these things, but I appreciate that he did. It's a support I didn't know I needed.

'Thank you,' I say huskily. 'So . . .' I swallow away the last of my hurt and anger. 'Do you want to keep us a secret?'

He raises an eyebrow. 'From the village? I think it's a little late for that.'

'It doesn't worry me. I don't care about gossip. But I know you don't like it.'

'I don't? Who told you that?'

I bite my lip, not wanting to give Aisling and what she told me about him away. 'No one. I just assumed you don't because you keep yourself so separate from everyone.'

He sighs. 'Living in a village has its own . . . peculiarities. Your life isn't your own, since everyone here knows all about it and has an opinion on it. And they're not shy about telling you.'

'Hey, I kind of guessed that. I've watched enough Hallmark movies to know.'

He smiles, once again causing my heart to leap about like a mad thing. 'I hate to disappoint you, but life in a small village is not like a Hallmark movie.'

'No. Because if it was, there would be a tall, dark, brooding stranger . . . oh . . . wait.'

He laughs and I feel like I've won the National Lottery, the sound of it raising delicious goosebumps over my skin. My God, it's sexy. I need to call the US President, tell him that one of his weapons of mass destruction is in an English village, taking the form of an illegally hot bookseller.

'I don't like pity,' Sebastian says after a moment. 'After Mum died, that's all I got. Pitying looks and lots of "poor boy" comments. Lots of "lucky you still have your father". It was too much, especially when I didn't actually end up having my father.'

I go very still. This is private and he's a very private man, yet he's giving me something, the way I gave him some of me. A little piece of himself, of his history. It's precious and important, and I don't want to say the wrong thing.

'Why not?' I ask carefully. 'What happened to him?'

'He preferred the bottle to me. Just like my grandfather preferred the track. I used to find empty whisky bottles hidden amongst the books on the bookshelves.'

My heart stops dancing and stands there holding itself, aching for a little boy who lost his mother far too soon and his father along with her. 'I'm so sorry, Sebastian,' I say. 'And this isn't pity, just so you know. It's sympathy.'

He searches my face for a long moment and I can't tell what he's thinking. 'The problem with a village is that there were plenty of people who had opinions, and yet no one lifted a finger to help. They all viewed it as none of their business.' He pauses. 'By the time I was twelve years old, Dad was drunk every night. I had to make my own meals, do my own washing. Get myself to school . . .' He stops. 'I'm not complaining. It was what it was. But it's very much a case of your business is our business until it isn't.'

Poor kid. He basically brought himself up. He must have felt so alone.

'Mum was on her own,' I say, wanting to share my experience, to let him know that I understand. 'It was just me and her.

She had to work a lot to keep the roof over our heads and I was left on my own much of the time. I had to learn to take care of myself because she wasn't around to do it.'

For a moment our gazes lock and we stare at each other, a moment of complete understanding flowing between us.

'The bookshop?' I ask, knowing already the answer to the question, because he told me once before. That's where he went to escape. To find companionship. To find the connections he wanted.

His mouth curls. 'The library?'

I smile back.

We know, the two of us. We know.

It was books. Books saved us.

He bends his head and his mouth is on mine, and then he moves. And I'm not thinking about books any more.

Only him.

Chapter Twenty

Who are you protecting? Him? Why?
When he doesn't protect you?

H

SEBASTIAN

I shut the bookshop door behind me, then cross the road to Portable Magic. Kate has changed the front window and it's full of fantasy books, with plenty of toy dragons posed appealingly and a couple of teddy bears that someone has fashioned armour and swords for. A big sign says: 'If you enjoyed *The Lord of the Rings*, you'll love these fabulous, fantastic fantasy reads!'

It's a great window. It compliments my *Lord of the Rings* one. I don't even mind the terrible alliteration or the exclamation mark.

I pause to admire it a moment, then pull open the door and step inside.

Kate is standing at the counter with the person we're meeting today.

Lisa Underwood.

Lisa is in her mid-fifties, short and wide, with straight white hair that hangs to her shoulders. She has a blunt fringe and her startling green eyes stare through the chunky, bright-green-framed glasses she wears. She's in a simple dress of kelly green, with a long, braided necklace of bright gold. Beside her stands a very tall, stern-looking man with sharp, hawkish features.

Lisa is talking to Kate and, as soon as I see Kate, the rest of the world vanishes, the way it always does when she is in the room.

Kate is smiling, shining like the ray of sunshine she is. She's wearing that white lace dress again that she wore to the pub that night, and, yes, her underwear is visible, and, yes, I can't look away. It's pink and pretty and delicate.

I watched her putting it on this morning, and told her to forget the slip, and then we were almost late to open up because I had to show her how much I liked it.

I still like it, but I also want to take it off and see what she looks like wearing that dress with nothing on underneath it.

Fucking hot.

Not that I should be thinking of Kate naked or otherwise just now, because Lisa Underwood is here – she wanted to arrive the week before the festival is due to start so that she could look around the village first, before all the crowds descend.

'Sebastian,' Kate says as I approach, and smiles as if I'm the best thing she's seen all day, and for a moment I can't breathe. 'This is Lisa Underwood. Lisa, please meet Sebastian Blackwood, owner of Blackwood Books, which you can see just across the road.'

Lisa gives me a startlingly charming smile and holds out her hand. 'Sebastian,' she says warmly. 'So lovely to meet you. This is my husband, Clive.' She indicates the hawkish man, who is standing close to her and regarding me suspiciously. He's protective of her, I can see that, and even though I'm no threat, I can't help but approve.

I take her hand and shake it. 'A pleasure,' I say. Then I take Clive's hand and shake that too, giving him a sharp, masculine nod, which he returns.

'So . . .' Lisa claps her hands together. 'Kate was just telling me that the two of you are the great-grandchildren of the writers of those letters. How spectacular. You can't imagine how excited I was when Kate got in touch about the festival, and then mentioned the letters.' Her expression becomes serious. 'She says that privacy is important to you, so I just want you to know that I won't use the real names of people or the village. Nor will I use the content of the letters, except as inspiration.'

I like her. She's very personable, and I like that she's straight up addressing any privacy concerns. I like that Kate mentioned that to her too.

'Thank you for clarifying that,' I say formally. 'I appreciate you thinking of it.'

'It's my standard disclaimer whenever I want to use real-life stories as inspiration. Also, I hope you won't mind, but I'd love it if you, and Kate here, could read a draft of the manuscript. I don't want to tread on any toes.'

'So, you're definitely going to use those letters, then?' I ask. 'For a book, I mean?'

She nods vigorously, her eyes shining. 'If that's all right. It's such a beautiful love story.'

'It's a tragic love story,' Kate puts in. 'I don't want to tell you what to write, Lisa, but it would be great if you could give them both a happy ending.'

'Such a romantic.' Lisa smiles, and gives her an indulgent pat on the arm. 'We'll see. Depends on what track the story takes. That's more important, as you know.'

'I want to thank you, Lisa,' I say. 'For coming to Wychtree. We're a small village and this festival was started by my great-grandfather in the early fifties. So, as you can imagine, it means a lot to the village and to me personally.'

Lisa's gaze is bright with interest. 'He started the festival, did he? How amazing. I'd love to hear all about him and your history. Perhaps at dinner tonight?'

'Certainly,' I say.

Lisa glances at Kate. 'Well. I love this little bookshop. It's absolutely perfect.'

Kate visibly glows at the praise. 'I'm so glad you think so. You should see Blackwood Books, though. It's amazing. Different vibe, but such a wonderful space.'

I can almost feel my chest inflate with pride at her words,

which is annoying, because I know my bookshop is amazing. I don't need her praise. Yet I find myself hungry for it all the same.

'It's a little tired,' I say, self-deprecating. 'But the readers find it suffices.'

There's a twinkle in Lisa's eye for some reason. 'Well, I'd love to see it. Would you show us around, Sebastian?'

I'm very aware of her hulking husband standing close behind her. He's less than an inch shorter than I am, and I am very tall. His gaze is definitely suspicious.

So maybe it's his suspicion that makes me reach for Kate's hand and thread my fingers through hers. 'Of course,' I say.

She blushes the most adorable shade of pink.

Lisa and Clive stare at our joined hands.

Clive relaxes into parade rest.

Lisa gives both Kate and me a delighted look. 'Oh, how wonderful! You two are together?'

'Yes,' says Kate.

'No,' I say, at the same time.

We glance at each other, but Kate looks away first. Her smile is still beaming at a hundred watts, but I can see that there's something else going on behind her grey eyes.

Did she not like me saying no? We're not actually together, that's the thing. We agreed last week, when we started seeing each other, that it was only going to be casual.

It's been going fine, too. We spend most nights with each other, alternating between her place and mine, and we have some truly sensational sex.

Not only that, though. We have great conversations too, mostly about books. Arguments as well, since we are who we are and neither of us likes being wrong. Also, she's been insisting on some ridiculous things for the festival – a cosplay cocktail party, for God's sake – that I've tried to veto. Emphasis on the 'tried'.

Because not only is she stubborn; she can also be very persuasive when she wants to be, usually in bed, and I've found myself swayed on more than a few occasions. Which means the cosplay cocktail party has unfortunately entered the programme, as has a 'date with a book' lucky dip. She even mentioned a couple of days ago something about a treasure hunt, but I pretended not to hear it.

So if sex, arguments and conversation can be termed 'being together', then, I suppose I was wrong and, yes, we are together.

I'm sure Lisa has picked up on our strange moment, because she's glancing at Kate, then me, and then back again, her gaze curious. I feel vaguely like an insect under a microscope.

I smile at Lisa, hoping it comes across as pleasant. 'What I meant to say is that we're together casually,' I say.

'How wonderful,' says Lisa. 'It's almost like fate, isn't it?'

Kate pulls her hand from mine and heads to the door of Portable Magic. 'Come on,' she says, tugging it open. 'It's just across the road.' Her smile is a tad fixed, but if Lisa notices it, she makes no comment.

Neither do I as we all troop across to Blackwood Books. Mainly because I have no idea what to say. I don't know what's bothering her, and I'm not sure I can offer anything even if I did. I thought she was happy with the way things were going, but the way she pulled her hand from mine, as if I'd burned her . . .

Clearly she's not and I'd like to know why.

She chatters away to Lisa as we go into the bookshop and then I take over, giving Lisa the grand tour. She's charmed and I can't help but feel smug. Blackwood Books is a calm, quiet oasis, an escape from reality, and that's the way I like it.

'I'd love for your Q&A to be here,' I tell her. 'It's small, but we can set up a video camera for streaming.'

She is nodding approvingly, looking around. 'Oh, it's perfect. Nothing worse than a large place with a small crowd. Much better to have a small place with a large crowd.'

'I'll have a desk set up for a signing.' I indicate where I'd envisaged putting it. 'Over there should be a good spot.'

'Oh,' Kate says, looking pointedly at me. 'I thought we'd agreed that Lisa would do a signing at Portable Magic.'

I frown. I don't remember us discussing that. 'Did we? I'm not sure we did.'

Lisa once again looks at me, then at Kate, then glances at her husband. 'Clive, why don't we go upstairs? I'm sure I saw an atlas that you might like.'

Clive, clearly a man of few words, nods and follows his wife up the stairs, leaving us staring at each other uncomfortably.

'We discussed it,' she says stubbornly. 'I remember.'

'I don't.' I'm irritated now. 'It makes more sense to have her Q&A here and then the signing here too. No one wants to go across the road.'

'It's not a hike up Everest, Sebastian. It's a two-second walk.'

'I know that, but think of the logistics of people going out and coming in.'

Temper flashes in her eyes. 'I don't care about the logistics. This is in aid of Portable Magic too, you promised. And after all, I was the one who brought her here.'

'Yes. But for *my* great-grandfather's letters.'

My voice has risen and, if it rises any more, Lisa is going to know we're having an argument about her, which will be desperately uncomfortable for all concerned.

'They're not *your* great-grandfather's letters,' Kate shouts back. 'Not all of them, at least. Some of them are my great-grandmother's too.'

I feel bizarrely enraged and I don't know why. I don't even know why we're arguing, because this is a ridiculous thing to argue about.

No. Actually, I *do* know why we're arguing and it's got nothing to do with where Lisa signs her books. It's about the expression I saw in Kate's eyes just before, when Lisa asked if we were together. She didn't like me saying it was casual. She looked . . . unhappy. And the reason I'm angry now is that I care about her feelings. It matters to me if she's unhappy. It matters if she's sad. It matters if some pathetic waste of space, who has the gall to call himself a man, hurts her.

She told me about said pathetic waste of space, she trusted me with her feelings, and it matters. Her feelings matter. They're important and I . . . I don't like it. I don't want to care about them. Because once you start to care, you're fucked.

Caring is difficult and painful, and sometimes it feels pointless, because caring doesn't change things. It doesn't make cancer disappear or cure alcoholism, or make people stay when you want them. It only makes everything hurt more.

Not caring is so much easier, so much simpler.

I'm angry that I've lost that.

Kate stands in front of me, grey eyes flashing, her chin jutting out in that stubborn way I've come to recognise. She's so beautiful, so free and honest with her emotions, while I'm the opposite.

I want to go cold. Freeze my anger. Lock it down. Find my way back to the man I was before she wrecked me, but that's impossible now. She's worked her way under my defences like a sapper under a castle wall, and I'm not sure how I can get her back out again.

All I can think is how strong she is. How brave. That bastard she was with tried to beat her down and yet here she is, standing in front of me, arguing with me. No fear, not a scrap. She's amazing.

'This is a stupid thing to argue about,' I say flatly. 'Lisa can sign wherever she wants, but what I want to know is why you went quiet when she asked if we were together.'

Her mouth opens. Shuts. Then she glances away and is silent so long I think she's not going to answer. Then she says, 'You said "no". Then you said "casually".'

I wasn't wrong, then. I don't know whether to be pleased I was right or annoyed about it.

'Yes,' I say. 'That's what we agreed on.'

She bites her lip, keeps her gaze turned away. 'We did, that's true.'

'I can hear a "but".'

She sighs and finally looks at me. 'It's fine, forget I said anything.'

'I have read that when a woman says it's fine, you're on the point of being decapitated.'

The anger fades from her eyes as quickly as it appeared and she gives me that little quirk of her mouth that I know is a reluctant half-smile. The kind where she doesn't actually want to smile, but she can't help herself.

I'm addicted to that smile.

'Close,' she says. 'But I don't think we're at decapitation yet. A light strangling maybe.'

'Kathryn,' I say, indulging myself with her full name. 'Is it fine? Is it really?'

'Do you care?' she asks, half-joking.

'Yes.' I don't smile. This is serious. 'I'm not another Jasper. I don't want to hurt you. That's not what this is supposed to be about.' I reach for her hand and pull her close and she doesn't resist. 'Was there something wrong with casual?'

She looks up at me and there is painful honesty in her expression. 'No,' she says. 'Nothing. That's what we agreed on, and that's what I want. I'm not ready for anything more.'

This is exactly what I want to hear and yet the words scrape over my skin like steel wool, and I don't know why. Casual is fine for me too. Seeing someone in the village is new for me. Seeing anyone more than once or twice is, frankly, new for me.

And I don't want to promise her anything I may not end up being able to give.

The last thing in the world I want to do is hurt her.

'Good.' I ignore the tight feeling in my chest that suggests that 'good' might not be the right response and that 'casual' is not the right word for what we have. Instead, I lift my hands and cup her face between them, bending to kiss her gently. 'Now, tonight after dinner. Your place or mine?'

'Yours,' she says promptly. 'I like your shower. The water pressure in mine is awful.'

'Glad to know someone's got their priorities straight.'

'Also,' she says, the look in her eyes soft. 'Just so you know, you're nothing like Jasper. Nothing like him at all.'

I'd like to think I wasn't, but you can never tell. And, honestly, I'd decapitate *myself* if I was anything like that prick.

So I kiss her again, already impatient for this dinner to be over.

Already impatient to have her where she belongs.

In my bed.

Chapter Twenty-one

*Please, don't let's argue. He's going down to London
tomorrow. I can come to you then.*

C

KATE

We've finished dinner and are sitting in the Wychtree Arms
dining room: me, Lisa and Sebastian, the notes between the
first Sebastian and the first Kathryn stacked neatly on the
table.

Lisa's husband, Clive – a darts fan, apparently – has
gone to try his luck against Mrs Bennet, while Lisa discusses
the love letters with us, jotting down notes in a pretty note-
book she bought from Portable Magic.

I'd been looking forward to her arriving and to our dinner,
so I'm not sure why I feel so . . . restless. Why all my attention
feels consumed by the man sitting opposite me.

'Casually', he said when Lisa asked us if we were together, and casual was what we agreed on. It was what we both wanted. Sure, I had a little moment when he first said it to Lisa and felt stupidly hurt. And that argument in his shop about Lisa's signing . . . Sebastian was right. It was a silly thing to argue about, especially when that wasn't the problem.

Except I don't know what the problem was. The word 'casually' hit me wrong, and maybe that's because the intensity of our connection doesn't feel casual to me. But . . . I don't want it to be more, so I don't know why I got so wound up. It's not as if I'm ready to hurl myself into a passionate relationship again, not after Jasper. Or indeed any kind of relationship.

Still, despite all of that, I'm not as okay as I thought I'd be with this middle ground Sebastian and I have been occupying the past week. I find it strange that he's willing to have this in-between thing with me, especially when he's such an all-or-nothing guy, and it makes me wonder why.

The sex is fantastic, so maybe that's the reason – he's a man, after all. Yet if sex was the only reason, then we wouldn't sit around talking and sometimes arguing about everything under the sun the way we have been.

It's so good between us that dangerous thoughts have started to slip in, such as what would it be like if we weren't casual, if our relationship actually matched our feelings . . . not that I know what his feelings are, yet . . .

But no. I can't think about me or my feelings. I can only think that trying for anything more with him would be a mistake. He'd throw himself into a relationship body and soul, and he'd take everything, and I don't have it in me to give him that. I don't want to give myself away again, not after Jasper. Maybe in a few years I might have the emotional bandwidth for it, but not now.

Sebastian is leaning back in the wooden chair at the table now, arms folded, his blue gaze on mine, his expression impossible to read. He's gorgeous again today, as he is every day, in a dark-blue shirt that emphasises the colour of his eyes.

'So, tell me more about the teashop,' Lisa says to me.

Over the past week I've been making visits to the local public library and looking at the historic village records, researching my great-grandmother's history. There's not a lot, but I did manage to find a few photos of the teashop in the archives.

'I've got these for you,' I say, reaching into my bag and getting out copies of the photos. I put them on the table and Lisa looks at them excitedly. 'It was called the Wychtree Tea Rooms,' I continue. 'Mrs Bennet in the craft shop said her husband made her give it up.'

Sebastian is looking at the photos too, a slight frown on his face. They're not new to him. I've shown them to him before.

'Ah,' Lisa says. 'That must have been awful for her. But these are great. May I keep them for reference?'

'Go ahead.' I pick up my glass of wine and sip it.

'Fantastic. And what do you know about your great-grandfather?' She peers over the top of her glasses at me.

'Nothing,' I say. 'Quite frankly, I don't care about him. He died in a car accident twenty years after the war ended, and I'm sure no one was unhappy about that.'

Lisa nods. 'And then . . . Kathryn disappeared, you said?'

I've done a bit of research into that too, looking at old newspaper articles about the search for her. 'She did. Around 1966, just after Rose turned twenty-one. She did leave Rose that note before she left.'

Lisa shuffles through the pile to find it. 'Oh, yes, so she did.' She frowns down at it and reads it again. 'Hmm. It's definitely a goodbye. Did the authorities ever come to a conclusion about what happened to her?'

'There was a coronial inquiry when she was declared legally dead,' I say. 'But, no, there were no real conclusions. Suicide was suspected.'

Lisa's frown deepens. 'If so, it's an awfully strange suicide note.'

Sebastian leans forward and studies it. ' "Know that I will be loved . . . that I will be happy",' he reads out. 'Perhaps she was talking about seeing her family on the other side. Or maybe God.'

I still find the note unbearably painful – I find all the notes my great-grandmother wrote unbearably painful – and I have to swallow the lump that's risen in my throat. 'Whatever happened to her,' I say. 'She thought she was going to a better place.'

Lisa nods solemnly and gives my great-grandmother a moment of silence. Then she glances at Sebastian. 'And your great-grandfather, Sebastian. His body was never found?'

Sebastian has told her about his great-grandfather's death.

'Never,' he says. 'There was an inquest, though. And the coroner's verdict was likely drowning, possibly suicide. He left no note, unfortunately.'

'What about your grandfather? What was his name? Charles? Did he have anything to say about it?'

'Other than being furious, no,' Sebastian says. 'He never talked about it, not to Dad and not to me.'

'Furious?' Lisa queries.

'Oh, yes. He was livid. Whenever the subject came up, he'd get tight-lipped and tense. The bookshop was in a bit of financial trouble and there were a few debts that my great-grandfather left behind. I'm assuming Charles thought his father took the easy way out.'

'How difficult,' Lisa murmurs in sympathy. Then she glances at me. 'What about Rose? Was she angry about her mother's disappearance, do you know?'

I shake my head. 'No. I never met her and Mum never talked about her. People in the village here have said she was a difficult woman. Then again, it can't have been easy for her being orphaned at twenty-one.'

'It must have been awful,' Lisa agrees. 'A troubled history on both sides, hmm? But now here you both are, descendants of the original Sebastian and Kathryn, and you're together. It's definitely fate.'

There are more similarities between me and my great-grandmother than I'd like – especially being with awful men – and talk of fate makes me uncomfortable.

'We didn't know our great-grandparents were having an affair,' Sebastian points out coolly, as uncomfortable with that idea as I am. 'We only found that out comparatively recently.'

'If you're trying to tell me that fate didn't have anything to do with it,' Lisa says, 'you're not making a convincing argument. You two not knowing a thing about each other and yet still finding love together.'

Love.

The word falls into the middle of the table like a rock dumped from a very great height, smashing through the easy atmosphere.

Sebastian's expression shuts down.

My discomfort intensifies.

Lisa notices the tension in the air and says hurriedly, 'Well, that's been so helpful, Kate. You don't mind if I do a bit of digging myself in the public library? I do love a library.'

'No, of course not.' I force a smile. 'We'll give you a tour of the village tomorrow so you know where everything is.'

'Good.' She gives me a smile back. 'Oh, it's so lovely seeing you. In fact, I've been wondering if I couldn't tempt you back to editing.'

A little electric shock goes down my spine. 'What?'

'I know you've moved here and opened your bookshop, but . . . You were such a fantastic editor, and this is partly your family's story. I'd love your input on it as I'm writing.'

This was *not* what I was expecting and for a minute I have no idea what to say. 'Um . . . Don't you have an editor already?'

Lisa waves a hand. 'Oh, yes. But I have a bit of clout these days. If I want a different editor and present the publisher with one, I'm sure they won't be able to say no.'

I'm struggling to process this. I loved editing. I loved being in publishing and helping writers make their stories come to life. But after Jasper and Mum, I had to leave, and my escape to Wychtree had felt irreversible. I swore to myself that I wouldn't be back, that I was going to make a new life for myself, a better life. I hadn't ever thought that door would open again, and now . . .

Abruptly, Sebastian shoves back his chair and stands. Lisa and I look at him in surprise, but his expression remains impassive. 'If you'll excuse me,' he says, in the most insufferably formal tones. 'I'll leave you two to your discussion. I have a few things to do. Let me know if you need any more help, Lisa.' He glances at me, his blue eyes glowing, but says nothing. Then, before I can speak, he turns and departs.

'My, my,' Lisa murmurs. 'He's an intense one.'

I watch as he strides out, wondering what on earth made him leave, because something did. Was it the talk of love or was it the mention of editing? And does that mean he doesn't want me to come back to his place tonight?

Lisa glances at me. 'I put my foot in it, didn't I?'

I hope my feelings aren't plastered all over my face. 'Oh no, not at all,' I say, unconvincingly.

'I shouldn't have said "love", should I?' Lisa is far too astute for her own good. Then again, writers are good at observing people.

I fiddle with my dessert spoon. 'Um . . . Let's just say we're not quite at that stage yet.'

'Oh, but I thought . . . When you look at each other . . .' She stops, then mutters under her breath. 'He did say casual.'

'It's fine.' My face is getting hot. 'Don't worry about it.'

But there is understanding in her eyes. 'Difficult, yes? Him, I mean. I can tell. Men like that always are.'

I bristle, defensive of him. 'No, he's not difficult. Not at all. He's actually a really wonderful man.'

Lisa waves a hand. 'I'm not being critical, that's not what I meant. What I meant was that he's intense. Passionate. Men like him wear their hearts on their sleeve yet think they have the world's best poker face.' She picks up the cappuccino she's drinking and takes a sip. 'Clive was like that. Still is. They take a little bit of getting to know, but once you do . . .' She sighs and a warm, reminiscent smile turns her mouth. 'Well, they're loyal. Honest. Protective. And so loving. They're totally worth all the drama, believe me.'

I look down at my empty dessert bowl, my heart tight and sore. I know that already. I know he's worth it. But what I don't know is whether *I* am. He clearly wants me physically and we have great sex, but . . . What else do I have to offer him? What else that isn't endless sniping and argument? We both like books, it's true, but so far it's only been book talk and sex, and a relationship needs more than that.

Then there's the question of whether I'm ready for a full-on relationship. I wanted a life of my own, that I'm in charge of, that wasn't endlessly picked apart and critiqued, and where I'm not held hostage by my own emotions. Sebastian is strong, opinionated and demanding, and I'm not sure how I could cope with a man like that after Jasper. And I certainly don't want to go tying my heart to anyone, least of all him. 'I'm sure they are,' I mutter meaninglessly.

'Oh, they are. You know, I get the impression he's very much like his great-grandfather. You can feel the passion coming from those notes he sent Kate, and Sebastian radiates that same passion.' She pauses. 'Especially when he looks at you.'

My cheeks are now flaming and I concentrate fiercely on my dessert bowl like a silly teenager, not wanting to meet her eyes. She seems to think she's witnessing some grand passion.

'He might be like him,' I say eventually, putting my spoon into the bowl. 'But that relationship didn't exactly work out well.' I push the bowl away and finally lift my gaze and give her a direct look. 'Also, if you're hoping to use us as some kind of inspirational couple, you can forget it. Sebastian's right. We're only together in a casual way.'

She doesn't look particularly abashed. 'Sorry, love. You know a writer, always looking for grist for the mill. I hear you, but I think you're wrong. I think you're both wrong.'

I decide to change the subject at this point, because the thought of Sebastian looking at me with passion makes me want things I don't know if I'll ever be ready for, and I don't want to talk about it now.

We discuss other topics for a while and then, after reiterating that she'd like me to think about that editing offer, and agreeing on a time for us to do a tour of the village the next morning, she excuses herself and goes off to find Clive in the saloon bar.

I slip out of the Arms and into the warm, summer night.

My thoughts are flying everywhere and refusing to settle.

Sebastian. My bookshop. Editing . . .

I don't know what to do. I did love editing, but Portable Magic has always been my dream, and I've only been here for two months. I'm not ready to leave it. I don't have to sell, I tell myself. I could get someone to manage it for me if I returned to editing, but . . .

I don't want to do that. I like being in the bookshop, meeting customers and managing stock. Organising events and liaising with authors and publishers. I want to do all of that myself.

Then there is Sebastian and this casual-sex situation we've got going on. A situation where I'm afraid that my feelings for him are not the slightest bit casual. I knew that the moment he first kissed me.

My feelings for Sebastian have *never* been casual, and I'm afraid.

I'm afraid of what being with a man like Sebastian could do to me.

I'm afraid that I'll never be enough for him.

I'm afraid that, if I give him my heart, he'll take everything, like Jasper did.

I'm also afraid that my heart might be on its way to him already.

The high street is quiet as I walk down it.

Quiet, as I pause in front of Blackwood Books.

I told him earlier I'd be at his place tonight, but then he left the pub without a word and now I don't know what to do. Does he even want my company tonight? Will we have an awkward conversation about why he left? Will I have to pretend that Lisa talking fate and love in the context of us doesn't mean anything to me? And will I have to say yet again that casual is fine?

I don't know if I can do it. I don't know if I'm a good enough actress.

Because the fact is that casual isn't fine and it never was, and I've been lying to myself this past week.

I thought he'd be the one who wouldn't be able to manage the middle ground, but, as it turns out, he's not the problem.

The problem is me.

I turn from Blackwood Books and go home alone instead.

Chapter Twenty-two

*I wish you would talk about it with me. I wish
you would let me help you. I live for the day
when you come to my bed and stay there, and he
becomes only a memory.*

H

SEBASTIAN

I stare at the laptop screen as the post I've just written appears on the Wychtree Village Facebook group. It reminds everyone that Lisa's signing in Portable Magic is in just a few hours and that any villager who wants to attend gets first dibs on tickets to her session tonight. We had to move her talk from Blackwood Books to the village hall in the end, because we had too many people who wanted to come. I thought it would be possible to stream it, but the setup was tricky and difficult, and it was much easier to have it in the hall instead. I'm a bit disappointed, since having it here would have been great exposure. Then again, my disappointment is offset by selling far more tickets than we'd anticipated, due to having it in the hall.

We're allowing villagers special discounts and priority seating – Kate's excellent idea – and in the post I've also included a sign-up link to the new Blackwood Books newsletter.

I glance up from the laptop to check on my customers.

The shop is heaving.

All the World's a Page literary festival was officially launched last night with a party at the Wychtree Arms, and judging by the number of people in attendance – mostly out-of-towners – it's going to be one hell of a success.

It's not a long festival – a couple of days only – which is a good thing, because it's not only my shop that's heaving, but the entire village. Those with businesses are ecstatic. Those who hate outsiders are furious. But no one can deny that it's going to be good for the village coffers, and that, in the end, will silence the naysayers.

I've just presided over Augusta Heroine's poetry reading/performance, which had an excellent attendance. Quite unexpected for poetry. Copies of her verse novel are selling like hot cakes, which, again, is unexpected yet very pleasing.

I've got a newsletter form displayed prominently on my counter and already have a number of sign-ups from people, both local and not. It means I'll need to get my act together and put the finishing touches to my inaugural issue, but that will have to be after the festival, when I have time.

Right now, I should be mingling with the poets and festival attendees, yet I'm staring down at my laptop and thinking about the dinner last week instead. Thinking about Kate's face when Lisa said Kate and I being together was fate. How something had flickered in her eyes and how I didn't know what it was, only that it was something. Then Lisa offering her an editor position, and me . . .

Well. I left. I shouldn't have, but I did. Because the thought of her leaving the village altogether made me want to howl at the moon like a wolf, and I had to get out of there before I did something completely ridiculous like reach across the table and drag her into my arms. Not exactly the kind of atmosphere we wanted to project for Lisa's first visit to Wychtree.

I was almost glad Kate didn't come back to my place that night. She sent me a 'too tired' text, which was fine, because I wasn't in any state to have a conversation that didn't include me being a demanding bastard, and I figured she'd already had enough of that to last a lifetime.

I didn't see her until the following day. By then I'd calmed down and we didn't speak about the night before, but I've been thinking about it almost constantly.

It's not surprising that Lisa offered her a position. Kate's an amazing woman and the truth is that she's wasted here in Wychtree. She's managed to get her bookshop off the ground and be part of village life in only two months and that's an incredible feat. Where else can she go from here? She's reached the pinnacle of achievement in our tiny village and now there's nowhere for her to go. She should be out in the world sharing her expertise, not trapped here in a casual-sex relationship with her competition.

In fact, I've come to the conclusion that it would be better if she did go. She's taking up too much of my brain space as it is, and I think I'd be better off if she wasn't around. I should talk to her about it, but the past week has been fraught with festival preparations and we've been too busy to discuss anything else.

Yet even as the thought of her leaving passes through my head, an acid fury gathers inside me at the prospect. Again, mostly at myself and my complete inability to actually feel casual towards her. My emotions used to be much more controllable, much more ignorable, before she came, and now she's here . . .

Christ. I need to start thinking about something else.

I step back from the computer and pace restlessly over to the poetry section, threading through the knots of people still standing around after the reading. Augusta Heroine – tall, regal, tattooed and pierced – is talking to local poet Jim Macalister – late sixties, bushy-haired, wearing a tatty pullover full of holes. Jim is telling her about his modest success with his bird poetry while she listens intently.

I go to the shelves, ostensibly to check titles, though I don't need to. I know exactly what's on my shelves. But I can't pace around like a beast on a chain when there are customers filling the shop.

I fussily rearrange the books and grit my teeth, wishing I'd never crossed the road that night and gone into Portable Magic. Never gone upstairs to her flat. Never kissed her senseless in the first place. Because if I'd never done any of those things, I'd never have to consider the relationship I'm in with her, and how it's driving me round the bend, because all I want is more.

More of her. More of us together. More time to explore what we have and what the future might look like and—

Fuck. I can't start thinking like that. She's been through far too much already in the past year, and she doesn't need me demanding things from her that she can't give. Not that I want to anyway, no matter what my heart is telling me.

I *don't* want more.

What I want is to stay in my bookshop, ordering stock and talking to customers and looking at reviews and redoing the front window. Reading.

That's all my life has been so far and that's what it will be in the future and I'm fine with that. More than fine. It's all I ever wanted.

Maybe that's what I should tell her. Maybe I need her to know that she shouldn't concern herself with me and whatever our relationship is. That she can take that editing job and leave, go back to London.

Better she does that now, while things aren't serious between us, rather than later when it's more . . . difficult. Because they all leave in the end, the women in my family. They can't live with the Blackwood men, because, quite frankly, the Blackwood men never deserve them.

Sebastian left his Kate to the mercy of a man who abused her and then shirked his responsibility by diving into a river. My grandfather's commitment to gambling got in the way of him being a good husband to his wife and she left. Then there's Dad, who never much liked the bookshop either and decided to take up drinking instead.

I'm no different. I haven't had a relationship with a woman at all beyond a couple of days, let alone a serious one, and this casual business is doing my head in. Anything more will be a fucking disaster.

I pace back to the counter and check my newsletter sign-up list yet again. Another name. Excellent.

At that moment, a small golden-haired whirlwind comes charging into the shop and rushes up to the counter.

It's Kate. She's pink-cheeked, her hair up in a hasty, untidy knot on the top of her head, golden strands falling down all over the place. She's wearing some ridiculous rainbow of a dress that she must have borrowed from the Wychtree Dramatic Society's wardrobe – the thing has underskirts, for God's sake – and she looks like she's about to have a panic attack.

I'm surprised to see her. She should be getting ready to open the doors at Portable Magic for Lisa's signing, which is in exactly twenty-five minutes.

'Shouldn't you—' I begin.

'There are no books!' she bursts out. 'None! They didn't arrive. Lisa's going to be here in ten minutes and there are no books for her to sign.'

I frown at her. 'You only found out about this *now*?'

'I had so many boxes arrive from the supply company,' Kate says furiously. 'And there's only me unloading and unpacking them, and I followed the shipment of *Colours* up twice and they *said* they'd get them to me by this morning at the very latest.' She throws out a dramatic hand. 'But they're not. Fucking. Here.'

She is beside herself and I get it. It happens sometimes. You organise an author signing, and then the books don't turn up, and the author is left sitting at a table with nothing to sign. Uncomfortable and awkward for the author and financially devastating for the bookshop, especially if the author signing is a big name.

I glance out the window at the already massive queue that's formed outside Portable Magic. A lot of people. A lot of people who will want to buy signed copies of the global smash-hit book by Lisa Underwood.

Except there are no books to buy, which means Kate will miss out on a lot of money.

'Fuck, indeed,' I say, pithily and to the point.

Kate blinks rapidly. 'I don't know what to do. I've got two copies on the shelves but nothing out the back, and she'll be here at any minute, and this is a disaster. A total disaster!'

I don't blame her for panicking. She's only been running a bookshop for two months, not to mention throwing herself headfirst into helping me plan and run a literary festival. And when I had a small fit about James Wyatt pulling out, she helped me get a new headliner. So the least I can do is help her, and, luckily, I've been in this situation before, so I know exactly what to do.

'It's fine,' I say, projecting as much calm as I can. 'I have my stock out the back, so you can use that.' Lisa agreed to do a second signing at the end of the festival because of the demand, and it's going to be held here. I got my stock from a different supplier and it's already been delivered.

Kate is still breathing fast. 'But what about you? Won't you need—'

'It's fine,' I interrupt gently, coming around the counter and taking her hand in mine, hoping to calm her down. 'Nigel in Greenham will be able to courier over some more.'

Her fingers close instinctively around mine as if for comfort. 'Nigel? Greenham?'

'He owns Dusty Shelf Books. I've done a few favours for him recently and he owes me one. He'll probably have a whole lot in stock, because his shop is bigger and he'll be wanting to catch some overflow from our festival.'

Her eyes go very wide, panic receding. 'How will we get them here, though? Is there anyone with a truck who'll be willing to deliver on a Saturday?'

As it happens, there is. 'Len'll do it.'

'Len? As in Len's Quality Construction Len?'

'Yes.' I smile at her surprise. 'You wouldn't know it, but our Leonard has a taste for art and history, and I've just ordered him a very expensive title on Venetian architecture. I'm quite sure he'll be happy with doing a delivery in lieu of payment.'

Hope flickers in her eyes and I feel it in my chest, a growing pressure. Satisfaction that she came to me for help. Pleasure that I could help her. Desire to be the first one she turns to whenever she needs help in the future . . .

'Are you sure, Sebastian?' she asks, huskily.

I squeeze her hand and, before the pressure gets too much,

I let go of it. Before I hold on for grim life so she's never out of my sight.

'Go back to your shop. Open the doors. And let me handle it.'

She leans forward, then puts her hands on my chest and rises up on her toes and kisses me. It's only a fleeting brush of her mouth, but it pierces me like an arrow. For long moments I can't move or breathe.

'You're the best,' she says quietly. 'If you don't want me falling for you, you're going the wrong way about it.'

Falling for me? I think. *She's what?*

But she whirls around and is gone, leaving me standing there staring after her with my mouth open, probably looking very similar to a stunned mullet.

She's kissed me before, a thousand times, and it's never had this effect, yet I can't think about why right now.

Not when I have a damsel to save.

I text Dan to help me carry the boxes of books from my shop to Portable Magic, then I give Nigel a ring. He's more than happy to help out and has plenty of stock. We discuss the financials and, once that's sorted, I ring Leonard. He's got no issue with driving to Greenham and doing a pick-up for me, and can do it immediately. He's pleased at getting the book on Venetian architecture in return, and I tell him I'll also throw in a signed edition of *Colours* for his wife, who is a huge fan.

By the time I've made the arrangements with Nigel and Len, Dan arrives and we start gathering the boxes of books I've got in my back room, carting them over to Portable Magic.

Kate has Lisa's signing table all set up, with a poster of the book, some pens, a glass of water and a little bowl of peppermints. Lisa is standing behind it chatting with her, while Clive looms menacingly behind Lisa.

They all look up as Dan and I come in with the boxes, carrying them over to the table and setting them down beside it. Kate's face is shining as she looks at me and all I can hear is her telling me that I'm going the wrong way about *not* having her fall for me. All I can think is that her falling for me is exactly what I want.

Because I'm falling for her too.

Fuck.

'Nigel's sending some of his stock over,' I say, my voice hoarse-sounding. 'We'll have plenty for the signing at Blackwood Books tomorrow too.'

'Oh my God, that's amazing!' Kate exclaims, her smile like the sun rising. 'You're a hero, Sebastian Blackwood.'

No, I'm not. I'm an uptight bookseller who prefers books to people, and yet when she looks at me that way, there's a part of me that almost feels like a hero. *Her* hero.

I almost tell her. I almost open my fucking mouth and tell her that's what I want to be. I want to be her hero.

But luckily there's no time for that, because Dan is busy opening boxes, getting out books and stacking them on the table, and the doors are opening, and people are coming in, and the moment is lost.

A good thing.

I'm not anyone's hero, least of all hers.

Chapter Twenty-three

Don't do anything rash, darling H. If you do something to him, he'll hurt you back and I couldn't stand that. I'd also probably lose the teashop and I can't bear that thought.

C

KATE

I'm on the door at the village hall, taking people's tickets as they come in for Lisa's talk, and the queue is huge. Almost as big as it was at Portable Magic earlier today when she had her signing. We sold out of books completely and had to turn people away, and, honestly, it was the most thrilling experience of my life.

After the drama of the books was sorted out, of course.

Thank God for Sebastian.

The books were supposed to arrive in plenty of time, but there were delays and the supply company promised me faithfully that they would get them to me today. So when they didn't turn up, I almost had a panic attack.

I couldn't think of who to go to for help except Sebastian. Things have been awkward between us since that dinner with Lisa and me not coming to him that night – we didn't talk about it afterwards and I was glad, because I didn't want to, and then things got too busy with the festival – but . . . There's a strange distance between us now, and an awkwardness that wasn't there before.

Even so, I didn't think twice about going to him. He's more experienced in the bookselling trade than I am, and he has contacts, and he dealt with everything with calmness and authority.

He literally saved the day, and if I hadn't already fallen for him before, I would have done so the moment he took my hand in his big, warm one, looking at me steadily with those incredible blue eyes of his. Telling me everything would be okay, that he'd handle it.

It sounds pathetic to be so relieved by those words, because I really *don't* need a man to save me. But sometimes it's nice when one steps in and says, 'Hey, don't worry about it. I'll deal with it', and you know that he will. You know absolutely that everything will be fine.

That's what Sebastian did and, the moment he held my hand, I knew everything *would* be fine. That I could stop panicking and relax. And I did.

Except the problem is that now I know how reassuring he can be, I'm not sure I can do without that.

I'm not sure I can do without him.

I shove those thoughts away hard, though, as I take people's tickets, because I can't think about it now. After the festival is over we'll have to have that conversation, but I'm happy not to now. I don't like making emotional demands. Jasper told me I was selfish when I asked for his support while Mum was dying and again, afterwards, when I was grieving. He wanted me to pay more attention to him and, when I didn't, he'd punish me by ignoring me for days on end.

I know the problem was him, not me, but still, sometimes it's better not to push.

Anyway, at least the festival is doing well. Ticket sales are great. So many people are coming, in fact, that we've had to move Lisa's talk to the village hall, and it's filling up nicely.

I should be thrilled. We've got more people attending than Sebastian and I ever dreamed of and most of the panels and events are sold out. Yet I feel uncertain and on edge, as if the ground beneath my feet isn't rock, but swamp, and it keeps shifting with every step. It's a little too much like London and Jasper, when he used to act as if our relationship was always in some kind of jeopardy and expected me to fix it.

I hate that feeling.

I should be settled and happy in my new life here, but I'm not, and I have a horrible feeling it's all *his* fault.

A couple approach me and I give them a big smile and a 'Nice to see you, thanks for coming' as I take their tickets and usher them inside. Then I check the time. It'll be starting in a couple of minutes.

I take more tickets and the queue disappears, then I quickly put my head into the hall to see how things are going.

It echoes with the buzz of conversation and laughing, and the whole place is packed. Standing room only. The small stage down one end has a rug, a couch and an armchair on it, and Lisa's already sitting on the couch. Sebastian is sitting in the armchair and chatting to her. He's the MC for the evening.

I lean against the doorframe, staring at him, because I can't help myself.

He's wearing all black tonight and it suits him, the lights reflecting off his glossy black hair and throwing his perfect bone structure into relief. I was the one who suggested he be the MC, because I want the whole village to see how personable he can be when he chooses, though he took some convincing. He doesn't like being the centre of attention and thought I'd be a better bet, but I told him that he's far more calm under pressure than I am, and he is.

He's great eye candy too.

I let out a slow, silent breath, unable to take my eyes off him.

He's the reason I've been feeling unsettled and weird. Why there's been an ache in my chest and a longing in my heart for something I can't name.

No, that's wrong, I *can* name it. I just don't want to. And I don't want to because, the moment I do, things will change, and change irrevocably.

Once I've acknowledged it, said the thing out loud, there'll be no going back.

I want to keep pretending for a little while longer.

My time for that, though, is rapidly coming to an end, because I know he's already sensed something's up. He keeps casting glances at me and frowning, and sometimes he'll say, 'Are you sure you're all right?' He knows something's wrong, but he hasn't asked me straight out, which means he doesn't *really* want to know. He wants to keep pretending, like I am.

'Kate?' a familiar, masculine voice asks.

I turn around.

A man has stepped through the hall doors and into the foyer. He's wearing an expensive dark suit with a red tie, and his brown hair is brushed back from his forehead. He's handsome and slick and he's smiling.

He's also a ghost from my past and I blink. 'Jasper?'

His smile turns self-deprecating. 'Yeah.'

I go cold, struggling to process what he's doing here. Struggling to process his presence at all, because I was pretty sure I'd seen the last of him when I silently crept out of our flat with a suitcase, leaving him lying in bed, still asleep.

How did he find me? I didn't call him. I didn't text him. I didn't respond to any of his texts or emails or voicemails. I got myself a new phone and pretended he didn't exist, because I was afraid. Not that he'd physically hurt me – violence was never Jasper's way – but that he'd somehow get under my guard again, manipulate me, make it impossible for me to do anything but go back to him.

'What . . .?' I swallow then start again. 'What are you doing here?'

'Good question.' There's a touch of nervousness to him that I've never seen before. 'I saw an ad for the festival and that it was at your bookshop and so I . . . Well, I thought I'd come and say hello.'

The shock of seeing him here is still echoing through me. This man was emotionally manipulative and subtly controlling, and now he's standing in front of me with an intent look on his face and I have a horrible feeling I know exactly what he's going to say.

Indeed, the next words out of his mouth are, 'Look, Kate. I'm not going to get angry about you walking out. I know why you did it and I guess you had reason. But . . . I've been thinking a lot these past couple of months. I've been doing some work on myself, and I know I acted appallingly about your mum's anniversary. So I'm here to apologise and to say . . .' His familiar hazel eyes are full of hope – or at least what looks like hope. 'Well. I made a mistake. I shouldn't have said those things to you that night and I'm sorry. I want to know if we can . . . repair things.'

Repair things. Repair what things? He's talking now as if what he said was the only terrible thing he did, and that our relationship was only a little broken and could be fixed.

When he first came into my life, I thought he was everything I'd ever wanted. He was handsome, had a well-paid job in finance, and was charming. He seemed like a stable, secure choice of partner, and that's not to mention the way he initially treated me like a queen on every date. But then his true colours were revealed and now all I can think of is how he never called me beautiful the way Sebastian did when he first saw me naked. He never did anything to help me when I had a problem, the way Sebastian did when those books didn't turn up. Not that I would have gone to him if I'd had a problem anyway, because I already knew he wouldn't help me.

I didn't trust him then, and I don't trust him now.

Not the way I trust Sebastian.

There's something clarifying in that thought and it makes me lift my chin. 'What about all my friends you deleted from my contacts?' I ask.

He waves a hand in dismissal. 'I was helping you clear your contact list. But I acknowledge that I should have asked your permission first.'

My mouth is dry and my fingertips feel numb. 'So you came all this way just to fix things? How did you find me anyway?'

He nods. 'You always talked about how you wanted to own a bookshop and I . . . well, I confess I did a little digging and—'

'You always said I should aim higher.'

His mouth flattens. 'Again, I'm sorry. I know I shouldn't have said that. I was insecure. You had a dream and I didn't, and I didn't know how to cope with that.'

I think he means it. Then again, I could never trust anything he said and I can feel again the familiar state of uncertainty he kept me in beginning to rise. The acid in my gut beginning to bite.

'Jasper . . .' I begin.

'Please, Kate.' He takes a step forward, getting closer to me, his expression open and earnest. 'I made a terrible mistake and I want to fix it. I want to do better.' His hand comes out and before I know what's happening, he's taken mine in his. 'I miss you.'

My throat is tight. There were times when all I wanted was to hear those words and believe them, to be able to trust even one thing that he told me. But I couldn't then and I know I can't now, because now I know what the truth looks like. I see it every day in Sebastian's eyes.

'If he comes near you again, let me know and I will kick him all the way back to London.'

I swallow. I want to shout at him, scream at him in rage about all the things he did to me, but we're in public and I don't want to cause a scene.

'I left you, Jasper,' I say. 'I left you for a reason.'

'For the third time, I'm so sorry about what happened that night—'

'It wasn't just that night. It was the whole four years we were together.'

He gives a tight smile. 'Not the whole four years, surely?'

He's doing it again, minimising his behaviour. 'Yes,' I say. 'Apart from the first six months when you lulled me into believing you were a normal person and not a raging narcissist.'

'Kate,' he says gently, as if I've said something incredibly unreasonable. 'Come on. Don't be like that. Like I said, I've been seeing a therapist and I can see how awful I was to you. I just . . . want to make it up to you somehow.'

'It's too late for that,' I say, which is no less than the truth.

He sighs, runs a hand through his hair in a way that reminds me of Sebastian when he's agitated. With Sebastian the movement is sexy and I know what I can do to ease his agitation, but with Jasper?

I don't want to ease his agitation. I don't want to smooth his hair. I don't want to take his hand and plant a kiss on his palm, or wrap my arms around him and put my head on his chest. I don't want to pour oil on his troubled waters and keep our boat steady and level, anything to make sure he's happy.

I don't want to do anything with him at all.

'Please,' he says. 'Please, Kate. I . . . I love you and I always have and I just made the worst mistake.'

Does he mean it now? Again, I can't tell. I never could with him. But then it's not him I want and abruptly that becomes clear. Not that it wasn't clear already, I was just lying to myself. I was happy pretending.

I'm not happy pretending any more.

'Jasper . . .' I begin haltingly. 'I'm sorry, but—'

'Kate, you left me. You didn't even say goodbye. One moment you were there, the next you were gone.'

Reflexive guilt twists inside me, even though I know I shouldn't feel it. Even though I didn't do anything wrong. Making me doubt myself. 'I'm sorry,' I say automatically, even though I have nothing to apologise for. 'I didn't mean—'

'It's okay,' he interrupts again. 'I forgive you for that. But maybe I needed you to leave so I could realise what I'd lost.' His eyes shine again with hope. 'Come back to me, Kate. Please.'

He can't possibly think that forgiving me for something I didn't need to apologise for in the first place will make me come back to him. He can't, right? But it's clear that's exactly what he thinks. He expected to come here, tell me these things, and that then I'd fall into his arms.

I was always so insecure with him and he took advantage of that.

'I'm sorry, Jasper.' I say the words clearly, politely. 'It's still over.'

He doesn't move and he doesn't take his eyes from mine. 'For God's sake, I'm trying to be better. And I—'

'Kate?' Sebastian's voice cuts through Jasper's like a hot knife through cold butter.

It's a shock hearing him, because the last I saw him, he was on stage talking to Lisa. Yet when I turn around he's standing behind me, radiating hostility, his blue eyes cold. But he's not looking at me; he's looking at Jasper.

His manner is oddly familiar and I can't quite put my finger on why . . . and then all of a sudden it comes to me: he looks like Clive standing protectively behind Lisa, on the lookout for threats.

My heart beats faster. We're 'casual', aren't we? I know I told him what Jasper was like, and, yes, he was angry on my behalf, but now he's . . . looking at Jasper like he wants to skin him alive. He must have caught the tail end of our conversation, which means he'd deduced who Jasper is. Great.

'S–Sebastian,' I stutter. 'What are you doing? Isn't the Q&A starting in a couple of minutes?'

'Yes.' He stares fixedly at Jasper. 'I wanted to ask if you'd like to share the MC duties. Since this is *our* festival.' He says the word 'our' with a certain emphasis, as if he's hurling it like a stone at my ex.

Well. This is fun. The foyer is now practically drenched in testosterone, and I'm caught like a sock between two growling terriers. No, on second thoughts, Jasper's the terrier. It's Sebastian I have to watch out for, because Sebastian's a wolf, and even though he has no reason to be jealous or possessive, he's now both. With fury tossed in there for kicks.

He looks like he wants to tear Jasper's throat out with his teeth, and part of me wants to see him do it. Maybe I could even get in a few rips of my own, but with Lisa's Q&A starting any moment, a fight is the last thing this festival needs.

'Sebastian,' I say firmly, deciding that a polite introduction should set the tone. 'This is Jasper Price, an . . . old friend of mine. Jasper, this is Sebastian Blackwood. He owns Blackwood Books.'

'Pleased to meet you,' Sebastian says, with a smile that broadcasts 'I'm going to kill you the first opportunity I get'.

'Likewise,' Jasper says, his own smile implying 'Bring it on'.

Mine says 'Behave or I'll kill you both', and deep down I can feel anger gathering inside me, a rage that comes from the shock at Jasper's presence, and the horrible sense of invasion. That he should come *here*, to *my* village, the place where I was safe, and tell me he *loves* me and that he wants to fix things.

How dare he? How *dare* he?

I swallow my rage, though, and give them both a barbed

smile. 'Jasper, find a seat. I'll speak to you after the event.'
Then I turn to Sebastian. 'Yes, I'd love to help out with the
MC duties.'

His hostile blue gaze flicks to Jasper and then back to me,
and I meet it head-on. 'Excellent,' he says, through gritted
teeth. 'After you.'

Chapter Twenty-four

Leave him, C. I cannot bear him hurting you any more.

H

SEBASTIAN

Lisa's Q&A went off without a hitch and afterwards I stand on the village hall stage, managing the queue of people who have cōme up to talk to her. She's answering the stupidest questions with the patience of Job, and generally being a true professional. She's been a great headliner for this festival and we're very lucky to have her.

Not that I'm paying much attention to Lisa, because the majority of my attention is aimed squarely at the entrance to the foyer, where Kate is standing with her arsehole ex-boyfriend, aka Fuckface.

She called him an 'old friend', but I overheard what he said to her. He's the man who manipulated her, who hurt her. Who made her, the most intelligent woman I've ever known, feel stupid. And now he wants her back. Even if I hadn't overheard him telling her he loved her, I'd have known who he was and what he was after by the acquisitive look in his eyes. That look is not because he's desperate for a signed copy of *Colours*.

It's possessive. It's what I feel myself whenever Kate is around.

The urge to punch someone has never been stronger and my smile as I usher the next person along to talk to Lisa is probably more feral than pleasant – the woman rears back like I'm about to take a bite out of her, so it's more than probable, it's certain – yet I can't seem to control my face.

There's acid sitting in my gut, courtesy of the rage that rushed through me the moment Kate introduced me to him. I shouldn't be feeling this way about a woman. I *never* feel this way about anyone. I've never felt strongly enough about a person before to generate this kind of anger, yet here I am, wanting to plant my fist squarely in Jasper's face, then fulfil my promise to kick him all the way back to London.

Kate, in her rainbow dress, is talking away earnestly to him while he's staring at her like a dog with a bone. He might as well be drooling. I can't stand it. I'm incandescent with fury at how he treated her, at how he made her feel, and now he's back and he thinks he can just . . . what? Take her? Like she's his property? Like he's entitled to her somehow?

Fuck that.

The only thing he's entitled to is me punching his head in.

She'd never take him back anyway. She has more taste than that and a hell of a lot more self-worth, no matter what she thinks about herself.

Also, she's currently sleeping with me. Not that I have any claim on her either. This is casual. Casual sex. Casual conversation. Casual arguments. Casual making-up afterwards. Casual. Casual. Casual.

Yet no matter how often I say that stupid fucking word, nothing makes any difference to the intense burning in my gut. The ache, the anger, the need.

'Uh . . . Sebastian?' someone says.

'What?' I snarl, tearing my gaze from Kate and Fuckface to round on the person who dared to interrupt my internal ranting.

But it's only Dan. He's dressed up for the event – he's even wearing a bloody tie, which he never does – and he gives me a concerned look. 'You need to settle down, mate. You're scaring the guests.'

He's not wrong. There are only a couple of people waiting to see Lisa now, but they're giving me apprehensive glances.

I swallow my rage and try to look pleasant, but I don't think I succeed, because they take a few uncertain steps back before turning and leaving.

Bloody wonderful.

Without a word, Dan takes me by the elbow and urges me off the stage and over to the side of the hall, where presumably I won't frighten the masses. I let him, because even I know I'm being ridiculous.

'Okay, turn down the volume on the alpha werewolf vibes,' Dan says mildly. 'We want people coming back to Wychtree, not running for the hills.'

'Alpha werewolf?' I look at him. 'What the hell are you talking about?'

He shrugs. 'Nothing. Just a book I picked up from Kate's. But seriously. You look like you want to bite someone. Preferably the guy she's talking to.'

'It's her ex,' I say, watching them.

'Oh, interesting. What's he doing here, then?'

'I overheard them talking. He wants her back.'

'Ah,' Dan says sagely. 'Well, I wouldn't punch him if I were you. Not the best look to have a brawl at a literary festival.'

I grit my teeth. 'He deserves to be punched. He was emotionally abusive and hurt her.'

'Ah,' Dan says.

'It's *not* about her,' I insist. 'He needs to learn that he can't treat anyone that way, let alone her.'

'Right,' Dan says. 'I mean, if it was only that he's an abusive tosser, then yeah, have at. I'd want to get in a kick myself. But you look like you want to actually kill him for her.'

'Nonsense,' I snap. 'The relationship Kate and I have is casual.'

'Uh huh.' There's a world of scepticism in his tone.

I don't like it and glower at him. 'What?'

'Don't take this the wrong way, Bas, but I'm not sure you can do casual.'

I stiffen. 'Bullshit. That's exactly what I'm doing. I've been doing nothing but casual for the past two weeks.'

'Yeah, but a casual relationship doesn't usually include punching people.'

A muscle flicks in my jaw. 'He hurt her, Dan. Do you really think I'm going to stand idly by and let him do it again?'

'No, I'm only saying that your reaction is a little . . . intense.'

I'm barely listening to him, because I've gone back to staring at Kate and Fuckface.

She puts a hand on his arm and he puts his over the top. He's a prick. I hate him. I want to punch his stupid face and then strangle him with his tie. Not enough to do serious damage, but enough to make sure he goes yelping back to London with his tail between his legs.

'You should tell her,' Dan says.

'Tell her what?'

'That you have feelings for her.'

'I don't,' I lie. 'It's just sex, nothing more.'

Fuckface is touching her shoulder lightly. I want to break his fingers. He manipulated her, he made her feel stupid, he *hurt* her, and now he has the gall to come here. Does he think she'll fall into his arms? Does he really think he can take her away from me?

Then a jagged shard of doubt pierces my rage.

It's arrogance to think that I have the higher ground here. That I'm so much better than him, when I've hurt her, too, with my insistence on casual. When I know she wants more and that I can't give it to her.

How can I? The history of the Blackwoods is what it is,

and I might not be a gambler or a drunk, but I'm a difficult man. I'm reserved and aloof and I don't like people. I prefer my connections with books. Kate deserves better than that.

She deserves better than me.

Except . . . I want to be there for her.

I've never had a relationship before, not one, and that's because I've never wanted one. Caring is hard work and complicated, and after Mum died and Dad left, I've been happy with easy and simple, yet . . .

I want to know what it's like to have her make-up in my bathroom, her clothes in my wardrobe. I want to know what it's like to share a living space with her. To cook dinner with her. To come home after work with her and have a glass of wine as we talk about our day. To argue over how to stack the dishwasher or whose turn it is to clean the loo. To laugh over a private joke that only she and I understand.

I don't have that, yet suddenly I want it. I want it badly.

Except . . . I can't. Not if I want her to be happy too.

'I don't think it's just the sex, Bas,' Dan says. 'You're always talking about her. In fact, you never bloody shut up about her.'

'It's casual,' I repeat, and I know I've said the word too many times, because now it sounds meaningless. Hollow. 'You know I don't do relationships.'

'Right,' says Dan. 'But you're lying to yourself, mate.'

I turn sharply. 'What do you mean?'

He gives me a long-suffering look. 'Bas, you're in love with her. You've been in love with her for at least the last month.'

Utter horror goes through me.

Love. I'm *not* in love. Why would I be? When love is the very last thing in the world I want? Love is hard. Love is difficult. Love has destroyed the men in my family and I want no part of it. I never have.

'Jesus Christ,' I say, with as much emphasis as I can. 'I'm *not* in fucking love, Daniel.'

'Sure. Just like you don't care at all if Kate's horrible ex-boyfriend is here, possibly wanting to get back with her.'

He's being a prick and I shouldn't rise to the bait, because I'll only reveal myself. I have never been one to protest too much. Yet now all I can think about is Fuckface and how he hurt her, and how he wants her back, and no matter how much I believe a leopard can't change his spots, maybe he has.

Maybe he really is a better man, maybe he's changed, and maybe he'll convince her to go back to him. He might. And she might, too, mightn't she? I don't know what she wants and I don't know how she feels, because we haven't talked about it.

Something inside me plummets, but I ignore it. Hard.

'Even if he has changed, she won't want to go back to him,' I say, mostly for my own benefit, even as my brain is going flat-out on a mouse wheel, around and around, jealous and angry and desperate all at the same time. 'She's too intelligent for that. But it's her decision, so if she does, I won't stop her.'

'Of course you won't.'

'Have you ever been in love, Daniel?' I growl.

He screws his face up, thinking. 'Once. With Carole.'

'The school secretary? When you were six?'

He shrugs. 'She was kind to me.'

'My point being that you're talking through a hole in your head.'

'Fair. But I know you, Bas. You've never been like this with another woman in your entire life.'

'I'm not listening.'

'What would be so wrong with admitting it?' he asks, persistent as a fucking mosquito. 'She feels pretty strongly for you.'

Does she? Does she really? She wants casual too, that's what she said.

'If I felt it,' I say, 'I'd admit it.'

'No you wouldn't,' he scoffs. 'You're about as emotionally open as a potato.'

I stay silent a moment, resenting like hell being compared to a potato, all the while struggling with the cascade of feelings inside me. We don't admit what we feel, the Blackwood men. We keep it properly repressed.

Fuck. Maybe Dan's got a point about the potato.

'I can't,' I say eventually, every word feeling like it's been dragged from the pits of hell. 'Love is the . . . very last thing in the world that I want.'

Dan gives a gusty sigh. 'I suppose that's fair too. It's not as if you've had great relationship role models in your life.'

'The Blackwood men are flawed. We're addicts and we fail those we love and—'

'Yes, yes,' he says impatiently. 'You've sung that song before. But have you ever thought that maybe your dad and granddad weren't so much flawed as not very emotionally aware? And didn't know how to deal with their feelings?'

It was not, actually, something that I'd ever thought about. 'No,' I say in a gritty voice, because now I *am* thinking about it, and, again, he's got a point. Dad finding solace for his grief in the bottle. Granddad turning to the horses to deal with his fury about his father.

'You should,' Dan says. 'Because you're not any different. You come across as cool as a cucumber and everything under control, but underneath you're one giant exposed nerve and you always have been.'

I do not like this analysis. Not one bit.

'So?' I demand sullenly. 'Stop comparing me to vegetables.'

Dan shakes his head. 'So, you feel stuff, but you tell yourself you don't. You convince yourself you don't, because feeling stuff, and caring about it, actually fucking hurts.'

He's not wrong there. It does.

I glance over at my pretty rainbow girl once again, standing with Fuckface, and he's still holding her hand.

'Tell me something I don't know,' I snarl.

He notices the direction of my stare. 'Bloody hell, mate,' he mutters. 'Stop acting like Mount Vesuvius about to erupt and do us both a favour. Go and talk to her. Tell her how you feel. And try to do so without being a dick about it.'

Kate and Fuckface are now walking towards the door, still talking.

I don't want to talk to her. I don't want to tell her how I feel. I want to keep chasing the lie I've built this little castle of casual on: that I don't care about her, that our relationship could end today and I'd be fine.

But I won't be fine, and I have to admit it. I have to own it. And it's probably too late for me to end it with her without earning myself a mortal wound, yet I have to. I can't live in this constant state of 'casual', and any other kind of relationship is out of the question.

All or nothing, and I've decided on nothing.

It's easier that way.

'Fine,' I say to Dan. 'I'll tell her.'

Chapter Twenty-five

You know I can't leave, H. Where would I go? And what will everyone in the village think? I would lose the teashop and that's the only thing apart from you that keeps me sane.

C

KATE

Jasper and I come out of the hall and into the gravelled car park outside. Most of the people who attended Lisa's session have gone, with only a few stragglers left, standing by the parked cars and chatting.

The session turned out wonderfully. I was hoping that no one would pick up on the tension between Sebastian and me, and no one did. Thank God. Or, if they did, no one said anything.

Jasper waited for me afterwards, as I asked him to, and now he wants to resume our little chat at the pub, though I'm trying to decide if it's better to break the news again to him there, so he can drown his sorrows, or tell him now and get it over and done with. Not that I care about his feelings; he never cared about mine.

He hasn't changed. That much I do know, because if he had, he'd never have arrived unannounced. He'd have texted me or rung me or something, and he wouldn't have said he wanted to 'fix' things. He would have said he was sorry for the hurt he'd caused and that he'd understand if I wanted nothing more to do with him.

But he didn't. He turned up out of the blue, telling me he'd changed, that he loved me, that he wanted me back, thinking that I'd drop everything and throw myself into his arms.

That's not happening in my lifetime and I know that now, because his presence has crystallised something for me, something I hadn't wanted to face.

It's not him I'm afraid of and it never was. He's a weak, petty, selfish narcissist and he was never any danger to me.

It was myself I was afraid of. Afraid that I was weak, that I was stupid, that I was somehow complicit in the way Jasper treated me. That my emotions were weaknesses that he could use against me, and even that I deserved it somehow. But I didn't. No one deserves to be treated that way.

When I got here, I thought I was done with men for good, but, as it turns out, I'm not as done as I thought.

There is one man I'm not done with and I'm not sure I ever will be.

A man who is the opposite of Jasper in just about every way.

A good man, no matter what he thinks about himself. A

caring man. A passionate man. A man who might be aloof and reserved, a bit arrogant and a touch grumpy, but who has his heart in the right place.

He's honest, always says exactly what he means, and even if he lies to himself sometimes, he doesn't run me down or build himself up at my expense. He doesn't make me feel as if I'm broken in some way or that everything I do is wrong.

He doesn't make me doubt myself.

I always thought I loved Jasper and he loved me, but that's not what love is, and I know that now.

Because now I've fallen in love with Sebastian Blackwood and I know better. He builds me up, while Jasper only pulled me down. He gave me back the pieces of myself that Jasper took. He makes me glad to be the person I am, not afraid. Not ashamed or embarrassed or guilty.

He told me the problem wasn't me, that I didn't deserve to be treated that way, and he made me believe it.

I would have loved him for that alone.

I don't know if telling him how I feel is the right thing to do, because telling him will change things between us, and those words, once spoken, cannot be unsaid.

But one thing I'm sure of right now is that I don't need to be afraid of myself or the love that I feel. I'm stronger than that. I'm strong enough to see Jasper for who he really is, strong enough to walk away, and now I know that I'm strong enough to tell him I will never – *ever* – go back.

'A drink, Kate?' Jasper asks, and then, teasing a little, 'Or do they not have the prosecco you like?'

Prosecco. I never liked prosecco. Jasper *told* me that's what I liked and so that's what I told myself too. I did everything he told me, because I was insecure. Because all my life I've never known who I was or where I belonged, and so I needed someone to tell me.

But I don't need that, not any more.

I know who I am and I know where I belong.

I had a dream when I came here, but I wasn't sure if I could achieve it, yet I did. I have my bookshop and, even though it's early days, it's going great, and I'm making friends with people in the village. I'm even finding out what I can of my own family history.

I'm in the building my great-grandmother owned and I'm running a business, just as she did. And I'm also in love with the bookseller across the road. But, like the first Kate Jones, I had an emotionally abusive partner.

She had a child, the first Kate, so that's why she couldn't be with the man she loved, but I don't. She called herself a coward, but I don't think she was. She was brave to stay for her daughter's sake.

But I do need to find some of her bravery for myself, because I think I need to talk to that bookseller across the road. I actually think I need to tell him how I feel. I don't want my life to end the way hers did, with a box of unsent letters and a broken heart.

He might not feel the way I do, and I'll have to deal with that if he doesn't, but I can't not say anything. I can't get myself stuck in the same pattern I was in with Jasper, too afraid to push.

This boat I need to rock is my own. And maybe that'll involve me getting tipped out and getting wet, but I have to take the chance.

I have to. For me.

'I'm not into prosecco,' I say to Jasper. 'I never was. I prefer scotch and the Arms doesn't have the Islay malt I like.'

He gives that laugh I know so well, the one he always gives when he thinks I've said something silly that needs correcting. 'No, you don't. You like prosecco, the sweet kind. That's what you always have.'

In the past when he said stuff like this, I laughed too and gave in. I never wanted to make a fuss over a drink. But now I give him one of Sebastian's own gimlet stares. And I don't laugh.

'No, Jasper,' I say very calmly, and with a certain amount of condescension, as if I'm talking to a child. 'I hated prosecco. I only drank it because you told me I should and I was too insecure to disagree. But I'm not now. I'm a different person and I have a different life, and I don't love you. I never did. And I don't want to "fix things". You haven't changed. You're still the same self-centred narcissist you always were, and even if by some miracle you'd actually become a better person, I still wouldn't go anywhere with you.'

He frowns as the words penetrate and temper flashes in his eyes – he's never liked being denied. 'Kate, I went to therapy, for God's sake. I worked on myself. I made myself a better man for you.'

'Right. So you're only here to make your therapy sessions worthwhile.'

'No, that's not what I said.' He smiles, but it's tight, impatient. It's the one he always used when he thought I was being obtuse. 'I did all this work for you and made a special trip to come here. I had to rearrange my schedule. The least you can do is consider it.'

Of course. It's all about him, just as it always is.

I stare at him, putting all of Sebastian's trademark chill into my gaze. 'No, Jasper.'

He mutters a curse and steps towards me. 'Come on, one drink. Just one. Let me try and convince—'

'She said no.'

Sebastian's voice is hard and cold, and both Jasper and I turn.

He's standing behind me and how he got there without either Jasper or me hearing him, I have no idea, but he did. Now he's got Jasper in his sights, and I can see we're heading for another stand-off.

'None of your business, mate,' Jasper says. 'You're not her boyfriend.'

I open my mouth to tell him that Sebastian is my casual lover, but Sebastian gets in first. 'Actually,' he says, 'as a matter of fact, I am.'

For a second I'm so surprised I can't think of a word to say.

'Is this true?' Jasper looks accusingly at me.

'Yes.' Shock drags the word out of me. 'It's true.'

Sebastian comes up beside me and I think he's going to stop there, but he doesn't. He strides past and straight up to Jasper, and before I can say a word, his arm goes back and he punches Jasper full in the face.

Jasper drops like a stone, going to his knees, his hands over his nose. 'What the fuck?' he demands in a thick voice. 'I'll fucking bring charges.'

'No, you won't.' Sebastian stands over him like an angel of God. 'You're going to go back to London and you'll never bother Kate again. Because if I ever see your face in my village, I'll kick you straight into the river.'

I don't need a man to defend me and I don't condone violence. But seriously? Jasper deserved that punch and Sebastian has saved me the bother, and you know what? It's nice to be defended. It's nice to have someone stand up for me, because I've been doing it by myself for four years and I'm tired of it.

'Kate,' Jasper says hoarsely, still clutching his nose. 'You can't let him—'

'Sorry,' I say, coming to stand beside Sebastian, looking down at my sad excuse for an ex. 'I can't control what Sebastian does. And you'd better listen to him, because being kicked into the river is mild in comparison to what I'll do to you if I ever catch you here again.'

Jasper stares up at us both then scrambles to his feet.

'Oh, and Jasper?' I say, sliding in the knife. 'Even if I hadn't met Sebastian, I'd rather be alone for the rest of my life than ever see you again.'

Sebastian slides a possessive arm around my waist, pulling me against him. 'You heard the lady,' he says to Jasper, his voice dripping with ice. 'Run along now, there's a good chap.'

Jasper eyes him for a long minute, spits blood ostentatiously onto the ground, then turns on his heel and walks away in the direction of the Arms.

As soon as he's gone, I turn and look up at Sebastian 'That was very satisfying,' I say. 'Thank you.'

His gaze is sharp, intense. 'That arsehole's lucky he only escaped with a punch. Sorry if I beat you to it.'

He's not sorry, I can see that, and neither am I. 'It's okay. You're stronger than I am, so it'll probably hurt him more.'

Sebastian raises a hand and his fingers brush my cheek with a fleeting touch. 'Are you okay? Did he hurt you?'

I turn my cheek against his fingers, unable to help myself. 'No. I didn't let him.'

His hand drops, an expression I can't read in his eyes. 'Kate,' he says softly. 'We need to talk.'

I already know what he's going to say. It's there in his eyes, in that look I can't read, in his arm around me, slowly losing tension and slipping away. In the distance that wasn't there before that is now suddenly appearing between us.

I could stay quiet. I could let him say the words that are going to break my heart, but I decide to speak first. I let Jasper dictate my own feelings to me. I let him twist them, turn them into weapons to use against me. I let him make me feel as if the problem was me, when it never was.

Sebastian told me I didn't deserve that and it's true, I

didn't. I don't deserve what he's going to tell me now, either, but that's his choice. His problem. It's not mine. So I'm going to tell him what's in my heart. I'm going to take charge by being vulnerable, by opening myself up. I'm going to be brave and let him know how I feel and, if nothing else, I'll always have that. And so will he.

'Kate,' he says.

'Sebastian,' I say at the same time.

He inclines his head, because, at his heart, he is a gentleman. 'You first.'

I put steel in my spine, and my heart is in my eyes as I meet his gaze head-on. 'I don't feel casual about you, Sebastian,' I say, putting everything I'm feeling into my voice as well. 'I never have. I thought I hated you at first, probably about as much as I wanted you, which was a lot. And then . . . I began to realise that it wasn't hate that I felt. You got under my skin with your passion for books and your honesty and your willingness to bend when I know you didn't want to. With the way you looked at me, the way you saw me. You got under my skin in a way no one ever has.'

The expression in his eyes has changed, turning into that electric blue that I love, and his hands have curled into fists at his side. The lines of his face have gone taut. They're not welcome, these words, but I already knew that. And I'm not upset that I said them, I'm not ashamed. I think, for the first time in a long time, I feel as though I'm being honest, as though the weight of those unspoken words has been sitting inside me all this time, and now I've said them, I'm lighter.

Now I've said them, I'm free.

'Kate . . .' he says again, so much regret in the word.

'I knew I was falling for you,' I go on, speaking my truth. 'The danger was always there, and now it's happened. I *did* fall for you.' I take a breath and it feels as if it's the first one, my chest expanding, my lungs filling with air. 'And there's nothing casual about it. I fell all the way in love with you.'

A muscle flicks in his jaw and he gives me the grace of his attention, not looking away as I say the words, even though I know he must be dying to. He doesn't speak.

We're standing close, facing each other like cowboys ready for a gunfight, and I'm the one who shot first. And I missed, I know I did.

For a second, though, I allow myself to think that maybe I didn't. That I hit my target and that he's going to surrender to me. That he's going to tell me he loves me too and all he wants is for us to be together.

A vain hope.

Sebastian draws his weapon and shoots.

Clean through the heart.

'I'm sorry, Miss Jones,' Sebastian says. 'Love is the one thing I can't do. Not with you.'

Chapter Twenty-six

I know you're afraid, but I will protect you. We could leave the village, go somewhere else. Not Europe, not now, but perhaps America? We could go to New York. It's a big city, we could lose ourselves there.

H

SEBASTIAN

Kate's face is white and I hate myself even more than I did already.

Dan was right all this time. I'm in love with her.

I had to admit the truth, the second I walked out and saw her talking to Fuckface, glowing in her rainbow dress, looking like an angel fallen to earth. Even if just to myself.

I've always seen her this way, right from that first moment

when the sun caught in her hair as she peered through the window of what would become Portable Magic.

Fate, Lisa called it, except I don't believe in fate. I don't believe in past lives or serendipity. I don't believe I'm my great-grandfather and she's her great-grandmother, and that we're destined to play out the same tragic love affair that they had.

I don't believe I was destined to love her; I just did. But that's the problem. I know people believe love is a positive force in the world, and maybe it is for some. But not for the Blackwoods, and not for me.

I mean, for Christ's sake, the first thing I did when her ex hove into view was to punch him in the face, which is *not* acceptable behaviour these days. That didn't stop me, however, and perhaps that's the problem. Perhaps I should have been born in an earlier time, at an earlier date, when duels were acceptable.

Except it's not the violence that disturbs me so much as the feeling itself. The relentlessness of it. The force of it. The way it takes away your self-control, makes you crazy, turns you into someone you don't even know.

It's like an addiction, and the only way to handle addiction is to go cold turkey. Cut it off at the root and ride out the consequences.

Dad never did. He's no doubt still drinking where he lives in Bournemouth, still sipping from the bitter cup that love left him. I will not be him. I refuse. I won't drink from that cup, and so this relationship/situationship/casual thing I have with Miss Jones has got to come to an end.

It's too late for me to escape unscathed, yet I thought – I hoped – it wouldn't be too late for her. But it is now.

She loves me.

The words are arrows, each one hitting its target – punching clean through my heart.

It makes everything so much worse. It makes me know the truth, that I'm no better than Fuckface. I hurt her too, and if this goes on any longer, I'll keep hurting her, keep disappointing her, because that's what the men in my family do.

'I'm sorry,' I say, because there's no other way out of this and I'm trying to find the words that will explain to her how much this whole thing disturbs me. 'I've never been a violent man, Miss Jones, you have to understand that. Yet I punched your fucking bastard ex in the face, because he hurt you. And I don't like feeling that way. I don't like feeling as if I'm not in control of myself, and that's all I've been feeling since you came to Wychtree.'

She stares at me, but I'm not sure what she's looking for. 'Why?'

I hold her gaze, every part of me tense. She told me her truth and I want to tell her that she shouldn't have said anything. That she's made everything so much harder, but it was important to her to say it, I can see it in her eyes. And I didn't stop her. I had to be different from Fuckface in at least one way, and that was to honour what she needed to say.

Even if I can't say the same and give her my own truth. It will only make things ten thousand times worse.

'I don't know,' I say, lying through my teeth like a

politician. 'I don't understand myself. I've never felt this way about any other woman, yet the first time I saw you . . .' I bite down hard on the words. 'It's not important, though. What's important is that I can't do casual, Miss Jones. Not with you. Not now. And if it's not casual, then I can't do it at all.'

She's still white but there's something calm about her, something serene. 'Why is what you feel not important?'

'Because feelings don't matter.' I inhale, trying to calm the painful beat of my heart. 'They change nothing.'

Her eyes glow silver in the night. 'You're wrong. They change everything. I was afraid of Jasper, afraid of what he might manipulate me into doing, but then I realised it wasn't him I was afraid of. It was myself and my feelings. And once I realised that . . . It made me brave, Sebastian. I never loved him and I know that now, because what I felt for him wasn't what I feel for you. It wasn't anything like it.' She takes another step, getting into my personal space. Her cheeks are pink in the light from the hall, her hair a glorious messy fall down her back.

She's beautiful and I love her. Which is why none of this can work.

'You gave me pieces of myself back again,' she says, her voice slightly hoarse. 'You made me believe in myself, and that's what love should be, Sebastian. You taught me that. You showed me that.'

The words are a punch to my chest, directly above my heart.

Terrible news. Devastating news. Suddenly, I'm incensed,

furious that she should feel this way about a man who will do nothing but further the hurt her ex has already caused.

'Why the hell,' I demand, 'would you fall in love with me?'

'Because you're amazing,' she says. 'You're not cold or reserved or aloof, or any of the things everyone here says you are. You're warm and generous and caring and protective. You're the most passionate man I've ever met. No one else makes me feel the way you do, not one single person.' She takes a breath, her dress a glowing rainbow. 'You gave me back some of my family history, a story that I lost, and you made this village feel like home. And I feel as if I've known you for ever and that you're . . . you're part of me.' She takes another breath, looking up at me as if she's staring into the face of God and not just into the face of a lowly bookseller. A lowly bookseller who is going to break her heart.

He has no choice.

He's none of the things she thinks he is and he can't be. He's an exposed nerve, as Dan says: a seething pit of rage. A child whose love wasn't enough to save his mother or make his father give up the bottle.

A man who gave up a potential career in medicine to stay home and read.

To stay home and sell books to people who weren't much interested in the first place.

A man who is nothing compared to a woman who had her mother die and another man treat her like shit, yet who found the courage to come to a new place, start a new business, meet new people, build a new life and not just thrive in it, but own it.

A man who can commit to nothing and no one except his bookshop.

A coward, no better than Fuckface.

'I'm sorry, Miss Jones,' I say, forcing the words out, because no matter how deeply I know it's the right thing to do, it's hard and it's painful. It's agony. 'But you've got the wrong man. I'm none of those things and I never will be.'

Then I turn on my heel and I leave.

She doesn't stop me.

Chapter Twenty-seven

I can't, H. Please don't ask me any more. Let it go.

C

KATE

It's Sunday, the last day of the festival, and Portable Magic is having a romance panel, consisting of my book-club attendees, festival-goers interested in knowing more about the genre, and some authors I managed to pull in.

The bookshop is packed.

I have my brightest smile pinned to my face and the 'good thoughts' mantra on repeat in my head.

Anything to blot out the memory of Sebastian the night before, striding away from me, no looking back, no hesitation. If he was Orpheus and I was Eurydice, I'd have come back from the underworld alive and well and singing hallelujah.

I watched him go, his tall figure wavering, and even

though I expected it, my eyes were full of shocked, painful tears.

I told him I loved him and it wasn't enough in the end, and if I was the strong, modern woman I'm supposed to be, I'd laugh and say 'Good riddance' and get on with living my strong, modern life.

But there's no laughter left inside me and I don't feel strong. I feel broken, and all I can think is a bitter 'Of course'. Of course he doesn't want me.

Men have always let down the women in our family and why would I think he was different?

I don't regret what I said, though, no matter how it hurts.

The truth is important and I was done with lying.

'Isn't that right, Kate?' someone says.

I blink and realise I'm supposed to be managing this panel, not vaguing out and staring into space, brooding over my poor broken heart.

I take a deep breath and force away the pain. 'Yes,' I say to Mrs Abbot, who was the one who spoke, though I have no idea what she actually said. 'Who else has a question?'

A woman by the door raises a hand and I point to her.

'Happy endings,' the woman says. 'Are they mandatory in a romance?'

A Greek chorus of shrieking from the book-club regulars erupts in response, and the noise rises as lots of people leap in with opinions, talking over each other.

No. It's a good thing that we're not together any more, and I have to tell myself that. It's better if he walks away, because if he doesn't want what I do, then I'm better off without him.

It's too soon after Jasper anyway, and Sebastian is a lot to handle. He's moody and intense, a dark cloud, while I prefer the sunshine.

We argue a lot. We're too different. He's too arrogant and he likes his own way far too much, and I'm stubborn. I don't like being told what to do.

Basically, even if he *did* feel the same way I do, it wouldn't work out between us, so there's no point being hurt about it.

It's all for the best.

'Not always,' I say to myself, because sometimes grand romances *don't* have happy endings.

An elbow suddenly digs into my side and I startle.

Every single person in the packed bookshop is staring at me in surprised silence. The festival-goers have interested looks on their faces, while the book-club attendees express nothing but betrayal.

'Oops,' Aisling murmurs from her seat beside mine. 'That's not what you were supposed to say. You're the convener, Kate. You'd better start convening.'

Happy endings. Are they even possible in real life? When reality is so full of pain and tragedy? Right now I can't think of one love story I know of that ended happily.

Including my own.

'Um,' I say, intelligently.

'Do you really think so, Kate?' Mrs Abbot frowns ferociously at me.

But my attention is diverted. I'm staring out the window at the preparations going on across the road for Lisa's second signing session in Blackwood Books. At the queue extending out of the bookshop and down the road.

At Sebastian standing in his front window, looking out at Portable Magic. Looking out at me.

We haven't spoken since last night and he hasn't sent a text. Neither have I. But I feel all of it again in my chest, a heavy, solid ache. Not that the pain ever went: it's been there since he walked away from me and I think it'll probably never leave.

He looks at me a second longer and then turns away.

Everyone in this stupid panel about stupid romance is still looking at me, expecting me to talk intelligently about happiness and happy endings when inside my heart is breaking. And no number of good thoughts is going to help, I know that now.

I stand jerkily. 'Mrs Abbot,' I say, my voice sounding strangled. 'Would you take over for me? I'm not feeling the best.'

Before anyone can say a word, I shove my chair to the side and I flee for the door to my flat and stumble up the stairs. And when I get to the top, I allow myself a couple of little sobs. Then I scrub fiercely at my face.

I don't care, I chant inside my head. I don't care about him.

'Kate?' Aisling's voice floats up from the bottom of the stairs.

Really, I'm pleased and thankful for all the friends I've made since coming here, but right now, I'm wishing they'd all bugger off.

'I'm fine,' I say, hoping I'm convincing enough. 'Just a little headache.'

I move away from the stairs, go into my kitchen, and stand at the sink with a glass. Turn on the tap and fill it.

'I don't think you're fine,' Aisling says, appearing in the doorway, evidently having followed me up the stairs.

So . . . not convincing, then. Great.

'It's just a headache, Ash,' I say determinedly, because if I say it enough times, then maybe it'll be true.

'Really? It must be more than that for you to leave one of your favourite events.'

She is, alas, not wrong.

I take a bracing gulp of the water I didn't even want to start with, then try yet another meaningless smile. 'Sebastian and I are over,' I say lightly, even though saying the words out loud makes me want to cry. 'I told him I loved him and he told me he can't do casual. So, there you have it.'

Aisling frowns. 'Wait, what? You told him you loved him? Since when did you love him?'

'Since he first kissed me, probably,' I admit. 'And please don't give me any pity or say "I told you so". I couldn't help it and it's obviously a disaster, and, really, the best thing is just to forget it ever happened.'

Aisling folds her arms and gives me a stern look. 'I would never say I told you so and you know that. Same with pity. And love, well . . . You can't choose it. Sometimes it just happens, and at the worst possible moment with the worst possible person.'

I swallow and put down my glass. 'I would never have chosen him. I would have chosen . . . well . . . anyone else.'

'You told him, though.'

'A stupid thing to do.'

Aisling shakes her head. 'Uh, no. A brave thing to do. If he can't handle that, then he's not worth it.'

My throat has a lump in it the size of Scotland and nothing I do will make it go away. 'Tell my stupid heart that,' I say.

Aisling lets out a breath and, before I can stop her, she comes around the counter and gives me a giant hug. I resist a moment, then I relax and let her hug me, the warmth of feminine support and comfort strengthening me.

'My ex arrived last night,' I say, the words spilling out. 'He saw the festival advertising and decided to make the trip up to see me. He told me he loved me and that he wants me back.'

Aisling releases me gently, then goes about the very British business of making emergency support tea. 'That's not what you want?'

I'm not going to tell her the details about Jasper, not yet. But I will.

'No.' I lean back against the counter, feeling a bit better. 'He was . . . not a nice guy when I was with him. Anyway, he told me he's been working on himself.'

'Hmm,' Aisling mutters as she puts on the kettle. 'One of those.'

I sigh. 'I used to think I knew what love was, but then he turned up and I knew it wasn't him that I loved. I loved Sebastian.'

Aisling gets down the teapot from the cupboard, finds the tea and puts in the leaves. 'And Sebastian was being an oblivious dick, I take it?'

'I told him I loved him and he said I couldn't, that he'd only disappoint me and that it was better if we weren't together.'

'Oh dear,' Aisling murmurs, as the kettle boils and switches itself off. 'He really is the stupidest man in creation.'

'He's not stupid,' I say, though I don't know why I'm defending him. 'He just isn't in love with me.'

Aisling stops her tea-making. Turns. Gives me the world's flattest stare. 'Are you kidding? That man has been in love with you since you got here.'

A shock courses through me. 'What? Why would you say that?'

'It's obvious. Every time you're in a room he can't take his eyes off you.' She pours the water into the teapot. 'It's like you're the only thing he's conscious of. Everyone's noticed, believe me.'

I don't know what to say. 'But . . . he was angry when I told him how I felt.'

'Of course he's angry. He's an emotionally illiterate man who doesn't know what to do with his feelings, and you know men. Well, some men. When they have a problem they don't know how to fix, they get angry. Especially if that problem concerns their emotions.'

I remember Sebastian's face from last night. The tension in him. The fury in his blue eyes. The emphatic way he said 'I am none of those things' when I told him who he was to me.

'*Why the hell would you fall in love with me?*'

'I don't know, Ash,' I say. 'I gave him all these reasons why I thought he was amazing and he . . . he was so angry about it. I think he doesn't see himself the way I see him.'

'No, he probably doesn't.' Aisling gets out the teacups. 'He probably saw your reasons as a whole lot of expectations he can't meet.'

'They're not expectations,' I protest. 'He's already met them. He already *is* all of those things. He doesn't have to try being them.'

'Does he know that?'

'I don't know. He didn't give me a chance to explain. He just walked away.'

'Hmm . . .' Aisling puts the cosy on the teapot. 'You didn't go after him?'

Slowly I shook my head.

She frowns. 'Why not?'

It's hard to say, but I force the words out. 'Because I didn't think it would make any difference. He's clearly decided.'

'And so have you.'

Another shock goes through me. 'What?'

'You've clearly decided that you're going to let him go.' She goes to the fridge and gets out the milk.

'I haven't,' I protest.

'Haven't you? You let him walk away without a fight.'

'All we've done since we met is fight,' I say, because it's true. 'I don't want to fight any more.'

She eyes me for a long minute. 'Strange. You dig in and

fight with him over the most petty bullshit, yet the one time it really matters, when it's really important, you give up almost immediately.'

I feel like she's sunk a knife into my side. 'That's not how it is.'

'Isn't it?' Aisling gives me a stern look. 'You were so angry when he didn't include you in the festival and you fought hard to get Portable Magic involved. You wouldn't take his no for an answer. Yet the moment he says no thanks to your declaration of love, you let him walk away.'

I swallow, my throat tight. She's right and I know she is. 'I didn't think it would make any difference,' I say. 'He was so emphatic and so . . . angry, that I didn't think fighting for it would help.'

'Are you sure?' She's facing me and her green eyes are very direct. She's not going to let me get away with this. 'Or was it just that you didn't have the guts?'

That hurts. It hurts a lot. But she doesn't know about Jasper and what he did to me, so it's not her fault. Also . . . she's probably right.

She catches the look on my face and sighs. 'I'm sorry, Kate. I didn't mean that. But how important is this to you? How important is *he* to you? You're afraid, I get that. Being in love is scary. But if he's worth fighting for then you have to fight for him.'

My eyes feel dry and prickly, and it's true what she says. I *want* to fight for him. I want to fight for us and what we could have, but I'm afraid it won't be enough.

'I would,' I say. 'But I don't want to fight on my own. He's got to fight too, and I'm not sure he's going to.'

Aisling is silent a moment. Then she picks up the teapot. 'Come on. Let's have a cup of tea and discuss how we're going to get Sebastian Blackwood to pick up his sword and head the fuck into battle.'

Chapter Twenty-eight

Did you get my last note? You returned the book, but you didn't answer. Is there something wrong, C? Please respond.

H

SEBASTIAN

It's the cosplay cocktail evening, the last event of All the World's a Page festival, and the pub is full of people in costume.

I was not a fan of the event and made no bones about it to Kate, but she insisted, so here I am, in a roomful of people in stupid costumes apparently having the time of their lives.

There are even literary-themed cocktails. A Virginia Woolf. A William Faulkner. A Nora Roberts and, of course, a Lisa Underwood.

I'm standing by the bar and *not* sipping a themed cocktail. I have a tumbler of single malt, because while I am participating to a certain extent, I draw the line at drinking a cocktail called Nora Roberts.

By the fireplace, Lisa is being mobbed, a shifting mass of costumed festival-goers and locals surrounding her. I can't help scanning the crowd for Fuckface, because, if he's here, I'm going to have a word. Luckily he must have realised what's good for him, because he's not. Good fucking riddance.

I don't stop scanning the crowd, though, because naturally it's not Fuckface I'm actually looking for.

I'm looking for Miss Jones, and she's not here either, and I feel her absence like a missing limb, phantom pain and all.

I don't know why I'm looking for her. I made my stance clear last night, and now I have, I should be living my life as if nothing has happened.

I can't, though. I'm still achingly conscious of her presence in the village, even when I can't physically see her, and if this goes on, I might have to do something.

Maybe I might have to leave Wychtree entirely.

'Who are you supposed to be?' someone says from beside me.

I don't turn because I know who it is. Dan.

'An independent bookseller,' I say, my attention restless as I look in vain for golden hair.

'Wow,' Dan mutters. 'The likeness is uncanny.'

I glance at him.

He's dressed in some kind of floppy white shirt and tight trousers, with a scarf that I think is supposed to be a cravat.

It's not so much a concerted attempt at period costume as a half-hearted, casual nod in the direction of something that might, if you squint hard, be period costume.

He looks ridiculous, and I tell him so.

Unbothered, he produces a lacy white handkerchief from somewhere and flourishes it at me. 'The Scarlet Pimpernel, at your service.'

That doesn't deserve a reply, so I don't give him one. I go back to restlessly scanning the room instead.

'Did you tell her?' Dan asks, not picking up on the 'Fuck off' I'm putting out.

'Tell who what?'

'Don't be dense,' he says, exasperated. 'Kate. Did you tell Kate you have feelings for her?'

'No,' I snap. 'Can we have this discussion later?'

'Why didn't you?'

'Oh, for fuck's sake.' I turn to him yet again. 'She told me she's in love with me.'

'She did? Oh, mate, that's fantastic!' Dan looks delighted at first, but then he picks up on my expression. 'That's not fantastic?'

'No.' I bite the word out. 'I don't want anyone to love me, Daniel. I never did. Especially when I can't love them back.'

'What absolute bullshit.' He looks annoyed now. 'You're an idiot, Bas. You've got this amazing woman in love with you and you told her what? That you didn't want her?'

'That's the problem,' I force out through gritted teeth. 'She *is* amazing. And I am not. And I can't give her what she wants, and I never will.' I pick up my scotch, drain the contents, slap it back down.

Dan stares at me like I'm a fool. 'Sebastian, I knew you were a stupid bastard, but I didn't think you were *that* stupid.'

He's going to give me some kind of psychoanalysing lecture, I just know it, and I'm not in the mood. I'm not in the mood for this wretched party either, especially if Miss Jones isn't here. Not that I want her to be here.

Christ. I don't know. I don't know anything.

I don't give Dan a reply. I turn and thread my way through the crowds to the exit, then head out of the pub, stalking down the high street, back to Blackwood Books and home.

I should stay and thank people. Raise a glass to next year's festival and say a few words. But I've got no stomach for it, not tonight.

Things feel . . . grey. Dismal. And I wish I could tell myself I don't know why I feel this way, but I do. I know.

It's her and what I said to her. It's her and the hurt that flashed across her face when I told her I couldn't love her, the lie I told her.

It's the feeling I'm missing something vital to my well-being and that, without it, I'm slowly dying.

There's no other choice, though, not for me.

I survived well enough before her. I can survive well enough after her.

I stop outside Blackwood Books and I tell myself I won't turn and look at Portable Magic as I unlock my own door.

And I'm strong. I don't, which is excellent. That's the first step out of this hell I've made for myself.

I open the door and walk into the shop.

And come to a sudden stop.

Someone is standing near the counter, doing exactly what I was strong enough *not* to do, which is stare at the bookshop across the road.

Someone tall, in a ratty black coat. His hair is grey and swept back from his forehead, and he glances at me as I enter.

For a minute I'm rooted to the spot with shock.

'Hello, Sebastian,' my father says, and smiles.

I do not smile back. 'What the bloody hell are you doing here?' I demand, because he is the very last person I need, or want, to see in the entire world.

'Well,' he says. 'I let myself in. Obviously I still have a key.'

'Obviously,' I bite out. 'But that doesn't answer my question.'

He glances out of the front window to Portable Magic again. 'I saw an ad for the festival. Thought I'd come along to see it.'

'You're a bit bloody late, aren't you?' I growl. 'You weren't even at the cosplay cocktail night.'

He ignores this. 'Your great-grandfather would have been proud of you.'

A curious feeling that I can't pinpoint winds through me. I shove it away. 'I didn't do it for him,' I say acidly. 'I did it because you left me a lot of debt to pay back.'

Dad sighs. 'I know. Neither I nor your grandfather were any good at managing this place.'

I don't expect the admission and it interrupts the anger building in my gut. Still, I'm not willing to let him off the hook. 'No,' I say, not bothering to hide the belligerence in my voice. 'You weren't.'

He doesn't respond for a long moment, still staring across the road at the pretty little bookshop sitting there, owned by the pretty little bookseller I gave my heart away to, and who doesn't even know it, because I'm a fucking coward. Like all the Blackwood men.

A silence falls, a lead curtain of quiet.

'I'm staying with Jean Abbot,' Dad says eventually, not looking at me. 'I didn't think you'd want me here.'

'Jean? Are you—'

'You probably don't want the answer to that question,' Dad interrupts. 'But yes, it's exactly what you think it is.'

I don't know what to say. I haven't spoken to him for months, possibly years, but apparently he's been having a life, all while I've stayed here, cleaning up the mess he left me.

The thought makes me even angrier than I am already. I open my mouth to say something pithy and cutting, but then he says, 'She told me you're seeing the great-granddaughter of the original Kate Jones.'

I feel as if I've been punched hard in the gut.

Fucking village telegraph.

'I was,' I force out. 'But I'm not now.'

'That's a shame. I thought history might repeat itself.'

'What history? You mean like Mum nearly leaving you?

Like Grandma left Granddad? Hardly. Thought I'd skip all that nonsense and go straight to—'

'Cutting yourself off from everyone?' Dad says calmly.

The words slice through me, sharper than a scalpel.

'We all thought we weren't good enough for the women we loved,' Dad goes on. 'And that, I've now learned, made us self-fulfilling prophecies.' He sighs. 'The only one of us who ever had guts was your great-grandfather.'

'Guts? Him? I read the letters in that box, Dad. He left the first Kate in a violent marriage and then he killed himself. No fucking guts there.'

'Hmm.' Dad nods, still looking out the front window. 'That's one ending, certainly. But there is another.'

'What are you talking about?'

'Your great-grandfather didn't kill himself.'

Shock pulses down my spine. 'But there was an inquest and his body was never found. There were clothes by the side of the river . . .'

'Yes, that's what it *looked* like. But that's not what happened.'

I stare. 'What happened, then?'

'If you read the letters, then you'll know that he had a secret love affair,' Dad says. 'With a woman who was married. Her husband was abusive, and she was afraid to leave. When your great-grandfather came back from the war and saw that her shop had closed, he tried to get in contact with her, but she never replied. She had a child by then, and he thought that's why she stayed.'

I'm very still as he tells me all about H and C. But I know all this already. 'Yes, yes,' I say, impatient. 'And then she disappeared a few years after her husband died.'

'Her husband's car went off the road,' Dad murmurs. 'And into the river. He drowned.'

I blink. 'Went off the road?'

'Yes.' Dad's voice is very level. 'You'll also note that your great-granddad disappeared not long after her husband died. Then she disappeared too.'

My brain won't work. 'Spell it out, Dad.'

'Tell me, is there a postcard upstairs in that box? A postcard from Sicily? There's nothing written on it, except an H and a C.'

An old postcard that I put to the side because I didn't think it was relevant.

I stare at him, unable to speak.

'Your grandfather received that a year after Kate disappeared. He knew already about the letters, because he found them in Sebastian's personal effects after he supposedly drowned. He told me that he thought your great-grandfather might have had something to do with Kate's husband's death, though he couldn't be sure. And then maybe, to avoid repercussions, he faked his own death. Dad suspected he spent a couple of years establishing himself abroad, making sure the authorities weren't able to track him down, then he got Kate to join him. Dad thought your great-grandfather, Sebastian, wanted him to know he and Kate were still alive, hence the postcard.'

I can't believe it. I don't believe it. It's impossible. 'They . . . were together? In the end?'

Dad nods slowly. 'Your grandfather thought they were. He was positive. He still never forgave his father for leaving him with the bookshop, I think, or for letting him think he was dead, but, yes, he believed Sebastian and Kate were together.'

I struggle to process what he's just said. 'How did you know C was Kate?' I ask, the first question that comes into my head.

'Rose, Kate's daughter, had some unsent letters that she found in her mother's effects. She spoke to Dad about it and he showed her the ones Sebastian had kept. She got a postcard too. They both decided no one should ever know about it. Dad only told me just before he died.'

It makes sense, at least that part makes sense. The secrecy of it. The scandal of a married woman, the abuse, and then running away together . . .

I still can't get my head around it. 'So, what? That's why you're here? To clear up some old family mystery that doesn't matter?'

Finally, he looks straight at me. 'Among other things. There's too much unsaid in our family. Too much that's hidden. So many stories that haven't been told, because people have gone to their graves with too many secrets and too many lies.' His blue eyes, so like mine, glitter in the light. 'The stories *do* matter, Sebastian, that's why I'm here. You need to know them. They're where you came from and they're part of who you are. You're part of me, and you're all I have left of your mother, and . . .' He lets out a breath. 'My story isn't over yet and I want a happy ending. An ending that includes a reconciliation with my son.'

'What is this?' My whole body is rigid with tension and shock and anger. 'One of the steps in your twelve-step programme?'

Dad moves slowly over to where I'm standing. Once, I used to think he was a tree or a giant, he was so tall. Now, I'm taller.

He searches my face. 'I'm sorry, son. I am so sorry for what happened, especially after your mother died.'

I'm not ready for his words; my hands clench into fists.

'It wasn't you,' Dad continues. 'The drinking. It was the grief, and I didn't handle it well, and I regret it. I regret not being there for you.'

He means it, I can see, and yet I don't know what to do. I don't know what to do with this feeling inside me, a growing pressure. Anger, shock, pain, grief . . . everything. Then again, I've never known what to do with any of my feelings other than to force them away.

'Mum was going to leave you,' I tell him, again saying the first thing that comes into my head. Perhaps to hurt him. Perhaps to push him away. 'She told me she wanted to.'

He doesn't look hurt and remains unpushed. 'She wanted to stay in the village and I wanted to go, and we had some difficulties with that, not to mention my drinking. But we were in the process of working our issues out.'

I don't want to accept that; it puts everything I thought

about my childhood into doubt. My mother, the wronged woman who died too young, and my father, the drunk who nearly drove his wife away. That's the story I told myself, and now he's telling me it was wrong?

'She wouldn't have,' I say. 'None of the Blackwood men can keep a woman. They always let them down, always.'

Dad is silent, eyeing me. 'Is that something that's actually true?' he asks. 'Or something you just want to be true?'

It's an excellent question and I hate it.

'It *is* true,' I say. 'Sebastian and Kate—'

'Found happiness in the end. Me and your mother would have got there in the end too.'

'What about Granddad, then?' I demand, furious for reasons I can't articulate. 'Grandma left him.'

Dad nods. 'Yes, she did. Your granddad was very angry about his father's disappearance. He didn't want to run the bookshop. He wanted to do other things, and was looking for buyers, but . . . then he met my mother and things were good for a while. Mum was a restless spirit, though, and she didn't want to stay in one place so . . . she left. Dad didn't want to leave me or sell the bookshop then, because he wanted to hand it on to me, so he stayed.'

'That doesn't sound like a happy ending to me,' I say. 'Not if Grandma left him.'

Dad sighs. 'Like I said, he was very angry about his father's disappearance, and I don't think he ever got over it, not even after I was born. He didn't have a head for business, which didn't help, and he played the horses far too much for his own good. But it wasn't as if he never saw Mum again. She didn't like being married, I don't think, but she did enjoy coming to visit, which she did quite a bit.'

I don't know what to say now. I don't know what to think. The Blackwood men can never hold on to the women they love, that's my family's history, and yet . . .

'They stayed together, then?' I ask stupidly.

'They never divorced, if that's what you mean,' Dad says. 'That was their version of a happy ending. And your mother and I would have had ours if she hadn't been ill.'

'So, it's all wrong, then.' My voice is hoarse. 'What they say about the Blackwood men?'

Dad rolls his eyes. ' "They"? Who's "they"? I suppose, if you're talking about the village, then, yes, it's wrong. That's just the story they made up about us. But the reality is always much more complicated than that.'

I run a bookshop; I know all about stories, and I should know that too. Yet, somehow, I missed this lesson, and now all I can think is that everything I've been telling myself is wrong. Even my own story is a lie.

A strange electricity runs through me and I turn away, staring out through the front window to the bookshop across the road.

Where Kate is.

If my story is a lie, then what is the truth?

But I know the answer to that question. The truth is the same. That I'm a coward who can't handle the feeling in my heart, and I've been using this lie to protect myself. The

Blackwood history is a castle I've built, with guards on the parapets and a drawbridge I can pull up to close myself off, because . . .

I'm afraid.

I'm afraid I'm not the man Kate thinks I am, that I'm not enough for her. And I'm afraid to even try.

'I know,' Dad says after a moment. 'It's a lot to take in, but I—'

'I'm in love with her,' I say hoarsely, the words a pressure I can't keep inside any more. 'I'm in love with Kate Jones. She owns the bookshop across the road.'

'Ah,' says Dad. 'Jean was right, then.'

I turn to look at him. 'I told her it was over.'

'Why did you do that?'

'Because I'm a fucking coward.' I can feel the muscle in my jaw leap with the tension screaming inside me. 'Because love fucking hurts and I hate it.'

Dad looks at me a long moment, and then, strangely, he smiles. 'Yes,' he says. 'Yes, it does.'

'Why are you smiling?' I demand. 'I fucked it up. She told me she loved me and I told her that loving me was a mistake and I walked away. I ended it.'

'That doesn't mean you can't begin again, Sebastian. It's not over unless you want it to be over.' He raises a brow. 'So . . . do you want it to be over?'

'No.' The word comes out immediately and without my conscious thought, every cell of my being joining in. 'No, that's the last thing I want.'

Dad's smile turns wistful. 'Ah, son. You always did feel things so very deeply. But that's not a bad thing – you know that, don't you?'

'No,' I repeat, the only word I seem able to say. 'No, I don't.'

'It hurts, of course, and no one wants to be hurt. But the pain is how you know it's important. It's how you know it matters.'

'But I don't want it to matter, Dad,' I say, sounding like a child as the truth hits me like an atom bomb, destroying everything inside me.

I don't want it to matter, but it does. She does.

And it hurts to love her, but she's important.

My father takes another step towards me and puts a hand on my shoulder. 'You can't fight love, Sebastian. Believe me, I tried. But the happiness that comes with flinging yourself bodily into it . . .' His smile turns warm with memories. Good memories. 'It's worth any price.'

I want to tell myself that I don't need my father to tell me about love, that I don't need his pep talk, but I don't pull away. 'I'm afraid,' I say, with an honesty I wasn't anticipating. 'I'm fucking terrified.'

Dad squeezes my shoulder and the ghost of the boy I used to be feels better. 'We all are, son,' he says. 'Remember, though. Your story isn't over. And the only person who gets to write your happy ending is you.'

Chapter Twenty-nine

*This is the last note I'll send, C. I'm going to
be called up soon, but I don't want to go. I
don't want to leave you alone with him.
Give me a sign, a nod, a look, anything, so I
know that you want me to stay.*

H.

KATE

The shop feels empty the day after the festival, though, to be honest, I'm enjoying the peace. I have boxes to unpack and a new window to plan; I've got plenty to do.

I'm just coming out with a box when I notice the book sitting on the counter. I put the box down and go over, pick the book up.

It's *I Capture the Castle* by Dodie Smith. My favourite book as a kid.

It's not an edition we have in the shop here and I wonder where it comes from. I pick it up and leaf through the pages, only for a note to slip out. The piece of paper flutters in the air and lands on the counter upside down.

A strange, electric feeling gathers inside me.

I turn the paper over. There's writing on it, in blue ink. A firm, slashing hand.

> *You don't have to reply. I'm not expecting anything. I just wanted to tell you that I'm in love with you and that walking away from you was the biggest mistake of my life.*

There's no signature. Only an H.

My throat tightens, a lump rising in it, and the blue ink on the paper wavers. Oh my God. Are those tears? I swore a man wouldn't make me cry any more and yet here I am, crying.

My chest feels sore and for long minutes all I can do is stare at the book on the counter and the piece of paper.

He wrote me a note. Just as Sebastian did for Kate, all those years ago . . .

Part of me doesn't want to reply. He told me it was over and, if he's having second thoughts, then that's his problem. I should do what the first Kate did and keep the book, not return the note . . .

Yet is this him fighting for me? For us? Is this him picking up his sword? If so, then he's absolutely going the right way about it. The pen truly is mightier.

I can't not pick mine up too.

I let him walk away from me two days ago, but I'm not going to walk away from him.

I pull out a piece of paper and choose my own sword – red ink, of course – and I write back.

How dare you not expect anything of me? You should expect something. You should expect everything.

C

I put the note back in the book and, when Mrs Abbot comes in to collect an order, I ask her if she'll take it across the road to Blackwood Books.

She gives me the oddest smile, but does so.

Five minutes later, the door to Portable Magic bangs open and Sebastian strides in. He's dressed in black and his eyes are glowing bright blue.

There are customers in the bookshop, but he looks only at me. 'Out,' he commands, and I know he's not speaking to me.

The customers flee, and I don't protest. There's only one person in the world worth bothering about in this moment and he's standing in my bookshop, staring at me.

He shuts the door, locks it. Then strides over to the counter.

I'm standing behind it, my heart beating its way out of my chest. 'How dare you?' There's no heat in my voice. 'Those were my customers.'

'I don't care.' He is fierce. 'Tell me what I should expect, Kathryn.'

I love the way he says my name. I love how sure it sounds in his mouth.

I love him.

'A happy ending, Sebastian,' I tell him. 'That's what you should expect. That's what you deserve and it's what I deserve too. The happy ending that Sebastian and Kate never got.'

'What if I told you they did?'

I open my mouth. Close it. 'But they—'

'There should be a postcard in Rose's effects,' he says. 'I'll show you later. But you should know that they were together in the end, and I think that's what we should be too. Together.' He moves towards me, coming around the counter to where I'm standing, and I can't breathe. The electricity pouring off him, the fierce burn of his eyes pinning me to the spot like a butterfly on a board.

I brace myself, waiting for him to reach for me, but he doesn't. He stays where he is, keeping some distance between us.

'I love you, Kate,' he says. 'I loved you the moment I first saw you.'

'But you walked away.' I don't want to argue with him, but of course I'm not able to stop myself. 'You told me we couldn't be together.'

'I know. But I was wrong. And I was a coward. You told me all those things you thought I was and I . . . I didn't think I could be any of them. I didn't think I was good enough, and it was easier to walk away than to try.'

My throat closes and I have to swallow. Hard. 'You don't have to try, Sebastian. You already are that man. You were him all along.'

He doesn't move; his hands are clenched. 'I don't feel like I am. When my mother died and my father drank, I closed myself off. I closed myself down, because it was easier. And I never learned how to deal with any of these . . . fucking emotions.' His expression is taut and he's breathing fast. 'I still don't and I'm . . . I'm fucking terrified. But . . . Kathryn, my beautiful Kate. I can't live without you and I don't want to. And you can't go back to Fuckface and you can't go with Lisa . . . You just can't leave me. I won't have it.'

He's struggling, this all-or-nothing man, who's apparently decided he wants it all. And I can see his fear. If easy was what he wanted, he'd never have written me that note, never have charged across the road and burst into my bookshop. But here he is, standing in front of me, fighting for what he wants.

Fighting for me.

I can't stand the distance between us now. It feels wrong, and he's made it this far, so I'm the one who closes the final gap. Who crosses that last piece of distance, which ends up being no distance at all.

It's me who reaches up to lay my palm against his warm cheek. 'Then I won't leave,' I say simply. 'I'll stay here. With you.'

He reaches up to my hand and covers it with his own, holding my palm against his skin. The look in his sharp blue eyes is painful. 'Are you sure? I'm not an easy man. In fact, I can be fucking awful, ask anyone here.'

'I've already asked most people here, and they say you're aloof sometimes and reserved sometimes, but you're also a good man.'

A muscle flicks in his jaw. He's so tense. 'Fuck . . . I don't know what to say now. I've never been in love before. I've never even had a proper relationship before.'

I smile, love filling my chest, inflating my heart like a balloon so that it presses painfully against my ribs. 'Well, I have,' I say. 'And I can help you with that.' Then I put my hand on his chest and rise on my toes, and I kiss him.

And the magic happens. The same magic that's always happened between us.

'I'm sorry,' he whispers against my lips. 'I shouldn't have walked away.'

'And I shouldn't have let you go. I should have gone after you, but you're not the only one who was afraid.'

His hands drop to my hips and, before I can protest, I find myself being lifted and sat on the counter. Then he lets go and puts his hands down on either side of me, looking down at me, and I love his closeness. I love his warmth and his scent. 'What are you afraid of?' he asks.

'That I'm not enough for you.'

He pushes a curl behind my ear, his fingers brushing my skin and making me shiver. There are flames in his eyes now and I feel consumed by them in the best way. 'I know you, and I think you're the most incredible woman. You're smart and passionate and fierce and loyal. You're everything I didn't know I needed.' He takes my face between his hands and his mouth covers mine and he kisses me for a long, long time.

Then, finally, when I'm breathing far too fast and far too hard, and I'm wondering when he's going to take me upstairs and whether we can even make it, he lifts his head and says, 'The first time I saw you, I thought you were like sunshine.'

My heart inflates a little more. 'Really? I thought you were an arrogant dick.'

Sebastian Blackwood smiles at me then, warm and full of tenderness, and it's the best smile I've ever seen from anyone ever. 'Guilty as charged,' he murmurs, insufferable as always.

I smile. 'Is this it, then? Is this our happy ending?'

'Oh no,' he says, pulling me close. 'This is not the end of our story, Miss Jones. Not while we're still writing it.'

We're writing it still.

And – spoiler alert – it's still happy.

Piha Beach,
Auckland,
New Zealand

1985

SEBASTIAN

I watch my Kathryn walk across the sand to me, the sea breeze making a banner of her hair. She wears it long and I like it like that, even though these days all the gold in it has gone.

I don't see the lack, though. I don't see what age has taken from her. I only see what it has given: a smile that lights up the world. Lines around her eyes and mouth that tell of heartbreak and joy, loss and happiness, of a life lived well and fully, with everything in her. A wisdom in her grey eyes that have been my compass since the day I first met her. A body still healthy and strong that carries the soul of the person I love more than anyone else on this earth.

It's a strange place to end up, us two, here on an isolated beach with strange, black sand, way down the bottom of the world and so far from where we came from. But it suits us. We have created a little family of our own down here, and we have many friends.

Yet we still carry our losses, she and I.

Her daughter, Rose. Her teashop. My son, Charles. My bookshop.

We couldn't go back, we both knew that, and we chose not to.

We chose each other.

Our story was done in Wychtree and we decided it was time to let another story take its place.

We've had everything we've ever wanted: years of love, years of joy, years of happiness together. I don't know how much time we have left, but, in the end, that doesn't matter.

We know what we had and have still, and that's enough.

Kathryn's painted her toenails in rainbow colours and, as the wind whips her hair around her head, she laughs.

We have our happy ending here in this moment.

And in every moment to come.

HEADLINE
ETERNAL

FIND YOUR HEART'S DESIRE...